Jeanne Whitmee studied speech and drama, followed by a career in the theatre, until her marriage and the birth of her two daughters. Before turning to full-time writing, she taught speech and drama. She is the author of over thirty books, some written under pseudonyms, many having been issued in large print and translated into various languages, both European and Eastern. She still takes an active interest in the theatre and arts and her hobbies are watercolour painting, gardening and cooking. She lives in Cambridgeshire with her husband, and has four grandchildren.

TRUE COLOURS

Frances, Sophie and Katie meet again at a school reunion and discover how their lives have changed. Katie is a successful fashion designer; Frances has a young son and a wealthy husband; Sophie has a happy marriage and a dream home. They resolve to keep in touch, but gradually each of them realises that her friends' wonderful lives are far from perfect . . . Katie is working in a small boutique and struggling to succeed; Fran's marriage to a controlling man is deeply unhappy; Sophie is on the point of bankruptcy and divorce. But old friendships die hard and each of them needs to learn to pocket her pride and reach out for the help and support of her friends.

Books by Jeanne Whitmee
Published by The House of Ulverscroft:

JEANNE WHITMEE

TRUE COLOURS

Complete and Unabridged

CHARNWOOD
Leicester

First published in Great Britain in 2012 by
Robert Hale Limited
London

First Charnwood Edition
published 2013
by arrangement with
Robert Hale Limited
London

A catalogue record for this book is available
from the British Library.

ISBN 978–1–4448–1739–3

Published by
F. A. Thorpe (Publishing)
Anstey, Leicestershire

Set by Words & Graphics Ltd.
Anstey, Leicestershire
Printed and bound in Great Britain by
T. J. International Ltd., Padstow, Cornwall

This book is printed on acid-free paper

1

Katie was late — as usual. No matter how hard she tried or how firm her intentions, something always seemed to get in the way of her being punctual. She'd really meant to be on time today too, so it was doubly annoying.

First, she hadn't been able to find her one pair of earrings — mainly because she seldom wore them, but today was different; today she wanted to create a good impression. By the time she'd found them (for some weird reason at the back of the bread bin) she'd missed the bus, which led to missing the train to Wellmead and now here she was, twenty minutes late for the head's welcoming speech, hot and perspiring, her red hair dishevelled even more than usual and her feet aching. A far cry from the cool and serene image she'd hoped to present.

Snatching a glass of plonk from a passing waitress, she gulped it thirstily and scanned the crush of people milling around in the hall of her old school, Simon Elmo Comprehensive. It hadn't changed much in the twelve years since she'd last been here. It even smelt the same — an odd mixture of floor polish, damp gym kit and yesterday's shepherd's pie.

She'd been surprised to get an invitation to the reunion of her year. She still received the school's annual newsletter but this was the first time it had featured a reunion for her old

1

classmates. She'd accepted, mostly out of curiosity but now, glancing round at the sea of faces, her first impression was that there wasn't a soul here she recognized. Somehow she'd expected them all to look exactly the same as they had back in 1996 but that was ages ago — fifteen years in fact, and of course people change. Had she? Did she look different, she wondered. Looking at the same face in the mirror every morning it was impossible to tell.

'*Katie!* Hi! I was hoping you'd be here.'

She turned at the sound of a voice behind her, surprised to see her old school friend, Sophie Bamber. Katie would definitely have recognized her had she seen her first. Not because she hadn't changed — of course she had after all these years — but Sophie stood out in any crowd and always had. She'd *developed* rather than changed, Katie decided. She looked sophisticated in an inventive kind of way; her long dark hair hung loose over her shoulders and her make-up was dramatic, all kohl eye liner and lipstick in the shade of sherbet pink that would have made Katie look like a Victorian consumptive. Sophie's outfit, that would have looked way over the top on anyone else, somehow looked exactly right on her. Katie put down her glass and hugged her.

'Soph! You look fantastic!'

'You look marvellous yourself — if a little stressed.' Sophie took in the unruly red hair that never would stay in place and smiled to herself. Same old Katie. She grabbed herself a glass of wine and took a sip. 'I can't wait to hear what you've been up to all these years. It's nothing short of criminal that we lost touch. That's why I thought I'd organize this reunion.'

Katie stared at her. '*You* organized it?'

Sophie laughed. 'Yes. You needn't look so surprised.'

'No — I'm not,' Katie stammered. 'It's just that after all these years . . . '

'I know. Someone should have done something about it years ago. The years fly past don't they? Life gets in the way.'

'I suppose it does. Anyway, I'm glad you did. It's great to see you.' Katie glanced at the elegant long skirt and beaded top Sophie was wearing and surreptitiously unbuttoned her jacket so that the missing button she'd meant to sew back on wouldn't show. 'Look at you, you're so slim and elegant,' she said. 'You put me to shame. I don't know how you do it, but then you always did look great, even in that ghastly school uniform. I put a pound on if I so much as *think* about a bar of chocolate. I suppose it must be all the sitting down.'

'Ah, you work in an office?' Sophie assumed.

Katie bit her lip. 'Well no. I meant I don't take enough exercise. But never mind me, what do *you* do? You stayed on after we'd left and got your A levels. Did you go to art school after that like you wanted to?'

Sophie nodded. 'Art school and then a poly,' she said. 'Got a teaching diploma. I teach in a comp' very similar to this but I do private commissions as well.'

'Wow!' Katie was duly impressed. 'I always

3

knew you'd do well.' Her eyes raked the crowd of women filling the room, all chattering away like magpies. 'Have you seen anyone else you know? Is Fran here?'

Sophie shook her head. 'No — to both. Disappointing, I was only really interested in seeing you and Fran again anyway.'

'Yes, me too. The three musketeers, remember? It would have been such fun reminiscing. What a shame she isn't here.'

Sophie took her arm. 'Come on, there's a buffet over there and your glass is empty. You're not driving, are you?'

'No.'

'Good, then come and get a refill and something to eat.'

The buffet consisted of some rather tired looking sausage rolls and several almost empty plates of curling sandwiches. Sophie pulled a face. 'Looks like the others have been here before us.'

'I was late,' Katie said, helping herself from the depleted buffet. 'For some strange reason I find it almost impossible to be on time for anything, no matter how hard I try.'

Sophie laughed. 'No change there then.'

They found a table and sat down with their glasses and plates. Katie looked at Sophie's left hand. 'Oh, you're married.'

Sophie nodded. 'Yes, I'm Sophie Turner now.' She grinned. 'Great name for an artist, eh?'

Katie took a bite of her sandwich. 'So — tell me all about him — Mr Turner. How long have you been married? What's his name and have you got any children?'

'He's a commercial artist, an illustrator. We met at college. His name is Rex and we've been married six years.' She took a sip of her wine. 'And no, no kids.' Sophie raised an enquiring eyebrow. 'What about you?'

Katie shrugged. 'I'm still waiting for that someone special to turn up — if he actually exists, but I'm not all that bothered. I quite like being on my own.'

'And what did you say you were doing?'

Katie hesitated. This was going to be difficult. She was well aware that the stories she used to make up at school had earned her the reputation of fantasist (a kinder word for liar) but those days were long gone. Surely she wouldn't still be tarred with that particular brush. 'Well, as a matter of fact I'm a fashion designer,' she said.

Sophie took in Katie's crumpled outfit and general air of dishevelment.

''Course you are.' She laughed and patted her arm. 'Good for you — same old Katie.'

Katie's heart sank. The old label had stuck fast then.

Sophie put her plate with its discarded sandwich down and glanced round. 'Look, it's like the parrot house in here. I've said hello to everyone I wanted to, so why don't we go and find ourselves a nice quiet little café somewhere?' She held up her glass and pulled a face. 'This stuff's pretty vile, isn't it? Overtones of paint stripper. I don't know about you but I could murder a cup of tea.'

Katie grinned. 'Me too. I slept in and I didn't

have time for any breakfast.' As they walked out through the main entrance into the car park she took a deep breath. 'Phew! Great to breath fresh air again. I'd forgotten that suffocating school whiff. It awakens some of the memories you'd rather forget.' At that moment an open sports car drove in through the gates and both girls gasped. 'Wow!' Katie said. 'Look at *that*! Someone from our year seems to have done well for herself. I wonder whose it is.'

'It sure as hell puts my old banger in the shade,' Sophie said. 'She would have to park right next to it, wouldn't she?' She indicated the battered Ford Focus next to the shining newcomer. 'I wish I'd put it through the car wash now,' she added wryly.

The scarlet Mercedes coupé pulled smoothly into a vacant space and drew silently to a halt. The driver pulled off her headscarf revealing exquisitely cut and highlighted hair but as she took off her shades Katie heard Sophie draw in her breath sharply.

'My *God*, I don't believe it!'

Katie peered at the car's driver, now opening the door and extending a shapely leg. 'Why? Who is it?'

Sophie clutched her arm excitedly. 'Don't you recognize her? It's *Fran*!'

'No, *really*?' Katie stared in amazement. The Frances Garner she remembered had been a quiet, rather mousy girl, small and thin for her age and, although cleverer than both herself and Sophie put together, always the last to speak up for herself. When out of school uniform she'd

6

always worn drab jumpers and skirts in beiges and greys as though she was trying to merge into the background. If it hadn't been for Sophie's recognition Katie would never have known her.

They hurried across to greet Fran as she climbed out of the car and there were squeals of delight, hugs and exclamations all round.

⋆ ⋆ ⋆

Facing one another round the table in the Pickwick Tearoom on Wellmead's High Street twenty minutes later, Katie looked at her two old school friends. Both of them had obviously done well. Both were married — apparently happily and, if Fran's chic designer outfit was anything to go by she seemed to have landed squarely on her feet. She told them she had been married for nine years to a businessman whose secretary she had been. His name was Charles Grayson and he was quite a bit older than Fran by the sound of things. He owned and ran his own electronics business. She had an eight-year-old son called Harry, whose photograph she proudly showed them.

'What a good looking boy,' Sophie remarked. 'So you're a stay-at-home mum now then?'

Fran nodded. 'I am at the moment but Harry is off to boarding school next September. I'll be at a loose end so I might go back to working with Charles again.'

'If I had kids I'd never let them go to boarding school,' Katie put in. 'I'd want them round me all the time.' The minute she'd said it she wanted to take it back. She was always putting her foot in it and Fran's slight wince didn't escape her notice. She forced a laugh and tried to backtrack. 'But hey, what the hell do I know? Spinster of this parish and all that jazz.'

Sophie smiled. 'We all idealise motherhood till we have kids of our own,' she said. 'I'm no different. But I imagine there comes a time when you want to move on and do your own thing again. And I bet Harry can't wait to go to his new school.'

'Probably,' Fran said wistfully. She looked up. 'What about you, Katie — how has life treated you?'

Sophie cut in before Katie had time to speak. 'Our Katie is a fashion designer, no less,' she said with a smile.

Fran's eyebrows rose. 'Well, well. Good for you, kid. You were always good with a needle, weren't you?' She looked at Sophie. 'As for you . . . it was always a foregone conclusion that you'd take up art if you could. I've never seen a more typical artist. I bet you're married to one too.'

Sophie nodded. 'Rex is an illustrator. We met at college. I teach art at the local comp' but I take private commissions too. At the moment we're up to our necks renovating a Georgian house — doing most of the work ourselves.'

'Yourselves? Wow!' Fran pulled a face. 'Brave of you.' She helped herself to another scone. 'So — no family?'

Sophie shook her head. 'Haven't had time for that yet.' She took a sip of her tea. 'But who knows? Maybe one day.'

'What was the head's speech like, by the way?' Fran asked. 'It's not still Miss Bowler, is it?'

Sophie laughed. 'Good God no! Hattie must be at least a hundred and ten by now. It's a Mrs Kirsty Aitken now. She's new — a trendy Scotswoman from Edinburgh, a dead ringer for Miss Jean Brodie. About forty I'd guess. I got to know her over the phone while I was organizing the reunion. I only caught the end of her speech but she clearly has ambitious plans to stir up the old place.'

'Not before time!' Katie chipped in. 'Unfortunately, I slept in — missed my train and arrived too late to hear any of it.'

Both the other girls laughed. 'Same old Katie!' It was the second time Katie had heard that remark today and she winced inwardly. Had she really always been seen as hopelessly pathetic? Sophie laid a kindly hand on her arm. 'But we wouldn't have you any different, would we, Fran?'

Fran shook her head. 'Many's the time you cheered us up with one of your outrageous stories. It's so reassuring to know that you haven't changed.'

'And you still live locally, Fran?' Sophie enquired.

'Yes. Well, a little way out. We live in Melford. When we married, Charles bought the Manor House and we had it restored. It took two years and a lot of angst, so I sympathise with your project. I can't imagine what it must be like doing the work yourself. It was bad enough

9

supervising the professionals. I have to say it was worth it in the end. We have almost two acres of ground, half an acre of lovely old English garden and an acre and a half of wildlife garden. We have foxes and badgers and all kinds of birds. You must both come and see it.' She frowned. 'Where do both of you live?'

'I'm in London,' Katie told her. 'I keep meaning to get a car but driving in London's a pain and the train only takes an hour.'

'And I'm only about an hour's drive away, on the outskirts of Leicester,' Sophie put in.

'Oh well, neither of you is too far away,' Fran smiled suddenly. 'Oh, it's so lovely to be together again. Why on earth did we lose touch? Now that we've got together again we must make sure we don't let things slip.' She looked at the other two. 'I know life must have changed for us a bit. It'd be strange if it hadn't after all these years, but basically we're just the same. Do you remember when . . . ?'

There followed half an hour of reminiscences and gales of laughter as they reverted to their schooldays until Katie looked at her watch and realized that it was almost time for her train.

'I should be going too,' Sophie said regretfully, gathering her belongings together.

'I'll give you both a lift,' Fran said. 'And on the way we'll exchange addresses and phone numbers. Being together again has been wonderful!'

★   ★   ★

As Fran's car was only a two seater the girls had gone into town in Sophie's Focus and in the end it was she who dropped Katie off at the station. Katie stole a look at Sophie as they drove and thought that her old school friend looked slightly pensive.

'Who'd have thought that Fran would have turned out so posh and glamorous?' she remarked.

Sophie nodded. 'She's obviously done well for herself; no shortage of money obviously.' She turned to glance at Katie. 'But did you notice that although she had photographs of her son she didn't have any of her husband?'

Katie shook her head. 'It didn't occur to me. Do women usually carry photographs of their husbands?' She looked at Sophie. 'Have you got one of yours?'

'As a matter of fact I have.' Sophie drove into the station forecourt and parked the car. Switching off the engine, she rummaged in her handbag and came up with a small leather wallet which she opened and took out a snapshot which she passed to Katie.

'It was taken on our honeymoon, in Italy — Catolica, on the Adriatic.'

Katie looked at the photograph of a smiling couple on a beach. Sophie wore a bikini and her hair was wind-blown. The tanned, handsome young man with his arm around her shoulders had dark curly hair and gleaming white teeth. They looked happy and in love. Katie felt a small twinge of envy.

'He looks great. Very dishy,' she said. 'Did you

11

say his name was Rex?'

Sophie nodded. 'Ghastly, isn't it? More like a dog's name. But somehow he couldn't be called anything else.'

Katie was about to make a joke about collars and leads but bit her tongue just in time. Somehow her jokes all seemed to come out sounding wrong. 'And you say he's an illustrator. Does that mean he works from home — freelance?'

'Yes.'

'Like me,' Katie volunteered. 'It's pretty precarious if you don't have a day job too. I work as a sales assistant in Fantaisie, in the King's Road. Do you know it?'

'No.' Sophie said. Her face coloured. 'Rex doesn't need a day job. He can hardly keep up with all the work he's offered. He's very much in demand.'

'Oh, I'm sure he is.' Katie winced inwardly, noticing Sophie's heightened colour. There she went again, putting her foot in it. She looked at her watch. 'My train's due,' she said. 'I'd better get on to the platform.' She reached for Sophie's hand and squeezed it. 'It's been so lovely to see you again and have a good old gossip,' she said. 'You will get in touch again, won't you?'

Sophie nodded. 'Of course. Give me a ring any time if you want a chat. Take care, Katie. I've really enjoyed today.'

Katie got out of the car and stood waving as Sophie drove away. The three of them had exchanged addresses and phone numbers but now she wondered rather wistfully whether she would in fact ever see either of them again. They

12

were poles apart — Fran in her restored manor house with her son and wealthy husband, Sophie with her arty lifestyle, all loved-up with her handsome other half. They had always been poles apart of course but back in the old days they had had school in common, plus the fact that they'd all had problems at home like most teenagers. They'd been the Three Musketeers — all for one and one for all. She sighed and walked through the ticket hall and on to the platform just as the train came in.

2

SOPHIE

After I'd dropped Katie off at the station I headed for the motorway. If there wasn't too much traffic I reckoned that I should be home by six. But as I drove down the slip road and merged into the stream of traffic it began to rain which was bound to slow things up.

On the whole I didn't regret organizing the reunion. It had been lovely to see my old school friends again but talking to Katie and Fran had been quite an eye opener. Who would have foreseen that shy little Fran would blossom into the glamorous wife of a successful businessman? As for Katie — endearing little Katie; she'd always been one to embroider her life with glamorous fantasies but *fashion designer*! That took some swallowing, like all the stories she was always spinning. The thing was, she managed to make her outrageous fibs sound so much fun that we let her get away with it. She'd always been quite clever with a needle of course. I couldn't help smiling, remembering the way she'd earned a few pence to augment her pocket money by subtly altering those awful uniform skirts we had to wear, turning up the hems and whittling down the side seams to give the more clinging look we all craved, to enhance our budding teenage curves. Oddly enough, none of

14

the teachers ever seemed to notice, or if they did they must have decided to turn a blind eye.

But now the day was over and as I peered through the streaming windscreen through the mist thrown up by the endless stream of vehicles, I wondered what was awaiting me at home. Would Rex have begun working on the kitchen? It was doubtful — with football on the box. I couldn't help wondering, not for the first time, if buying Greenings had been an enormous mistake.

I remembered how excited I'd been the first time I'd seen the house. It had been a showery spring afternoon much like this one, almost two years ago. At the time we'd been living in a poky little flat in Leicester, quite close to the school where I taught. It was hopelessly cramped. There was nowhere for Rex to set up a studio so he'd been working in the living room and I was sick and tired of his drawing board and other paraphernalia cluttering the place up. We'd been talking of getting a foot on the property ladder for some time but the weeks kept passing and we hadn't got around to doing anything about it.

It was on a Sunday afternoon and we were out for a drive. We'd promised to look in on my parents to see their new house and we'd stopped to ask directions to the village where they lived when I spotted the house. The rain had stopped and, getting out of the car to stretch my legs, I spotted an agent's 'For Sale' board leaning drunkenly by tall wrought iron gates almost obscured by foliage. Hidden behind a screen of tall silver birches on the edge of a village, the little Georgian house seemed to beckon invitingly. If I'd thought about it at the time it might have occurred to me that the lurching agent's board, stained green with algae, and the general air of neglect was a sure sign that the house had been on the market for some time, but at that moment I was too enchanted to think practically. While Rex was asking a passerby for directions I unlatched the squeaky rusting gate and peered inside. The gravelled drive was weed infested and overhung with tree branches but I could glimpse the house, its windows winking in the sunlight. Solid and square, it looked like something straight out of Jane Austen, the kind of house I'd always seen myself living in. I felt excitement quicken my heartbeat as I rushed to get Rex.

He had been maddeningly cautious. 'Ye-es, it's attractive, I grant you, in a distressed kind of way, but it looks as if it's been empty for ages. It's probably falling to bits. It'd cost a bomb to put right.'

'Not if we did most of the work ourselves,' I argued. 'It seems like fate that we stopped in this very spot today, like an omen. Aren't you excited?'

He pulled a face. 'Not really, no.'

'Well, let's at least get in touch with the agent and take a look round?'

'Oh God, must we?' Rex groaned. 'Hey! Wait a minute, what are you doing?' I'd already fished my mobile out of my bag and was punching in the agent's number that was printed on the 'For Sale' board. 'You're wasting your time, it's Sunday,' he wailed.

'Estate agents are always open on Sundays,' I pointed out, already listening to the number ringing out at the other end. 'It's when they do most of their business.'

A few minutes later it was all arranged. We had an appointment to view the house on the way back to Leicester later that afternoon.

My parents had bought their new house in the country to retire to. I'd been surprised when they told me their plans. I thought they'd never retire from the chain of hairdressing salons they'd created together, let alone bury themselves in a village like Little Penfold, miles from the bustling city life they'd always enjoyed. Since Rex and I married I'd been on slightly better terms with them than before. When I was a kid they literally never had time for me. I was what's known as a latchkey kid. When I was little there had been a kindly woman who had collected me from school and given me my tea. She'd wait with me till Mum came home, hopefully in time to put me to bed. I'd envied kids like Fran, whose mums were always there, waiting for them at home time, taking them to the park on the way home, buying them sweets or ice creams. By the time Mum got home she was always too tired to read me a story or even talk to me much. When I went on to secondary school I was given my own key which I wore on a ribbon round my neck so that I could let myself in when I got home. It was impressed on me that having your own key and being trusted to get your own tea was a very grown up thing and I should be proud of the responsibility they were trusting me with.

Sometimes I'd be allowed to invite Katie and Fran for tea on Sundays. We'd always play in my bedroom afterwards because Mum and Dad would be busy catching up on their paperwork in the study downstairs and mustn't be disturbed. The girls had always been impressed by my pretty dresses and expensive toys, and more especially by the fact that I had my very own telly. I never drew their attention to the fact that I'd realized long ago that these things were only really meant to keep me out of the way. I'd much rather have had parents who found time to play and give something of themselves to me. I let Fran and Katie envy me because even at a young age I'd latched on to the fact that envy was preferable to pity and that material things were better than nothing.

College was a revelation. For once I felt like a real person, not just an inconvenience to be tolerated. I guessed that Mum and Dad were relieved to see the back of me, even though they put on a show, insisting that they would miss me. Most of the students' parents drove them to college at the beginning of that first term, seeing them settled in before driving home. Mum took an hour off to come to the station with me, pressing a cheque for a hundred pounds into my hand as I boarded the train. 'For emergencies — or treats,' she said with a slightly apologetic smile. As the train drew out I watched her walk across the platform, slim and elegant in her high heels and designer suit. As she returned my wave I could almost hear her sigh of relief.

I met Rex almost at once. He was a mature

student, seven years older than me. He'd decided to study art after serving a plumbing apprenticeship. He told me that his working class parents had always been hard up and he hadn't had the chance to go to university, but his grandmother had died and left him a legacy which had enabled him to break free and do what he'd always wanted to do. He had plans to become an illustrator and he certainly had talent. I loved the way he took charge, making decisions for me, planning surprise outings for us, concerts and exhibitions to go to, arranging things to do that I'd never have thought of myself. Some girls might have resented having decisions made for them, but I couldn't believe that someone actually thought me important enough to spend time with, saw me as a worthwhile person and not an irritating inconvenience. I suppose it was inevitable that I'd fall in love with him.

We were married in our last year at college. Mum and Dad put up no objections, even paying for our honeymoon in Italy. They seemed to approve of Rex but I suspected that they'd have approved of Quasimodo if he'd offered to take me off their hands.

At the end of my course I went on to study for a teaching diploma while Rex began the tortuous task of getting a foot in the door as an illustrator. We lived in a tiny bedsit and worked in bars and clubs in the evenings to keep the wolf from the door, but we were happy — perhaps happier than we'd ever been, before or since. What a pity we never realized it at the time.

On that spring afternoon, when we first viewed Greenings, Rex had been appalled at the state of it. 'It's even worse than I thought,' he said. 'It wants knocking down if you ask me.'

I glanced hopefully at the estate agent. 'It's a very fine example of eighteenth century architecture,' he said, encouraged by my enthusiasm. 'And, all things considered, it's in quite good condition.'

Rex looked at him, one cynical eyebrow raised. 'Really? I dread to think what you'd consider *bad* condition.'

I was scarcely listening. The hallway was already working its magic on me with its enchanting arched ceiling and elegant curving staircase. There were three reception rooms on the ground floor and a well proportioned drawing room that looked out on what had once been a pretty garden. It had a beautiful Adam fireplace and lovely cornice work on the ceiling. There was also a dining room and what I suppose had once been called a morning room.

'This would be perfect for your studio,' I enthused. 'It faces south so the light would be perfect.' Rex grunted.

The agent led the way through to the kitchen and I stood in the doorway enraptured as I pictured how it would be. 'This flagged floor is great. It only needs a bit of elbow grease and we could have an Aga over there,' I said, pointing to where a black cast iron range crouched in a recess. 'And a big round table in the middle, a dresser over there with willow pattern china and a big squashy chintz sofa under the window.' I turned to Rex. 'Oh, can't you just picture it, reclining on the sofa with a glass of wine while I cook dinner?' But when I looked at him I could see that he saw only what was before his eyes, an empty square room with a dirt-ingrained stone floor, cobwebs festooning the window and peeling chocolate brown paint. 'Oh, for heaven's sake use your imagination, darling,' I said exasperatedly. 'We could make it absolutely wonderful.'

'At a guess I'd say that the windows would all have to be replaced,' he pointed out, prodding the rotting woodwork. 'Then there's the wiring. No supplier would risk his reputation by connecting this place to the local electricity supply. It'd plunge the whole neighbourhood into darkness. There's no central heating so it'd be like living in an ice box in the winter and as for the plumbing . . . ' He turned on a rusting tap in the adjoining scullery and threw up his hands. 'It must have been put in in the stone age!'

'But darling, you're a qualified plumber,' I reminded him. 'If you did the work yourself it would save us a small fortune!'

'You're kidding!' He laughed. 'In your dreams!'

But in the end after a lot of wheedling I managed to talk a reluctant Rex into buying Greenings. My chief argument was that it would be a fantastic investment once we'd done it up. It had been empty for three years and I think that

21

the thing that kept him teetering was the price, which was incredibly low. As a last resort I daringly suggested that we make an even lower offer and to my delight and Rex's astonishment it was accepted. I knew he was right when he said it needed a lot of work, but as I constantly pointed out, we'd save money by doing a lot of the work ourselves and we'd be well into pocket if we ever decided to sell. Once the house was all in order it would be worth a small fortune.

The rewiring and the window replacement were done before we moved in and I found a retired gardener in the village to prune the trees and shrubs and tidy up the garden. I was ecstatic, but as the weeks passed and our overdraft increased Rex grew more and more convinced that we'd made a huge mistake, and of course he blamed me.

Although I would never admit it, he was right. Everything was so much more expensive than we'd foreseen and there were peripheral things that we hadn't even thought of, like the second car we quickly realized we'd need so that I could commute to school and back, public transport being almost non-existent. One bus a week into town was all there was, which toured all the local villages and therefore took hours. I was grateful for my private commissions, mainly children's portraits which were well paid and for which I was becoming quite well known by word of mouth. I tried hard to convince Rex and myself that everything would be fine but he continued to be resentful about what he called the money pit I'd landed him in.

The trouble was, with me working school hours and weekends as well, I had very little time to spend on the house restoration. Being freelance, Rex worked from home so it was decided that he would do most of the work, fitting it in around his commissions, which was fine in theory but in practice was quite another matter. I worked solidly on the decorating all through the school holidays and usually instead of putting my feet up in the evenings I'd be wielding a paint brush as well as trying to fit in the preparation for the next day's teaching. Most of the time I was exhausted and the harder I worked the more excuses Rex seemed to find to get out of it. He argued that his work had to come first and that anyway, it was me who wanted the house. My resentment grew until at last I could contain it no longer and it erupted into a row when I came home one summer evening to find Rex sunbathing in the back garden, the grass almost up to his ears as he sat in the deckchair.

'Couldn't you even mow the grass? I stormed. 'Do I have to do everything round here?'

'I've been hard at it all day,' he protested.

'Hard at *what*?' I demanded.

'My work, of course. The stuff I earn my living by — remember that? I might not exactly be the bread winner around here but you know I've got to finish that magazine commission by the deadline if I want to get any more work from them. The bloody plumbing will have to wait.'

'Till when exactly?' I challenged.

'Till I'm bloody good and ready!' He glared at

me. 'Your trouble is that you've always been thoroughly spoilt,' he threw at me. 'I've been hard at it all day. You just have this maddening knack of walking in the minute I sit down for a break. Anyway, what about your share of the work?'

'*My share?*' I was appalled. 'I do far more than my share, on top of going to work all day.' I protested. 'And as for being spoilt — no one ever spoilt *me*!'

'Rubbish! Your parents overindulged you — gave you everything you wanted,' he taunted. 'You'd only to ask and they'd get it for you.'

Hot angry tears filled my eyes. 'Yes, to keep me quiet and out of their hair,' I snapped. 'Have you any idea what it's like to grow up feeling unwanted and in the way?'

'Aw, poor little rich kid.' He taunted. 'A house full of expensive stuff kids like me never even dreamed of. Well now you've got what you wanted and a load of debt to go with it so I hope you're satisfied!'

'I wanted this house because I knew I could make it into a home,' I choked. 'A home that was mine; the *real* home I never had.'

'Is that all the thanks your folks get? I hope if we ever have kids they'll be a bit more grateful than you! I said you were spoilt and you are.' He sat up and stared at me. 'You haven't got a bloody clue, Sophie. Have you ever gone to bed hungry? Or had to wear clothes your mum got at a jumble sale so that the other kids all laughed at you? You don't know you're born!' He stood up and threw down his newspaper. 'You wanted this rotting pile of crap. I tried to tell you what it'd be like but would you listen? No! You're too bloody used to getting your own way. You've landed us in this mess so now you'd better grow up and get on with it because I've had it up to here!'

My heart sank as I stared after him storming off into the house. It was the first time I'd realized how much he resented the gap in our respective backgrounds.

We made up of course — later, blissfully in bed, and Rex promised that as soon as his current commission was finished he'd get down to the work — on one condition. As soon as the house was finished it was to go straight back on the market. I was dismayed but I had no choice but to agree, though deep inside I reassured myself that I'd be able to talk him round when push came to shove.

* * *

I started the car again and drove round to the garage to put it away, promising myself not to say anything if Rex hadn't caught up with the work. I loved the house and I loved Rex too. And of course he was entitled to a break. After all, I'd just had a whole day away and he hadn't complained. When I got the idea of organizing the reunion he'd actually encouraged me to go ahead with it. Since the day we had the blazing row I'd told myself over and over that once we'd finished the restoration on Greenings everything would fall into place. Rex would have fallen as much under the house's spell as me and our relationship would return to what it was before. Our marriage was being tested. Like the house it needed patching up but we'd work it out somehow.

3

FRANCES

I put the car away and let myself in, standing for a moment in the hall. Even if I hadn't known that Charles and Harry were out, the house itself would have told me with its almost tangible silence. This was a taste of what was to come, I told myself as I made my way through to the kitchen. Once Harry had gone to school there would be a lot of empty hours stretching ahead of me so I might as well get used to it.

It had been great to see the girls today. Katie hadn't changed much. Sophie was different though. She'd had more education than Katie and me of course, staying on for A levels and then college. She, of all of us, seemed to me the most adjusted and fulfilled. She'd had a very privileged childhood — well-off business parents who clearly overindulged her. Still, it didn't seem to have spoilt her too much and clearly she'd worked hard to justify what they must have spent on her. I'd always envied all the time she had to herself, up in that luxurious little den of hers with her TV, her expensive toys and her seemingly endless collection of videos and CDs.

My parents adopted me when I was three weeks old and it felt to me as though they'd never left me alone for a minute from that day on. There she would be — Mum — standing at the school gates every afternoon, making sure I didn't get run over or kidnapped or, even worse, led astray by some of the kids from the council estate. Needless to say, she really disapproved of poor Katie.

Even when I went to secondary school she was still there, doggedly waiting every afternoon until I begged her to stop. I tried to explain to her that it was embarrassing, that I was already suffering from mild bullying because I was shy and introverted and if she continued to baby me I knew I was in for much worse, but she still managed to make me feel guilty, accusing me of being ashamed of her, of not loving or appreciating her any more.

Katie understood. That was the nice thing about Katie. She could always see my side of things. She didn't talk much about her own home life. I knew her mum had died when she was quite young and I wasn't sure what happened to her dad except that he wasn't around any more. There were a lot of children in her family, some of them had been left behind in Ireland with a grandmother. Katie lived with her elder brother and his wife. She never complained, though there were times when I'd noticed bruises on her arms and I wondered if all was well at home. But she always spoke fondly of her brother, Liam, so I never plucked up the nerve to ask. There was certainly no over-protective mum waiting to escort her safely home. I'd disappointed them of course, as I'd always known I would some day. No one could possibly live up to the standards and expectations they'd set for me.

I poured myself a glass of juice from the fridge and then went upstairs to shower and change. The house was beautiful. I was always telling myself I should be grateful for such a fantastic home. Our bedroom overlooked the garden and as I opened the window the scent of roses and lavender drifted up to meet me. Fitted wardrobes occupied one wall, their mirrored doors throwing back a reflection of the room — cream carpet, turquoise silk brocade curtains at the windows with the same material flouncing the dressing table and the hangings of the four-poster bed. A room most women would die for.

In the en-suite I showered and was just changing into jeans and a T-shirt when I heard Harry calling up the stairs.

'Mum! Come and see what I won at the fête.'

I walked out on to the landing to see him standing at the foot of the curving staircase, his dark hair tousled and his brown eyes eager as they looked up at me. He'd been to the village fête with two of his friends and it was clear that they'd had an enjoyable afternoon.

'Mum, can Paul and David stay to tea?'

'Of course.' I ran downstairs and hugged him, feeling him stiffen slightly in my arms. Charles had instilled into him that at eight he was far too old for hugs from his mother, too old for bedtime stories and certainly far too old for teddy, who had been put out with the stuff for the 'bring and buy' sale at the fête.

I let him go and looked around. 'So — what did you win — where is it?'

29

The cheeky grin that I loved so much lit up his face and he picked up a plastic supermarket carrier bag from the floor. Opening it he held it out for me to look inside.

'Tadaah!'

I could hardly believe my eyes. 'It's a teddy — your teddy.'

'I know. They'd put him on the tombola stall. I bought a ticket and I won him. Dad's got to let me keep him now, hasn't he?'

I wasn't so sure. 'Well — maybe we'd better keep him out of sight for the time being,' I suggested. 'Just in case. Where are Paul and David?'

'Waiting outside. I said I'd ask you first.'

'Well you'd better go and get them,' I laughed. 'Is fish fingers and chips OK?'

'Great!' he called over his shoulder on his way out.

As I peeled potatoes I thought about Charles, away at a conference. He was away an awful lot of weekends for one reason or another. The business, Grayson Electronics, was doing very well and it was the price one had to pay for success, or so he was always telling me.

Ever since we moved into Crayshore Manor he'd been urging me to engage a housekeeper or at least someone to cook and do the housework but so far I had held out against it. He refused point blank to allow me to go back to work for him, which is what I would have preferred. What else would I do with my time? With Charles working long hours and very often weekends and Harry off to boarding school soon life was going to be pretty empty and aimless.

There had been endless arguments about Harry going away to school. In my opinion he was too young.

'Why can't he go at eleven as he would if he stayed at home?'

Charles had laughed. 'That's Irish!'

'You know what I mean,' I argued. 'He'd move on to secondary school at eleven, so why can't he wait till then to go to your precious old school?'

His face set in the determined lines I'd come to know all too well. 'He's an only child and he's getting hopelessly spoiled.'

'No he's not!'

'Admit it, Fran, you baby him. Do you want him to grow up into an effeminate ninny?'

'Plenty of boys go to the local grammar school without growing up into ninnies.'

He threw down the newspaper he'd been reading. 'Maybe not, but they don't have you as a mother, do they?'

His words hurt. When Harry was born there had been complications and I was told that it was doubtful that I'd be able to conceive again so Harry was especially precious because of that. They must have known at the hospital that Harry wasn't my first child, but no one mentioned the fact, something for which I was infinitely grateful. When Mum came to see me and her new grandson she asked me if anyone had enquired about my previous pregnancy. I was surprised. After it was over it had never been mentioned again — till now. I told her nothing had been said and she was clearly relieved.

Obviously she wouldn't have wanted Charles to know about my guilty secret and she wasn't alone in that.

I was sixteen and in my GCSE year when it happened. Pete and I had known each other since primary school. It was only when we reached puberty that we started seeing one another as boyfriend and girlfriend. I adored him. He was such fun. His parents, unlike mine, both worked and were very free and easy with their kids. Lisa and Frank, his brother and sister were older than him and both at work so their house was often empty during the day. Sometimes after school I'd go to his house and we'd play videos or listen to music but then things grew more serious between us and one day we got carried away and things went too far. It was just the once, but as they say — once is all it takes.

I took it for granted that Pete would stand by me but when I told him I thought I might be pregnant, I was completely shattered when he refused to take it seriously.

'You can't be. It was only the once and everyone says it can't happen the first time — unless . . . ' He looked at me in a way that turned my heart to ice.

'Pete! You can't think . . . '

He shrugged defensively. 'Well, how do I know? If you did it with me how do I know there haven't been others?'

I was speechless with hurt as I watched him walk away. After that he ignored me, refusing to speak to me, even when I followed him home and begged him. It was the most miserable time of my life. I didn't know which way to turn. As the weeks went by I couldn't face telling my parents so I took the line of least resistance, trying to convince myself that if I ignored it maybe it would simply go away.

No one knew. Pete obviously hadn't told anyone and I didn't even confide in my best friends. I carried on at school and took my exams. To my relief nothing showed and by the time term ended and I was six months pregnant I was as slim as ever, but after that it gradually began to be noticeable. I made excuses not to go out, wore loose tops and stayed in my room a lot until eventually Mum's suspicions were aroused and she came upstairs and asked me outright if I had anything to tell her. It was then that I blurted out the truth, relieved in a way to get it out in the open.

My relief was short lived. Dad had to know of course and their reaction was even more awful than I'd anticipated. They sat in judgement on me, appalled that I could have behaved so immorally — let them down so badly after their careful upbringing, and they were furious when I refused to tell them who the father was. I wasn't protecting Pete. I was afraid he might repeat his earlier accusations and that my parents might believe him. It was made all too clear to me that I was an ungrateful child and an enormous disgrace and disappointment. It was also made clear to me that there would be no question of keeping the baby. As soon as it was born it would go straight for adoption. At sixteen and still living under my adoptive parents' roof I had no choice but to agree.

'*Mum! Watch out, the chip pan is smoking!*'

I spun round at Harry's alarmed warning and pulled the pan off the heat, smiling reassuringly at him. 'It's OK. I was miles away. Tea will be about ten minutes so the three of you just have time to wash your hands.'

* * *

Dad drove me down to Dorset soon after my shame was revealed. I was to stay with his sister, Aunt Mavis, until the baby was born. Mavis wasn't my real aunt of course and it was clear from the start that she resented having me to stay. I helped as much as I could with the housework and shopping. She wasn't exactly unkind but from time to time she spoke of how she had warned her brother and sister-in-law at the time not to take the risk of adopting. She would make snide remarks about 'bad blood', saying that adopted children were always 'a gamble' and an 'unknown quantity', reminding me of my obligations and how ungrateful I was to reward them in this way. Once she looked me up and down and shook her head. 'Who'd have thought it?' she muttered. 'A dowdy little thing like you.'

When I went into labour she drove me to the hospital and left me there. She picked me up when I was discharged and a week later I was on my way home, my baby girl no more than a fleeting memory of blonde hair as soft as

34

thistledown, heart-breaking blue eyes looking trustingly up into mine. I thought that the painful ache in my empty arms would surely kill me.

At home I wasn't encouraged to wallow in my wretchedness. 'It's over now, we'll forget it,' I was told. But I couldn't forget. At night I'd cry myself to sleep in secret, stifling my sobs in the pillow as I agonized about my baby. In my heart I'd called her Carolyn. Where was she now? Would she be loved as I would have loved her? How could I bear the thought of her growing up in the belief that I'd abandoned her? But in the daytime there was no time for regrets or dreams of what might have been. I'd had a lucky escape, I was told. I should be grateful for a roof over my head and good Christian parents. Now it was time to grow up, to train for a job and start to earn my own living.

I enrolled at the local college for a secretarial course. It was a new environment. My friends had gone — Sophie to sixth form college and Katie to some dead end job. I was too ashamed to seek them out. The other girls on my course seemed so young to me, so light-hearted and fancy free. They seemed little more than children and compared to them I felt a hundred years old. Occasionally one of them would invite me to join the crowd for an evening out, to a club or disco but I could imagine the scene if I dared to suggest it at home. I'd already learned that I was never to be trusted again.

★ ★ ★

35

The three boys ate their tea in the kitchen, chattering to each other about the fête, about football and swimming and all the other things little boys are interested in. Soon Harry would have to say goodbye to his friends and try to make new ones, just as I had all those years ago, but he wasn't shy like me. He had a friendly, gregarious nature and he had no shameful secret to cut him off from the rest. He surely wouldn't find it a problem. Oh, I hoped so *much* that he wouldn't find it a problem.

★ ★ ★

I qualified well at the end of my course and worked for a year in an insurance firm. When I saw the job with Grayson Electronics advertised, I applied. It was an up-and-coming firm and although the job advertised was only temporary, the money was good and I thought that even as a temporary job it would look good on my CV. I was anxious to be earning enough money to be able to leave home and get a little place of my own. I didn't think I had the remotest chance of getting the job and no one could have been more surprised than me when I got it.

The outgoing PA, who was leaving to have a baby, invited me to have coffee with her during which she filled me in on 'The Boss'.

'Charles is a lovely man,' she told me, leaning confidentially across the table in the little café round the corner from the office. 'He's a good boss, very kind and considerate, but he's in the middle of a rather acrimonious divorce at the moment so you have to make allowances for his mood swings.'

She told me she had loved the job and looked forward to returning to it when her baby was a year old. As it happened she never came back.

When I began working for Grayson Electronics, Charles was in his late thirties. He was the archetypal romantic novel hero, handsome, tall and well built, his thick hair attractively streaked with silver. His dark eyes were shrewd, summing up people and situations quickly and on my first day as his PA, I couldn't have been more nervous. When I made my third stupid mistake and was close to tears he smilingly put me at my ease.

'It's your first day, Frances. You're not going to get everything right straight away,' he said kindly. He explained that the reason he hadn't engaged an experienced PA was that she would have had to unlearn her old boss's ways and habits.

'I need to train you to my ways,' he told me. 'Can't do with someone who's always telling me how they did things at her old firm and how much better it was. I don't think you'll find me too difficult to work with,' he continued with a smile. 'I'm told that I do sometimes have a tendency towards sarcasm. If that happens just tell me to calm down — or chill out, or whatever it is you youngsters say these days. Right?' He smiled that thousand watt smile of his and won me over completely.

I learned quickly, loving the job and the environment. GE was a good firm to work for with excellent facilities. Charles had the mood swings I'd been warned about but knowing the circumstances I made allowances. Usually he'd be quiet. Sometimes he'd snap. I soon discovered that when he was like that it was usually triggered by a new complication in his divorce and I learned to get on with my work quietly and wait for him to come round.

A lot of gossip and rumours went round the office. The general consensus seemed to be that his wife was a complete bitch, bent on bleeding him dry. Once she turned up at the office on a day when Charles was away. She was very glamorous in her designer outfit and attractive in a hard way. She quizzed me about my background and education in a way that I resented and I guessed that the real reason for her visit was to look me over. Her husband suddenly appointing a PA half his age had clearly aroused her suspicions. Proof that he was having an affair would presumably provide a useful lever to extract more money from the divorce settlement. But she took one disparaging look at my clothes and hair, my pale face, devoid of make-up and clearly decided that I was not in her husband's league. It didn't do a lot for my ego at the time.

Six weeks later Charles arrived at the office one morning with a crate of champagne which he took to the canteen with instructions that everyone was to have a glass with their lunch.

'My decree came through at last,' he confided to me as he closed the office door. 'Couldn't let it go without some kind of celebration.'

I smiled. 'Congratulations.' Immediately I felt my colour rise. 'Oh! I mean — I really meant to say I'm sorry . . . '

He was laughing. 'I know what you meant and congratulations is very much in order so don't worry.'

I bit my lip. 'Well, I shall certainly look forward to my glass of champagne.'

'Oh, you're not getting one,' he said gravely. Seeing my crestfallen face he added with a smile. 'You're not getting anything in the canteen today because I'm taking you out to lunch, so your first job this morning will be to ring and book a table for two at Donnizetti's.' He looked at my startled face. 'Oh, don't you like Italian food?'

'Yes, I love it, but . . . '

'That's all right then. Shall we say one-thirty?'

That was the first of many so-called 'working lunches'. Over them Charles gradually learned more about me. He had a way of getting information out of you almost without your knowledge. He discovered that I was adopted and that I didn't get along too well with my adoptive parents and their Victorian attitude to life; he learned that I longed for a place of my own, for which I was saving. The lunches somehow turned seamlessly into dinners and eventually the pretence that we were working was abandoned. Charles told me that he'd handed over the marital home to Celia, his ex-wife and now he was living in a flat at the top of a large fashionable riverside block.

'It's very impersonal,' he said rather wistfully. 'I chose it because it was furnished — couldn't be bothered to go to all the trouble of buying furniture again. But it's not a home, just a place to crash, basically.' He gave me a wry smile. 'It takes a woman to make a real home.' His fingertips touched mine across the table. 'I bet you anything that when you get that little pad you're saving up for you'll make it a home instantly, even if it's just a bedsit.' He suddenly looked at me, his head on one side. 'Frances, do I pay you enough?'

I blushed. 'Yes. Why do you ask?'

He shook his head. 'I don't know. Forgive me, but are you going without things to save for your own flat?'

'No!' My cheeks grew even hotter. 'What kind of things?'

He shrugged. 'Don't take this the wrong way but, well, you know — stuff that most women like: clothes, hair dos, make-up.'

I hid my scarlet face in my coffee cup. 'I — I've never really gone in for all that.'

'You should, you know.' His fingers curled round mine. 'You're a very pretty girl. You could make so much more of yourself.'

I looked at him. 'You mean I'm plain. I know that. I've always known.'

'*Plain!*' He laughed. 'You're far from plain, Frances, believe me. You have beautiful eyes. They're the colour of the sea and so expressive. You have a lovely complexion and your hair . . . ' He reached out to tuck a stray strand behind one ear. 'It's a delightful corn colour. Some lighter highlights would do wonders for you. Why don't you try it?'

Suddenly I felt angry. 'I'm *me*,' I said brushing his hand aside. 'This is the way I am and anyone who doesn't like me the way I am can do the other thing.'

He looked surprised. '*Frances*! I've never seen you get feisty before. You should do it more often. Your eyes are sparkling and you have the most delightful colour in your cheeks.'

Being criticised was bad enough but I hated the fact that he was laughing at me. I gathered up my coat and bag and stood up. 'It's late. I have to go now.'

'Of course.' As he drove me home Charles broke the awkward silence between us. 'I've offended you. I'm so sorry, Frances. It was unintentional.' He looked at me. 'Am I forgiven?'

I nodded miserably without returning his look. 'Of course.'

But later in my room I thought about what he had said and made up my mind not to go out with him any more. It was unprofessional. Clearly he was sorry for me, after what he'd said tonight that much was all too clear. He realized that I had no social life and was trying to make my life a little more interesting — plus the fact that since his divorce he probably felt a bit adrift. Remembering his words I peered at myself in the mirror and asked myself if he could be right. I'd always been shy and, if I were truthful, I tried to merge into the background as much as possible. But would more fashionable clothes and a new haircut help my confidence? Should I buy some make-up and experiment? But those things cost money, I reminded myself. And I needed to save as much as I could if I was ever going to get that flat.

Oddly enough my parents made no objections to Charles taking me for the occasional dinner. It was only when the outings stopped that any concern was shown.

'You and Mr Grayson haven't fallen out, have you?' Mum asked me one evening when we were washing up after the evening meal. I looked at her.

'Of course not. He's my boss.'

'But you seemed to be getting on so well — er — outside of office hours.'

'We're still getting on well,' I told her. 'I think he was lonely after his divorce. Perhaps he's met someone else now.' Though I knew this wasn't true. Charles had asked me out repeatedly but every time I'd found some excuse not to go.

Mum looked disappointed. 'Oh. I was beginning to think that you and he . . . '

'I told you,' I snapped. 'He's my boss. He's also twice my age.'

'Your father is twelve years older than me,' she said. 'And you could do a lot worse. He's well off and you'd be well looked after.'

'Well, it's not going to happen.' I put the last of the plates away and closed the cupboard door.

'There's no need to snap at me like that.' She shot me a look over her shoulder. 'I hope you're not being too free with him,' she said. 'Just you make sure you let him know that you're not that kind of girl or you'll end up in the same mess you got yourself into before,' she said sharply. 'This time you've got a lot more to lose.'

She was never going to let me forget my teenage lapse — as if I ever would anyway. I didn't reply, just left the kitchen and went upstairs to look at my latest bank statement. The sooner I got out of here, the better.

The following week it was my twentieth birthday. Charles had arrived at the office early and was waiting for me when I arrived. On my desk was a massive bouquet of flowers and a card. As I opened it something fell out. I bent to pick it up and saw that it was a voucher for the local beauty salon; a very generous voucher. I looked up at him.

'Humour me,' he said with a smile. 'I just want you to achieve your full potential. I can see the radiance shining away there under the surface. Let the experts bring it out for you — just for me — please?'

I looked again at the card with its tempting offer of a top to toe make-over. 'I'd be there all day,' I protested.

'That's the idea. You've got the day off, you deserve it. And at the end of it I'm taking you up to town for dinner and the theatre.'

I stared at him. 'To London?'

'That's the city.' He took a step towards me and took both my hands. 'Come on, Frances, you can't refuse, can you?'

'I've never had a present like this,' I whispered.

'So, is that a yes?'

★   ★   ★

I couldn't believe my eyes when I looked into the mirror at the end of my make-over. On impulse I went to the exclusive boutique next door and blew a month's salary on a dress, shoes and bag to wear for the outing to London. When Charles saw, me his eyes shone.

'What did I tell you? You're beautiful! Would it ruin the make-up if I kissed you?'

'I don't think so,' I smiled as he held out his arms but what I'd expected to be a peck on the cheek turned out to be a full on kiss that left me breathless and trembling.

The evening was magical. I'd never known anything like it. At the end of it Charles told me he'd booked us in at a Mayfair hotel — two single rooms, though as it happened we used only one. The following morning he asked me to marry him and the rest, as they say, is history.

★ ★ ★

'Mum! Can Paul and David stay for a swim?'

Startled, I spun round. 'What? A swim?' I looked out of the window. 'Well, if you like but it's raining.'

'That's OK,' he grinned. 'I love being in the pool when it's raining. It makes the water feel really warm.' He paused halfway through the door. 'Why don't you come too?'

I shook my head. 'Not today, darling. I don't share your enthusiasm for cold showers.'

He pulled a face. 'Come on, Mum. Don't be a wuss.'

I laughed. 'That about sums me up. No, you go and enjoy yourselves but don't stay in too long and get cold.'

'We won't.' He rushed off excitedly and I sat down at the kitchen table with a cup of coffee. The swimming pool was relatively new. We'd only had it installed that spring. Harry adored it. Children were so easy to please at his age. In a few years he'd be into motorbikes and driving lessons. He'd be off to university and a new life — parties and girlfriends and God knows what else. I'd have lost him, I told myself miserably. If only I could have had these last few years of his childhood.

★   ★   ★

Our wedding was a quiet affair. Mum was disappointed. She'd been hoping for the full works — a church ceremony with me in a massive meringue and veil, a reception at a smart hotel and photographs in the local county magazine — all so that she could boast to her friends of course. Instead we had a brief register office ceremony and a meal at a restaurant for Charles's close friends and family. I knew that Mum and Dad felt a little out of their depth, especially with Charles's parents who'd flown over from France, where they'd lived since their retirement. Mum wore a serviceable navy two-piece, justifying the extravagance by assuring Dad that it would come in useful for other such occasions. Dad wore his funeral suit. They told me afterwards that they were selling up and going down to Dorset to live nearer to Aunt Mavis. I tried not to show my relief.

Sometimes I think back to my twentieth birthday and I see what I was too flattered to see at the time: it was the day that Charles began to take control of me. I often wonder what he would have done if I'd resented his offer of a make-over and refused it, if I'd come out of the beauty salon looking worse than when I went in, if my taste in clothes had been brash and common. Somehow I must have passed the test of potential trophy wife material.

It took me some time to see the truth, which was that basically we were both running away from something: Charles from enforced bachelorhood, which, to his surprise he had discovered that he hated and me from the crippling burden of my parents' relentless condemnation. Each of us thought we saw something in the other that would fill a gap. Charles needed a home maker, someone young enough to give him the son he'd always wanted, whilst I craved the love, warmth and approval I'd never known. Instead I got a husband who only saw me as a means to an end, a beautiful empty home and the cherished child I was now about to lose.

4

KATIE

The train was crowded and by the time I'd queued for the bus I was soaked. Who'd have thought that such a lovely summer day could turn out so wet? And of course I didn't have an umbrella with me. Actually I don't own an umbrella. Every time I buy one I leave it somewhere. I've lost count of all the umbrellas I've lost so in the end I gave up buying them and now I just leave it to chance.

It was a relief to get back to my tiny flat in Hackney Road, change out of my damp clothes and put my feet up with a cuppa to think about the day. I really enjoyed it. It was great seeing Sophie and Fran again. Of course all our lives have taken very different directions since we were all at school together, but I could tell that underneath they were still the same — like me. After the first few minutes the years seemed to roll back and we all reverted to our schoolgirl selves.

Going back over our natter I winced at the thought of some of the things I'd said. I really must learn to 'engage brain' as they say. Why on earth had I said I was a fashion designer? They hadn't believed me of course. They must have thought that nothing had changed and that I was still fantasizing — which is true to a certain extent. It's part of my nature. I've always done it, maybe I always will, though not to the crazy, outrageous extent that I did when I was a kid. Now it's more what I'd prefer to call exaggeration. Anyway, hearing all about their exotic lifestyles I had to think of something interesting to tell them about me, didn't I? Not that it was a total fib. I've been designing clothes for a while now. I just haven't managed to get anyone interested enough to buy any of my designs. But give it time, eh?

I work in a rather exclusive little boutique in Kensington called Fantaisie, and I have to admit that once or twice I've pinched the odd design for the dresses I make. I've always altered them a little, just to be on the safe side and anyway I only did it as a favour for customers who couldn't afford the real thing. Over the past few years I've worked up quite a nice little clientele with my dressmaking: evening gowns and bridesmaid dresses, outfits for the bride's mum and white dresses for little girls taking their first communion. About a year ago I was asked to make my first wedding dress. That was a big thrill, except that the bride didn't have a clue what she wanted. I talked to her, made a few sketches and got some fabric samples for her to see. We tried this and that and eventually I came up with something she was pleased with. At the wedding — to which I was invited — a lot of people asked who made the dress. I got several more orders through it. That was what gave me the idea of designing myself and so far it's proving quite popular, in a small way. Someone suggested taking some of my designs to one of the big fashion houses, but so far I've chickened out on that.

At the moment I'm working on a wedding dress which has to be ready for early August so I'd better get my skates on. I have to do my sewing work at weekends and in the evenings after work, which takes a lot of self discipline. Being at today's reunion meant I'd lost a whole day so I told myself that when I'd made myself something to eat I'd better get down to it.

This dress has a lot of beadwork on the bodice so while I'm sitting here sewing away I'm remembering the events of the day. When we were at school I was always aware that Sophie and Fran had very different situations at home to me. Sophie had parents who spoiled her with toys and clothes and everything a child could possibly want. Fran's parents weren't as well off but her mum was always there after school to pick her up and take her to the park or shopping. I envied them both but not in a bad way. I never felt spiteful towards them. They were good friends to me. They never made nasty remarks or bullied me, like some girls did, about my accent, my shabby clothes and unruly ginger hair. I loved them both for that.

I can't remember my dad. He was killed in some kind of fight in Belfast where we used to live when I was a baby. Mum did her best bringing up my four brothers and me, after she lost Dad. She wanted to move away from Ireland to get us away from the troubles but one of my older brothers was already working and the other two, who are twins, were in the middle of exams at school. As soon as they left school and started working Mum sent them to live with my gran and brought my brother, Liam and I to England. I was five by then and Liam was fifteen. She had a friend in Leicester who found us a flat in the same high-rise block where she lived.

Poor Mum worked so hard, going out to clean offices early in the morning while Liam and I were still asleep and then again to another job in a factory after we'd gone to school,

When Liam was twenty he married a girl he met at St Joseph's where he was a server. His wife, Shauna moved in with us after the wedding. Right from the start she never tried to hide the fact that she didn't like me. A year later, Mum — who'd never been very strong — got ill and died, worn out with worry and work. After the funeral Shauna suggested to Liam that he should have me taken into care but he refused point blank. After that she resented me even more.

When Shauna had baby Declan we were allotted a council house. It was nice for me because it was closer to school, but the minute I got home I had to look after the baby and make Liam's tea while Shauna went off to her evening job in the local pub. Declan was a miserable baby. He never stopped leaking — from both ends — and no matter what you did with him he cried non-stop. He was enough to put anyone off having kids for life. It was almost impossible for me to concentrate on my homework and I never seemed to have time to catch up. Saturday mornings I had to do the housework while Shauna went shopping and then Saturday evenings and Sunday mornings I had a paper round. The result was that I failed most of my GCSEs. The only ones I passed were art and needlework, my favourite subjects. Shauna said it was because I was thick and good for nothing. Liam just smiled sheepishly and said nothing. He never stood up for me. I know he sympathized but I think he was half afraid of Shauna's vile temper.

Of course I never let on to Sophie and Fran how bad things were at home. I was too ashamed. I painted an idyllic picture of life with Liam and Shauna, who I described as a glamorous model, and my angelic baby nephew. I made up stories all the time, some of them so outrageous that I knew perfectly well they wouldn't believe — like how I was really a princess who'd been changed with another baby at birth. Then there was the time I said I'd met Sean Connery — who was related to me of course — and he told me he'd get me into the next Bond film and make me a millionaire. Sophie and Fran knew it was all fantasy but it made them laugh and they always wanted to hear what came next because I made it sound so exciting. I never told them about the drudgery I endured or the crafty slaps Shauna handed out or the names she called me when Liam wasn't around, so I suppose that when I failed most of my GCSEs they must have shared Shauna's view that I was thick, not that either of them was mean enough to say so.

After school I sort of lost touch with the girls. Sophie went off to a sixth form college and then to art school and Fran just seemed to disappear. I got a job in a supermarket, stacking shelves. I saved as much as I could out of my meagre wages. It wasn't much because Shauna took rent off me as well as expecting me to carry on with the chores the same as before. As soon as I could I found a little bedsit of my own. It wasn't much but it was bliss to be able to come home and actually have some free time. There was a hell of a row when I announced that I was moving out. Shauna called me an ungrateful little — well, you can guess, but I know for a fact that it was only the rent she took off me and the free skivvying and baby sitting that she was going to miss.

I was eighteen when I decided to move down here to London. Once again it was to get right away from Shauna. My new-found freedom didn't last long. She was soon knocking on my door several evenings a week to beg me to babysit. There was always an excuse — she had to go out unexpectedly and couldn't find anyone to watch Dec, she'd booked a sitter but they'd let her down at the last minute. I knew she was lying of course. I'd heard that she was going clubbing when Liam was working nights and she was getting quite a reputation. I had a strong suspicion that she was cheating on him, but I had no proof so I didn't dare say anything. I could have refused to make things easy for her but by that time Declan was six and it was clear that she was neglecting him. At least if I went round to babysit I could give him a bath and read him a bedtime story, poor little scrap. I knew the marriage was in trouble and I could see things getting nasty. I hated the thought of getting involved in it all so finally I decided that the only way out of it was to move right away.

By this time I'd been promoted to the checkouts at the supermarket and I applied for a transfer to a new branch that was about to open in Hackney. To my delight I got the transfer and found the little flat where I still live. It's really a bedsit with an en-suite shower room and cupboard-like kitchen but it's cheap for London and it's part of what was once a lovely old house in Hackney Road. The bus for Liverpool Street station stops right outside so it suits me down to the ground.

I'd been here about a year when I saw the job advertised. It was for a sales girl at a boutique called Fantaisie in Chelsea. The name intrigued me. If ever a place was made with me in mind this had to be it! I applied and was offered an interview, I took a trip up to the King's Road to suss the place out and my heart sank a bit when I saw how posh and up-market it was, but having been offered an interview I wasn't going to pass it up. On the day I took a lot of trouble with my make-up, did my best to tame my horrible hair and searched my skimpy wardrobe for something suitable to wear but when I got there it was obvious that I couldn't hold a candle to the other applicants. I was totally gob-smacked when I was offered the job. I think what swung it for me was the GCSEs in art and needlework and the fact that I was willing and able to do customers' alterations.

So that's all about me. Not very exciting like Sophie and Fran, is it? I haven't found a rich, handsome husband and I haven't achieved any dreams — yet. But I'm happy with my job and my little sideline. I lost touch with my brothers back in Ireland when Gran died but now and again Liam comes down to London to see me. He and Shauna split up a few years ago. In the end she did a bunk with some guy she was working with. I think secretly Liam was relieved. He's with a lovely girl now and seems very happy. Sometimes he brings Declan with him. Dec's nearly twenty now and at Leicester University. He's grown up to be a very nice young man considering what a lousy start he had. He's not bad looking except that he's got my crazy red hair, poor kid, but he turned out to be quite clever and he's studying architecture. I often think how proud Mum would have been, God bless her.

* * *

By the time it was ten o'clock my eyes were beginning to smart so I put the sewing away and made myself a cup of cocoa. While I was drinking it I got the card out of my bag and looked again at the numbers and addresses on it. It would be fun to keep in touch with Soph and Fran. Did they really mean it when they said they'd like to meet up again? These things are easy to say in the heat of the moment, but after a few days back in their busy and eventful lives they might regret saying it and secretly hope they wouldn't hear from me again. I tucked the card back inside my bag. Oh well, time would tell, wouldn't it? And whatever happens it was lovely to see them both again.

5

'Good morning, Fantaisie Boutique, Imogene speaking. How can I help?'

Clearly the voice wasn't Katie's, as Fran had hoped it would be. 'I wonder, would it be possible to speak to one of your assistants,' she asked. 'Katie MacEvoy?'

There was a brief frosty silence at the other end of the line. 'May I ask what it is about? Is it an emergency?'

'Well, no. She's an old friend of mine and I've lost her number,' Fran paused. 'It's not really a personal call. I need an outfit for a special occasion and I know she works there. I was going to ask . . .'

'Oh, I see. Please hold. I'll see if she's free. Can I give her your name?'

'Of course. It's Frances Grayson.'

A few minutes later Katie's voice came over the line. 'Hi, Fran. How lovely to hear from you.'

'I'm so sorry to ring you at work, Katie, but I've somehow mislaid your number.'

'That's OK.' Katie tried to ignore Imogene's eyes boring into her. The boutique's owner was very strict about personal calls. 'Maybe I could ring you back in my lunch break. We're a bit busy at the moment and I'd love to chat.'

'Right. You've got my number?'

''Course. Talk later then. Bye.' Katie replaced the receiver and glanced apologetically at her

56

boss. 'Sorry about that, Imogene. She'd lost my number and . . . '

'So she said.' Imogene looked over the tops of her glasses. 'Katie, I hardly need to remind you of my rule about personal calls. It's most unprofessional.'

'Well *I* know that, but she didn't. I've said I'm sorry. I'm ringing her back in my lunch break.'

'She mentioned that she needed an outfit for a special occasion,' Imogene said. 'I hope you're not giving this number to your dressmaking customers.'

Katie winced. Her secret had been blown a few weeks ago when the mother of one of her brides had brought photographs of the wedding into the shop to show her. There was nothing Imogene could do about it of course but she'd been throwing out snide little remarks ever since.

Katie shook her head. 'Fran is married to a very wealthy businessman,' she said. 'If she's looking for a special outfit it'll have to have a designer label.'

The frost holding the corners of Imogene's mouth down thawed and they lifted slightly. 'Oh! Well, in that case I hope you'll do all you can to encourage her to buy it here. Have you any idea what the occasion might be?'

'I didn't get the chance to find out, did I?' Katie said. 'Maybe she'll tell me at lunch.'

In spite of what Katie had told Frances, the shop wasn't busy at all and she knew that Imogene was worried. The turnover had dropped alarmingly since the beginning of the year. So much so that the newest girl Imogene had taken

57

on as a junior had recently been let go. Plenty of people came in to look round but not so many were willing or able to fork out the prices Imogene charged any more. Katie had tentatively suggested stocking a cheaper range or that Fantaisie might start a hire service, mainly for hats and ball gowns, but the boutique's owner had thrown up her hands in horror at the very idea.

'Things aren't that bad! I sincerely hope that Fantaisie will never be reduced to *that*,' she said.

Katie said nothing but she knew that if she was running the boutique she'd do anything to keep it afloat. She also sensed that some of Imogene's friends, the ones she was so afraid of losing face with, were as hard up as she was and would welcome help with keeping up appearances.

In her lunch hour Katie usually went to a little fast food café near the underground station. Tucked into a corner with her panini and coffee she took out her mobile and the card with Fran's address and landline number on it and tapped it in. Fran answered almost at once.

'Hi, Katie. Thanks for ringing back. I hope I didn't cause any problems earlier.'

'No, don't worry. You mentioned making a trip to town for an outfit. When do you plan on coming?'

'Well, next week actually. I thought I'd ring Sophie and see if she's available to come too and the three of us could meet up — maybe have lunch?'

'That sounds lovely. I get the afternoon free on

Thursdays because normally I work all day Saturday. I was only able to come to the reunion because Imogene owed me some time off.'

'That would be great. Next Thursday would be fine for me and as it's the school holidays Sophie should be free too. I'll ring her right away and get back to you. I've got your number on my phone now.'

'OK. I'll look forward to seeing you both.'

Katie felt buoyed up as she walked back to work. She'd been hoping she'd see her two old school friends again and if Fran bought a nice outfit it would earn her a few brownie points with Imogene too.

★ ★ ★

By closing time on Saturday Fantaisie had suffered its worst week ever. Katie found Imogene in the office, her shoulders slumped as she pored over the boutique's accounts on her computer. In front of her on the desk was her calculator, a glass and a half empty bottle of wine. She looked up and hastily tried to adjust her expression as Katie looked in.

'Oh, Katie! I thought you'd gone home.'

'No, I was just putting the dust sheets on and having a tidy round.' She took a tentative step forward. 'You look tired. Shall I make you a coffee before I go?'

Imogene removed her glasses and pulled back her shoulders. 'I need something a bit stronger than coffee.' She closed down the computer with a flourish and threw her calculator into a drawer.

'Sod this lot! Let's go to the pub.'

'Oh!' Katie was taken aback. 'Well, OK if you like.'

'I do like, most definitely. I need to talk to you too, so get your coat.'

It was a pleasant warm evening and The Feathers, the pub round the corner from Fantaisie, had tables outside among a profusion of flower-filled tubs and hanging baskets. Window boxes overflowed with begonias and geraniums and the air was heady with the scent of dianthus. Imogene chose a table near the door under one of the striped umbrellas and disappeared inside the pub to return a few minutes later carrying two double gins and bottles of tonic water on a tray. Katie was mystified. She'd been working with Imogene for three years but this was the first time she had ever showed any sign of cordiality, let alone invited her to share a social drink. She looked at her boss speculatively. There had to be a snag. Was she about to get the sack? Was business so bad that the boutique was going into bankruptcy? She poured tonic into her glass, took a sip and waited.

Imogene sloshed a small amount of tonic into her gin and swallowed most of it in one gulp. Sighing deeply, she leaned back in her chair. 'Ah, that's better.' She looked at Katie, her face serious. 'You're a good little worker, Katie. I may not always show it but I do appreciate all your hard work.'

'Thanks.'

'And I'm sure I don't have to tell you that

we've just had our worst week yet.'

'I know we haven't sold much.'

'That's the understatement of the year!' Imogene sighed. 'We've got to the stage when something has to be done or I'm very much afraid we're going under.'

'I'm really sorry about that.' Katie took another sip of her drink, wondering what was coming next.

'We've been trading at a loss for the past three months now,' Imogene went on. 'And I don't mean peanuts. I've just had a bill through from the last buying trip. There was a letter with it. They won't deliver the stock until they receive payment.'

'Oh dear. I'm sorry.'

Imogene frowned. 'For God's sake stop saying you're sorry. You sound like a bloody parrot, Katie. I don't want your *sympathy*. I want you to come up with some ideas.'

'*Me?*' Katie stared at her employer. 'You wouldn't want to know about any of *my* ideas. You said . . . '

'Never mind what I said. These are desperate times.' Imogene blew out her cheeks. 'Bloody hell, I've got to have another drink.' She picked up her glass and looked at Katie. 'Another for you?'

Katie nodded. 'OK, thanks but just the tonic this time.' She indicated her still half full glass. Not having eaten much all day the gin was making her head spin a little but it also had the effect of making her more relaxed and confident. Imogene had asked for ideas, well, OK she'd got

61

plenty of those and if Imogene didn't like them
— well, *tough*. It looked as though she was the
one in the driving seat at the moment.

When Imogene was seated again, Katie took a
deep breath. 'I'll tell you one thing: if the boutique was mine I'd do anything to keep it afloat.'

Imogene pulled a face. 'Not *anything*, surely?'
She downed her second double gin without the
addition of tonic water and giggled like a schoolgirl. 'You're not going to suggest we open the
upstairs rooms as a knocking shop, are you?' She
giggled again and hiccupped, so loudly that a few
of the other customers turned to look at her.

Katie was embarrassed. How many glasses of
wine had Imogene had before she started on the
gin? 'Of course I'm not,' she said. 'What do you
take me for?' She tried not to meet the amused
glances of the other drinkers.

Imogene looked suitably contrite. 'Now it's my
turn to say sorry, Katie. I'm embarrassing you.
Fact is I've had nothing to eat all day and I think
I'm a tiny bit drunk. Pop inside and get me a
packet of crisps, there's a dear.'

The crisps seemed to do little to mop up the
alcohol Imogene had consumed but she calmed
down a little as she munched them. 'OK,
sweetie,' she said, crumpling the empty packet.
'Sock it to me. Throw me a life belt.'

Katie looked doubtful. 'Maybe you'd feel
more like brainstorming tomorrow when you
— you're . . . '

'Sober?' Imogene reached out her hand.
'Believe me, if I can't see any light at the end of
the tunnel tonight there probably won't *be* a

62

tomorrow. It's as bad as that. Just give me something to hang on to, Katie, there's a love.' She leaned forward confidentially. 'Look, I'll be straight with you; my ex-husband put up the cash to open Fantaisie. He always said I was a fool when it came to running a business and I can't let him be proved right, can I?'

Katie looked hopeful. 'I suppose he wouldn't help, would he?'

'What, Andrew the Almighty?' Imogene snorted. 'Like hell he would! I can just see his smug, gloating face if I went grovelling to him. He said when he walked out that I'd never survive without him.' Her eyes suddenly filled with tears and her lower lip wobbled. 'But I will, Katie. I bloody *will* if it kills me!'

Katie chewed her bottom lip. This was about more than money. Imogene's self esteem was at stake here too. 'I did suggest starting a hiring service,' she offered tentatively. 'I'm pretty sure a lot of your customers are feeling the pinch too but they don't want people to know. You could do designer ball gowns, wedding outfits, hats for Ascot — stuff like that.'

'But they could only go out once,' Imogene complained. 'I've got quite a small clientele of regular customers as you know. Most of them know each other and go to the same functions. It would be too awful for two of them to hire the same dress. It could ruin me.'

'You'd have to keep careful records of where the things had been worn and who by,' Katie said. 'But I'm sure it could be done.'

Imogene sat back and thought about it. 'I

suppose it might work if I could carry a large enough stock,' she conceded. 'But haut-couture costs a bomb and I might not be able to hire things out enough times to cover the initial cost.'

Katie thought for a moment. 'You would if you went downmarket with them after a few hirings.'

Imogene frowned. *'Downmarket!'* She spat the word out as though it tasted bad. 'You know how I feel about that.'

'I meant somewhere else, not at Fantaisie.'

'But that would mean renting another shop. More expense! I can barely afford the rent on Fantaisie the way things are.'

'You could let me have them,' Katie said with a sudden burst of inspiration. 'We'd have everything dry cleaned and I could do any repairs necessary, then I'd have them at the flat and let my customers have the benefit of them — at a cheaper rate.'

Imogene looked doubtful 'I'm not sure that it'd be legal for you to run a business like that from your flat. What about your landlord?'

'He knows I do a bit of dressmaking. It would just be an extension of that.'

'Would your customers have any need for designer clothes?'

'You bet they would! They've got just as good taste as your customers — just not the money. They'd jump at the chance to go to a wedding in something with a designer label.' She glanced at Imogene as another idea bubbled to the surface. 'Eventually we could even sell them second hand.'

Imogene looked stunned. After chewing this

64

idea over for a moment she looked at Katie. 'You know, I do believe you might have something there,' she said slowly. 'Of course we'd have to cost it all out.' Her eyes narrowed. 'What would be in it for you though? I mean, you clearly aren't planning to do all this for nothing.'

'Of course I'm not!' Katie said firmly. 'To begin with it'd do me out of a lot of business. *And* I'd need a bigger flat.' As Imogene's mouth opened, Katie held up her hand. '*But*, I happen to know that the ground floor flat where I live now is about to become vacant. It's got two bedrooms and a living room. I could use one of the bedrooms for the business.'

'You'd have to be completely up front with your landlord.'

'Of course. But I don't see why he'd object. Anyway, if it really took off we might be able to rent a little shop,' she added hopefully.

'Let's walk before we try running,' Imogene said wryly. 'I'd have to pay you considerably more than I do now for all this and what with one thing and another I don't know how I'd finance it all. I'm going to have a problem paying for the stock I've just ordered, let alone branching out into a new venture.' She shook her head. 'It sounds like a massive risk.'

'They say you have to speculate to accumulate,' Katie said. 'You could ask the bank for a loan.'

Imogene nodded thoughtfully. 'Or re-mortgage my house.'

'It all depends on what Fantaisie means to you and whether you're brave enough to take the bull by the horns.' Katie looked up suddenly. 'I know, why don't you let me do some research?'

'What kind of research?'

'Give me a day off on Monday and I'll go round all the dress hire places. I'll get them from the Yellow Pages, up *and* down- market places. I could see what they charge and do a bit of snooping.' She grinned. 'Who knows? We might even be able to offer a slightly cheaper rate . . . '

'Undercut? That's a bit of a cheek.'

'But not illegal.' Katie shrugged. 'Well, it's just a thought.'

'Katie, you're a treasure,' Imogene said with a grin. 'A devious treasure but a treasure nonetheless. OK, Monday is all yours. Go and do your darndest.'

★　★　★

The following Monday Katie hit the ground running. On Sunday she'd contacted her landlord about the ground floor flat, asking what the rent would be and securing his promise of first refusal when it became vacant. Then, with the aid of the Yellow Pages she made a list of as many dress-hire shops as she thought she could manage in one day and another list of all the important details she needed to find out.

Being naturally friendly and easy to talk to she had no trouble in engaging the assistants in conversation, no trouble either in creating a plausible reason for her seeking out the hire establishments.

At lunchtime she found a small park where

66

she sat and ate her packed lunch and made notes. She'd discovered that the cost of hiring an outfit with a good designer label was quite high and there was also a deposit to make as insurance against damage or loss, repayable on return — something she hadn't thought of. All garments were dry cleaned after every hiring, but she learned from one of the chattier assistants that they had an arrangement with a local dry cleaning firm who gave them special rates. She had a good look through the stock in each of the shops she visited and felt sure that Fantaisie could offer something more exclusive and, as she pointed out to Imogene later, with her able to do any repairs and minor alterations, they'd save money all round. (Nothing like making yourself indispensable, she told herself.)

Imogene was delighted and announced that she had been to the bank in her lunch hour to make a tentative enquiry and told to make an appointment to return with a business plan and financial projection the following day when her loan would be given consideration.

'So can you stay behind with me this evening and help me work out some kind of business plan?' she said. 'I'll treat you to dinner afterwards in lieu of overtime.'

Katie was stunned. Never in a million years would she have imagined Imogene putting so much faith in her. 'OK, if you like,' she said nonchalantly. 'I'm not doing anything else.'

'And I think you'd better come to the bank with me tomorrow as well,' Imogene added. 'You're so much better at talking than me. You've got the gift of the gab whereas I'm only articulate when I've got a few drinks inside me as you know.' She smiled ruefully. 'And somehow I don't think that'd go down too well, do you?'

'I think you're probably right,' Katie agreed.

★   ★   ★

They sat in the office after closing time working on the business plan. When it came to the financial projection Katie found that although she had failed her maths GCSE she was actually better at it than Imogene. Finally they had worked out something that was to Imogene's satisfaction. Before she began printing it out ready for the bank Katie decided to voice the idea that had been nagging at her all day.

'Imogene. Before you start there's just one thing.'

'What? Have I forgotten something?'

Katie cleared her throat. Her heart was thumping and her mouth was dry. What she was about to say might well ruin the whole thing. 'It's just, won't the advisor at the bank wonder why I'm there too.'

'I'll explain that you're my assistant.' Imogene shook her head exasperatedly. 'All right, I'll say it was all your idea if you like. Will that do?'

Katie took a deep breath. 'I'd rather you said I was a partner.'

Imogene stared at her. '*Partner?* You've got to be joking!'

It was the reaction Katie had expected and she stuck to her guns. 'No, I'm not. After all it *was* my idea. I could have started a hiring agency up on my own without saying anything to you. I'm having to take on a bigger flat and work longer hours and you said yourself you couldn't afford to pay me much more. There has to be more in it for me than that.'

Imogene sat back in her chair and looked at Katie for a century-long minute. After a moment she said. 'OK, you've got a point. So, how much cash were you planning to put into the venture, Katie?'

'Cash?' Katie's jaw dropped. 'I wasn't. I mean — I haven't got any.'

'Then how do you think you could have started up a business on your own?' Katie shook her head and Imogene went on, 'That's what being a partner means: equal ownership. Surely you can see that if I'm going to share the profits with you, you have to share in the initial outlay. That's fair, isn't it?'

'Yes, but my contribution to the partnership would be the idea.'

Imogene laughed. 'Oh! You see yourself as the brains of the business, do you?'

Katie thrust her chin out. 'If you want to call it that — yes!'

Imogene's smile faded and for a moment she sat back in her chair, a thoughtful expression on her face. Katie held her breath until finally Imogene looked up.

'I appreciate your candour, Katie, and yes, I agree that your idea might well save my business, so how about this: I make you a partner in the hire business. Not Fantaisie. My ex's name is

69

still on the lease of the shop and it could get complicated. But the hire business is something new. We could keep it completely separate. How about this: we give it — this partnership idea — a trial for six months, dividing the profits say — eighty/twenty until we have a proper contract drawn up legally. What do you think?'

'Seventy/thirty,' Katie countered. 'With a view to increasing it to sixty/forty once it's legally binding.'

Imogene gasped. 'I'm beginning to think I've underestimated you, Katie. You've got the bloody cheek of the devil! Look, shall we agree on seventy/thirty for now and see how things go? After all, we haven't got the loan yet.'

Katie held out her hand. 'OK, done,' she said.

★ ★ ★

When Thursday morning arrived Katie was looking forward to seeing her old friends for lunch and bubbling over to tell them her news. She'd had a call from Fran on her mobile when she was on the bus on her way home on Wednesday evening to tell her what she had arranged.

'I want something suitable to wear for Harry's new school's open day next week,' she said. 'I can't find anything I like locally so I'm hoping to find it at your boutique.'

'I'm sure we'll find something to suit you,' Katie said. 'What time are you coming?'

'You said it's your half day, so I'll come close to lunchtime,' Fran said. 'I've booked a table for three at a nice little Italian restaurant I know and arranged to meet Sophie there at half past one.'

Katie sailed through the morning on cloud nine. The meeting at the bank had gone well. The financial advisor had shaken his head when he saw the last six month's figures for the boutique but he seemed impressed with Katie's idea of a dress hire business and after studying the projected figures he thought it might have a good chance of saving the current business. Imogene had pointed out that they planned to rent a small outlet shop in the future in which to dispose of exhausted stock second hand and the advisor had nodded his head approvingly. Finally, after some consideration and a brief consultation with a more senior colleague, a loan had been agreed. Imogene had taken Katie out for dinner that evening to celebrate.

Fran arrived soon after midday and Katie was gratified to see that Imogene approved of her appearance and style. The outfit she wore was clearly of the quality Imogene favoured and she summed up her taste quickly which was what she was so good at.

In her turn Fran was impressed by the boutique's wide choice and was soon being ushered into one of the changing rooms with three outfits. Katie went with her but she had already guessed which one would suit her best. She was right. When Fran emerged from the changing room in the silver grey dress with its smooth, figure-hugging lines, Imogene beamed.

'That looks so elegant,' she enthused. 'Not many of my customers could wear something so plain,' she said. 'But then not many have your figure. On you it looks perfect. I'd suggest no jewellery except perhaps some rather special earrings. Now, what about accessories?' She looked at Fran, her head on one side. 'I think either cerise or kingfisher blue.' She looked at Katie. 'We've got just the thing, haven't we, Katie?'

Fran tried both and chose the blue accessories, which looked fabulous with her colouring: a stylish wide brimmed hat, matching sandals and a clutch bag. By the time she had paid for her purchases it was almost lunchtime. Imogene looked at Katie as she packed the outfit into one of the distinctive black patent carriers.

'You might as well go too, as you're having lunch with your friends,' she said.

★ ★ ★

Sophie was waiting for them at Napolitano, the Italian restaurant where Fran had booked. She looked a little flushed and explained that she'd almost missed her train because her car had a flat tyre.

'Don't these things always happen at the wrong time?' Fran said as the waiter ushered them to their table.

'That's one of the reasons why I haven't bought a car,' Katie put in as they sat down. 'Though with the way things are developing I might have to rethink that.' To her annoyance a waiter reappeared at that moment and handed each of them a menu, asking if they'd like to order drinks at the same time. Fran looked at the other two.

'Shall we have a bottle of wine?'

They agreed and the waiter departed.

They consulted the menu and agreed on their choice of food. Sophie looked at Katie. 'What were you saying just now — something about recent developments?'

Katie smiled. 'Yes. Imogene — she's my boss — has invited me to be a partner in the business.'

'Really? Well done you.' Sophie and Fran exchanged wry glances but before Katie could continue the waiter reappeared to take their order. Katie bit her lip in frustration. Their bottle of wine arrived at the same time, was duly uncorked, approved by Fran and a glass filled for each of them.

Fran raised her glass. 'To us,' she said. 'Long may we flourish.' She looked at Sophie. 'How are things with you? Is the house restoration going well?'

'Oh yes,' Sophie said. 'Rex is an absolute whiz at all the DIY stuff. Every time I come home I see a difference. And now that the holidays are here I'm helping as much as I can.'

'With moral support and lots of delicious meals, I expect,' Fran said.

'Of course.' Sophie surreptitiously hid her roughened hands and broken nails under the table's pristine white cloth. 'Have to keep his strength up.'

Fran took another sip of her wine and looked at Katie. 'What was that you said about a partnership?'

Katie cleared her throat. *At last!* 'Well, I

suggested to Imogene, the owner of Fantaisie, that we open a hiring service. She thought it was a fantastic idea and she straight away . . . ' Once again the waiter arrived with three steaming plates of lasagne. Katie longed to pick up her plate and empty it over his head. When he had once again withdrawn Sophie looked across the table at Katie.

'So, what about your designing work?'

'Oh, I'll still do that,' Katie told her, picking up her fork. 'We're going to open another shop eventually in East London and I'll be in charge. It's all so exciting.'

'It must be. Congratulations.' Fran and Sophie smiled at her and each other indulgently.

'I'm dying to see your new outfit, Fran,' Sophie said.

'She looks lovely in it,' Katie put in. 'It's to wear at your son's open day at school, is it?'

Fran nodded, lowering her eyes. Every time she thought about it tears threatened, a sight which irritated Charles intensely. She swallowed hard and looked up with a smile. 'He's looking forward to it so much,' she said. 'Charles and I will miss him so much but it's what's best for him after all so we can't be selfish,' she said, echoing Charles's words. 'And of course a whole new world will open up for me.' Again, Charles's words.

'You'll go back to work?' Sophie asked.

'I hope to,' Fran said. 'Being part of Charles's business will be so fulfilling.'

After lunch the three went to a film and afterwards Fran insisted on treating them all to afternoon tea at the Ritz.

They parted company, the three of them agreeing on a date for their next meeting and went their separate ways. On the bus on her way home Katie reflected on the day. Clearly her friends hadn't believed her when she'd told them her news. Why did they think she was still that pathetic, fantasizing schoolgirl from the past? She'd told the truth — well, almost. She had to admit that she'd made it sound just a little bit better than it actually was. She sighed. Maybe one day what was in her head and what came out of her mouth would coincide!

6

SOPHIE

Driving home from the station I couldn't help feeling depressed. It had been a lovely day and I really enjoyed seeing Katie and Fran again but for some reason being with them had made me feel sad. It wasn't their fault of course. They'd been great company, each with their stories of what life held for them in the future. No doubt Katie's bit of news about the partnership was exaggerated but nevertheless, life definitely seemed to be on the up for her. As for Fran — well, she had it made, hadn't she, with her wealthy husband and adored son? They both seemed so fulfilled and happy with life that I'd felt obliged to put on a brave face about my present situation.

It wasn't just that either. They both looked so fantastic. Fran was so *soigné* and well groomed. Even tear-away Katie had looked sophisticated today in the little black dress she had to wear for work, her wild red hair tamed into a neat French pleat.

After lunch, in the Ladies, I took a long hard look at myself in the mirror and decided that the time had definitely arrived when I must change my style. I looked long and hard at the reflection staring back at me and all at once I saw how ludicrous I looked — a thirty-something woman still dressing like an art student. I took in the maxi-skirt decorated with mirror embroidery, the gypsy top and sandals — all of which had seen better, not to say *younger* days. This morning I'd briefly considered making a trip to Fantaisie myself until Fran told me how much she had paid for her chic new outfit. I felt my jaw drop and tried hard not to gape in horror when she casually named the price. The kind of money I'd had to spare for clothes since Rex and I took on the restoration of Greenings wouldn't buy an outfit from a jumble sale let alone designer clothes.

Contrary to the scene I'd painted for the girls, Rex wasn't working on the house at all these days. True, he'd had a lot of commissions and, as he'd pointed out, that was where the bread and butter came from. (Rex is old fashioned about being 'kept' by a woman, even when that woman is his wife.) He's started spending several days a week away from the house, taking the early train up to London in the mornings and returning sometimes quite late at night. He says he needs to keep in closer touch with his agent and calls it 'keeping a finger on the pulse', says it's important to meet up with other freelancers and find out what they are doing. Of course I can see his point but his attitude isn't likely to get the house in order any time soon.

Since school broke up for the summer holidays all my time has been spent in old jeans and baggy tee-shirts; sandpaper, or a paint brush in my hand. My hair badly needs cutting and my hands are a disgrace. Commissions for the portrait work have fallen off too, no doubt due to the recession. I've only had two since May and although I still love the house dearly there are days when I wish we'd never set eyes on it. Bit by bit it's slowly taking over my life and undermining everything including our marriage. There's no time for leisure any more, no time for fun, no time to spend together — at least, not in the way we used to. When we are together nowadays we're always arguing, usually about money. Clearly we can't put the house back on the market until the restoration is finished and at the rate we're going that day grows more distant with every week. It's a 'catch twenty-two' situation.

As I turned the car in through the gates I wondered whether Rex would be at home. However, as I swung round the curve in the drive I saw that a large blue van was parked outside the house. My first thought was that we were being burgled. No doubt they had watched us both leave the house and then broken in to steal the new bathroom equipment, still waiting to be plumbed in. I stopped the car in the drive and got out, reaching into my bag for my mobile. At least I could block their way out.

Phone in hand I gingerly approached the front door, which stood open. I could hear men's voices coming from upstairs. Hastily I punched in 999 and asked for the police. After a moment a voice answered.

'Police.'

'I want to report a burglary.'

'Can you give me your name and address, madam?'

At that moment a man in overalls appeared on the stairs. When he saw me he smiled and called out, 'Hello there! Mrs Turner, is it?'

I nodded, speechlessly. 'Who — who are you?'

'Bob Harris from Harris and Jarrold, builders. Your husband said you'd be surprised when you got home.' He ran down the stairs and began to cross the hall, rubbing his hand on the seat of his overalls before he held it out to me. 'Pleased to meet you.'

I could hear the voice at the other end of the line repeatedly asking for my name. I raised the phone to my mouth again. 'I'm so sorry to have troubled you. It's a misunderstanding.' I switched off the phone and stared at the man.

'I thought we'd got burglars.'

He laughed. 'I warned your old m — er, your hubby that some ladies don't like surprises.'

'But — I don't understand. You say my husband engaged you?'

'That's right.'

'And you're here to do — what?'

He held out his hands. 'You name it. And believe me there's no shortage of jobs.' He began to count off the tasks on his fingers. 'Plumbing in the bathroom and the en-suite shower; tiling them both, *and* the kitchen, not to mention fitting the rest of them kitchen units. I could go on as I'm sure you know.' He smiled sympathetically at me. 'How you've managed with the place in this state all this time beats me. I reckon that old bathroom must've been put in by Adam and 'is mate!' He laughed loudly at his own joke. 'If you ask me, you deserve a medal.'

'Thank you,' I said weakly.

'We've cleared out all the old stuff. It's in the van.' He cleared his throat. 'Er, I know you've only just got in, Mrs T, but we'd really appreciate a cuppa.'

I looked at my watch. 'Isn't it time you were knocking off?'

'Normally it would be, yes, but your hubby wanted us to make a good start today so I said we'd do a couple of hours overtime.'

'I see. Give me a minute to put the car away and I'll put the kettle on.'

Driving the car round to the garage, I fumed. Where did Rex think the money was coming from to pay these builders? And how dare he go out and leave me to walk in on it without a word of warning?

In the kitchen, as I waited for the kettle to boil, I took out my mobile again and selected Rex's number. His phone was switched off and the call went straight to voicemail.

'It's me. I've just got home to find the house full of builders — engaged apparently by you,' I snapped. 'Will you ring me as soon as you get this and tell me what the hell is going on?' I hung up and threw the phone down on the worktop. How dare he do this without talking to me about it first? A voice behind me made me jump.

'Tea up, is it, Mrs T? Me and Jim are spittin' feathers.'

'Right, coming up.' I threw a couple of teabags into two mugs and got out the milk and sugar.

'Three sugars each,' Bob instructed. 'And if you've got any biccies they'll be gratefully

80

received as they say. Be a while before we get anything to eat tonight.'

Tight-lipped I got out a fresh packet of biscuits and a plate.

I sat fuming during the two hours that followed while Bob and Jim banged away upstairs, their portable radio booming out 'heavy metal'. Finally at about half past seven Bob appeared in the kitchen doorway again.

'Right, we're off,' he informed me. 'Broken the back of that bathroom a treat if I do say it myself. Should finish it tomorrow all bein' well as they say. We ain't left you with no lav so you won't have to get a bucket out.' He chuckled. 'We'll be back bright and early in the mornin' if that's OK with you.'

'All right. Thanks, Mr Harris.'

'Oh, call me Bob. Don't stand on ceremony, don't me and Jim. Night then, Mrs T. Have a nice weekend.'

★   ★   ★

After the men had gone I made myself a sandwich and tried to watch TV but I was too angry to concentrate so I switched it off. It was eleven o'clock when Rex finally arrived home. He had clearly had a drink and was in a jovial mood.

'Hello sweetheart. How's my favourite brunette then?' He planted a beery kiss on my cheek and began to take off his coat.

'Did you get my message?' I asked him.

He looked puzzled. 'Message?'

81

'I tried to ring you — about the builders.'
When he still looked nonplussed I sprang up.
'Rex! Don't play the innocent with me. What the
hell did you think you were doing, engaging
builders to do what you've had months to do
yourself? And doing it without a word to me!
Didn't you think it might have been better to
talk it over first?'

My anger seemed to sober him up. 'Talk it
over? Just look at you now and ask yourself why
I did it without telling you. You always bloody
overreact to everything.'

'It's not just a question of overreacting,' I
shouted. 'How on earth are we going to *pay* for
it?'

He turned away from me, his face sheepish. 'Is
there anything to eat or drink? I've had nothing
since lunch.'

'Rex! Answer me,' I demanded. 'Did you get
an estimate from these people? How much is it
going to cost, and just where is the money
coming from to pay for it all?'

He waved a dismissive hand. 'It's taken care
of so you don't have to worry.' He walked out of
the room but I followed him through to the
kitchen where he began looking in the fridge.

'Taken care of — *how?*'

'Is there any cheese?'

I put a none-too-gentle hand on his shoulder.
'Rex! Look at me. Tell me the truth. What have
you done? If you've taken out a loan . . . '

'I haven't taken out a loan — well, not
officially,' he mumbled.

'Go on.' I stood in front of him, blocking the

doorway. 'I'm waiting and you're going nowhere until you tell me. What have you done?'

He sighed and put down the can of beer he'd just taken from the fridge. 'OK. I asked your folks to help out.'

I stared at him. 'You *what?*' My heart was thudding and I felt my neck and face flushing. 'How *dare* you. You know how I feel about asking them for anything.'

He shrugged. 'They're loaded. And they've always given you anything you asked for.'

'Anything except real parenting, which is why I've always been so determined to stand on my own feet. I don't want to take anything from them ever again. I've told you how I feel enough times so why can't you understand?'

'Beggars can't be choosers,' he said calmly. 'This house is *your* dream project, not mine, and now it's time to admit that you've taken on more than you can cope with. We need help and they can afford to give it. Anyway they were only too delighted to be able to help out.'

'I bet they were,' I said bitterly. 'They've always thought they could buy my loyalty. This is their way of making me admit that I still need them — bringing me to heel. Now that they're retired a daughter is suddenly an asset, an adjunct to complete their idyllic lifestyle and show off to their friends. No matter that it's the child who used to be nothing more than an inconvenience to them.'

'Oh, stop being so melodramatic! You're overreacting again.' Rex pulled the ring-pull off the can of beer and took a long drink from it.

'And you wonder why I never asked you first.'

'You could have done the work that those builders have done today,' I said. 'In one day they've achieved more than you've done in three months.'

'I'm an artist, not a bloody navvy!' He was angry now. 'You say you want to stand on your own feet and show your mum and dad how independent you are, but would a nice little semi in the suburbs do? Would it hell! You just wanted to best them, didn't you? You wanted to kick them in the teeth and tell them what they could do with their money. Well I'm sorry but it's backfired. I'm not going to slave away at work I hate and let my new career that I worked so hard for go down the tubes just for some crazy hang-up of yours.' He glared at me. 'Get real, Sophie.' He swallowed the remnants of his can and tossed the empty can vaguely in the direction of the bin. 'I'm going to bed.'

* * *

It was an hour before I crept upstairs and into bed beside Rex, an hour during which I'd thought long and hard. He had a point.

Maybe I'd been unfair to him. It wasn't his fault that my parents thought cash could solve everything. His parents may have been poor but at least they loved their children.

Thinking he was asleep I slid into bed and lay still but after a few minutes he turned to me. 'Look, Soph, I'm sorry.'

I eased myself away from his reaching arms.

'No, listen, I've been thinking,' I said. 'You were right. I let us in for more than we could handle and I'm sorry. We'll let the builders finish the work then we'll put the house on the market. As soon as we've sold it we'll pay the loan back with the appropriate interest, then we'll look for the little suburban semi you've set your heart on. Happy?'

There was a pause then he turned over, away from me. 'Whatever you say,' he mumbled.

7

FRANCES

The open day at St Eldred's School was painful. I wore my new outfit, which Charles barely noticed, and a brave face, which he later said looked like a death mask. Harry, bless him, was delightfully oblivious of it all. He was excited to be getting a foretaste of his new adventure and when we arrived he was in his element. By the time the day was over he had already made several friends. I know I should be happy about that — and I am. I wouldn't want him to be miserable or homesick of course. But with every smile and handshake, every introduction to Charles's old school friends, their wives and assorted offspring, some of whom had been at the school for several years already, I felt the bond between Harry and me stretching to its limit — like an elastic band, just a snap away from breaking.

A selected few 'old boys' and their wives, including Charles and me were invited to take tea in the head's study and I found myself sitting next to one of Charles's old school friends. She looked at me sideways over the rim of her teacup.

'Will this be your son's first term?'

I nodded, trying to smile. She nodded sympathetically.

'He's rather young for boarding school, isn't he?'

I felt my heart contract again and tears begin to gather but I blinked hard and smiled at her. 'He is a bit. He's eight — nearly nine.'

She nodded sympathetically. 'It's all a bit traumatic, isn't it? But Richard, who starts next term, is our third and believe me once they've been away from home for a while you get used to it. See it as the beginning of new freedom. The long summer holidays will be so exhausting that you'll be glad to wave him off to school again every September.' She looked at my expression and laughed. 'Oh, you might not think it now, but believe me you will.'

I knew I never would.

As we were leaving, the head's wife, Mary Masterson buttonholed me. 'My dear, I've been meaning to have a word with you,' she said quietly.

She was a kindly woman in, I'd guess, her early fifties; the twin set and pearls type, with greying hair cut in a sensible short style and very little make-up. I took one look into her sympathetic blue eyes and felt my throat thicken again. She reached out and took my hand between both of hers.

'I've been watching you this afternoon. All this is rather difficult for you, isn't it?'

I nodded. 'He's so young to be going away to school.'

'Harry is your only child?'

I nodded.

'I thought as much. I agree he is a little young

87

but he seems a very well adjusted little boy. I really wouldn't worry about him,' she said. 'I make it my business to keep a close eye on the young ones and make sure they don't feel lost during the first few days. We have a very good Matron too. She's brought up a family of her own and she understands children. She's firm but very kind.'

I returned the soft pressure of her hand and withdrew mine. 'Thank you. That's very reassuring,' I said. 'It's just me being silly. Harry's really looking forward to starting here next month. I just can't help wondering how he'll feel when . . .'

'When the realization that he's actually left home behind kicks in?' She smiled. 'Call it a rite of passage. He'll soon get used to it. He seems a friendly little chap. He'll be in his father's old house of course and with so much to get involved in here he'll soon slip into the routine.'

I hoped she was right.

★ ★ ★

In the car on the way home Harry sat beside Charles in the front of the car. He chattered non-stop about his new school: the science lab with its state-of-the-art equipment, the sports facilities, including a rugby pitch and a super-size swimming pool and the 'dorm' where all the boys had their own small private space complete with wash basin. Clearly he couldn't wait for the new term to begin. I knew then that nothing between us would ever be quite the same again.

I cried myself to sleep that night, stuffing a corner of the sheet into my mouth so that Charles wouldn't hear. He'd enjoyed the day almost as much as Harry had

And he couldn't understand why I couldn't be happy for our son.

'He's going to get the best education money can buy at St Eldred's,' he said at breakfast next morning, looking exasperatedly at my red-rimmed eyes. 'Surely you don't begrudge him that.'

'Yes, Harry's bright,' I argued. 'So surely he'd do just as well at the local Grammar. In my opinion private schools are only for children who need small classes and special attention.'

'Oh, for heaven's *sake!*' he snorted. 'What a stupid, ignorant point of view. I suppose you can't help it, taking your upbringing into consideration. St Eldred's is one of the finest public schools in the country, not a school for children with learning difficulties. I hope to God you didn't voice your left wing opinions in public yesterday.'

'Of course I didn't.'

'Thank God for that!' He looked at me disdainfully. 'I never had all this nonsense with my mother,' he told me. 'In fact I think she was glad to see the back of me by the time I was old enough to go to St Eldred's. But unlike you she had a busy social life. You should get out more, Fran. What about voluntary work or a bridge club — both even? You spend too much time on your own, thinking and worrying about things.'

'That's why I'd like to come back to work,' I

ventured. 'You know I hate gossiping women and do-gooders. I'd rather be occupied with something productive.'

But as usual his patience snapped as soon as I suggested working for him again. 'Oh *Fran!* For God's sake! We've been through all this a hundred times.'

'Well why not? I was good at my job, wasn't I?' I knew I was pushing it too hard but I couldn't help it. 'I know you, and I know the firm. I could be really useful to you.'

He gave a deep, exaggerated sigh. 'Why can't you get it into your head — that part of your life is over and done with?' he told me. 'You are my wife and Harry's mother, not my PA any more. It's unprofessional to blur the boundaries.' He got up to leave but paused in the doorway. 'Anyway, I've already got a PA.'

I opened my mouth to argue but he was already gone. As I watched from the window I saw his car speed off down the drive, leaving me feeling frustrated and misunderstood.

There were times when I longed to ring Katie or Sophie and tell them how I felt — ask them what they would do, but I never did. Neither of them had children of their own. Katie wasn't even married. When we met I'd hidden the fact that I had a husband who seemed to have lost interest in me. I'd played up the fact that I had a beautiful home and plenty of money. They couldn't possibly know how it felt to have my son taken away — just as that other little one was taken from me? I could never tell them about that any more than I could tell Charles. So, with my sad secret and so much else locked up inside me there was no one I could turn to for advice. I had to face the fact that soon Harry would be gone, leaving me here rattling around the house like some useless, unfulfilled ghost to cope with it on my own.

★　★　★

On the day that Harry was to travel to St Eldred's, Charles refused to let me accompany him. He took Harry himself in the car, dragging him away from me as I gave him a final hug and speeding off without a backward glance. I guessed that Harry would get a lecture on the way about toughening up and not becoming a mummy's boy.

I wandered round the house for a couple of hours, feeling like a lost soul and dreading the empty weeks ahead. Then I caught sight of the swimming pool through the bedroom window. The blue water sparkled temptingly in the sunlight and on a sudden impulse I decided to have a swim. The pool had only been installed at the end of April and I'd hardly used it. Maybe that was one thing I could do with all this new freedom — improve my swimming skills.

It was a beautiful morning, warm and sunny without a cloud in the sky. As I opened the gate to the paved enclosure the boy who came daily to maintain the pool was just finishing. He raised a cheery hand to me.

'Morning Mrs Grayson. Fancied a dip, did you?'

'I thought it was about time I made use of it,' I said.

He rolled up his hose and vacuuming equipment and stowed it in the little wooden building that housed the heating element. 'Right. I'll be off then,' he said. 'Enjoy your swim.'

I shrugged off my robe and slid into the water. It felt cold at first but after the first length it was silky and refreshing. I rolled on to my back and did a length of backstroke, beginning to relax and enjoy myself. I was floating dreamily on my back, my eyes closed as the sunlight danced on my eyelids when I suddenly became aware that I was not alone. I opened my eyes to see a man standing at the pool's edge watching me.

'Oh!' I hastily swam to the side.

'Please, don't be alarmed,' he said as I clambered out of the water. 'I didn't like to disturb you as you were obviously enjoying your swim so much.'

I pulled on my robe and shook my wet hair. 'What can I do for you?'

He held out his hand. 'I'm Adam Fenn from Tropicalle Pools. I like to visit recently installed pools personally to check if everything is satisfactory.'

I shook the hand he offered. 'Oh, I see. How nice of you. I don't remember you coming before.'

He smiled. 'I don't install the pools myself. I own the company.'

I shook my head, embarrassed. 'I'm so sorry. I didn't realize.' Looking more closely I took in the well tailored suit and expert haircut. I should have known he wasn't a foreman or some kind of labourer. 'Look, please let me run inside and dress,' I said. 'I'll make some coffee. I'm sure you could drink a cup.'

'Please don't go to any trouble,' he called as I moved away.

'It's no trouble. I won't be a minute. Please have a seat and make yourself at home.'

Upstairs I hastily dried myself and pulled on a tee-shirt and jeans. Glancing out of the window I saw that instead of sitting down he was walking round the pool, crouching down around the edges to examine various things. I ran down to the kitchen and hastily made coffee. When I arrived once more at the poolside with coffee and biscuits on a tray he was just emerging from the room housing the heating system. I put down the tray on the table.

'Come and have some coffee.'

Smiling, he joined me. 'Well, I'm pleased to see that everything looks fine,' he said, sitting down. 'I only employ competent people but you never know. There's nothing like a personal check.'

'We've been very pleased with the pool,' I told him, pouring the coffee. 'My son loves it. He and his friends have spent all summer in it — till now.' I stopped speaking abruptly as I felt my throat thickening again.

He took the coffee cup I passed to him without a word but after a moment he asked quietly: 'Are you all right, Mrs Grayson?'

I forced a laugh. 'I'm fine. Take no notice of me. My son has gone off to boarding school this

93

morning and it's a bit — a bit . . . '

'A bit of a wrench?' he finished for me.

I nodded. 'I'm just being stupid, or so my husband keeps telling me, but he's our only child you see and he's only eight.'

He said nothing as I struggled to keep my emotions in check, hiding my face in my coffee cup. Eventually I looked up at him. 'Do you have children?'

He paused. 'I did,' he said at last. 'Twin girls, Amy and Angela. They would have been six this year.'

Would! I felt my heart sink. I wanted to ask what happened but I couldn't bring myself to probe. As though reading my thoughts he answered my unasked question.

'It was three years ago. My wife was taking them for a visit to the grandparents in Yorkshire. They were involved in a pile-up on the motorway.'

'And . . . ?' I whispered.

'The car was totally wrecked and they were all killed,' he finished the sentence matter-of-factly but I could see the pain in his eyes. He took a deep drink of his coffee. 'The only consolation is that it would have been instantaneous,' he added.

'I'm so very sorry,' I said, chastened. 'Here am I whingeing on about my son going to boarding school when you . . . '

'Let's not dwell on sadness on a beautiful morning like this,' he broke in. He took a deep breath. 'So, what are you going to do with yourself now that you're at a loose end? I expect you have some interesting prospect lined up.'

'No, I don't and that's the problem,' I told him. 'It's better for men. You have your work. All I have is this house to rattle round in all day.'

'Have you never worked?'

'Oh yes. I used to be a PA. That was how I met my husband. I'd go back to work for him tomorrow if he'd allow it, but he doesn't want me to.'

'That's a pity. What a waste of good experience and talent.'

I poured him a second cup of coffee. 'Have you always been in the swimming pool business?'

'No. I used to be a civil engineer but after I lost my family I needed a change. I sold the house — it had too many memories anyway — and put the money into 'Tropicalle'. I design the pools myself and as you know they have various safety features that other pools don't have, which is good for families with youngsters.'

'And it's taken off?'

'Even better than I could have hoped,' he told me. 'I thought it might be a risk, going into a luxury business in times like these but I think a lot of people are investing in a pool rather than spend money on expensive holidays.' He smiled. 'And having one is a boon in the school holidays as you've already experienced.'

'And having the boss himself checking that everything is satisfactory is certainly a bonus,' I told him with a smile.

'It's been great talking to you, Mrs Grayson. Thanks for the coffee.' To my dismay he began to get up and I hastily cast about for something

95

to keep him a few more minutes.

In a sudden panic I blurted out: 'You wouldn't have a job going for a bored housewife, would you?' The moment I'd said it I felt my face turning scarlet and I curled up inside with shame and embarrassment. He looked shocked and mortified by turn and I hastily made myself laugh. 'Listen to me! What am I like? Sometimes I have this warped sense of humour.' I stood up and held out my hand. 'It's been so nice to meet you, Mr Fenn. Maybe we'll meet again — if we have a problem with the pool, I mean,' I added hastily.

'Which I hope you won't.' He smiled. 'I hope your son enjoys his new school and you don't miss him too much.' He shook my hand warmly. 'Don't see me off the premises. I know the way. Maybe you could continue your swim. Goodbye.'

'Goodbye.'

★ ★ ★

Harry's first letter home was short and to the point. The boys were not allowed to email their parents but made to write proper letters. Harry's went as follows:

Dear Mum and Dad
It's great here. I'm in Hereward, Dad's old house, and my housemaster is Mr Merridew. He is nice. He's got glasses and a beard and a wife called Mrs Merridew. I've got two friends. Peter and James. We have prep after

supper and bed at eight so no telly. I think it's too early.
From your son Harry.

He didn't say he missed us and there was no way of telling whether he was happy or not. I asked Charles if they were supervised and if the letters were censored before being posted. He laughed.

'You make it sound like Stalag Seventeen.' He said. 'Of course they're supervised, for spelling mistakes, that's all. It's a boys' school, not some kind of corrective institution.'

I didn't argue, but it would have been nice if he'd signed off with the word 'love'. He was normally such an affectionate little boy. Would they turn him into some hard-hearted stoic? I asked myself. *Like Charles*, a tiny voice inside my head added.

It was about ten days later when I got the phone call. I was on my way out of the house to keep a hairdresser's appointment when the telephone began to ring. I hesitated before picking up the telephone. If I answered it I'd be late. After the customary four rings the answerphone cut in with its recorded message and then:

'Mrs Grayson? Adam Fenn here. When you get this I'd like you to ring me if you can. The number is — '

I snatched up the receiver. 'Hello, Mr Fenn. I was just on my way out. What can I do for you?'

'If this is a bad time I can ring again later.'

'No. It's fine. I'm not in a hurry.'

'It was just . . . ' He paused and cleared his throat. 'I've been thinking about something you

97

said the other day. Were you serious when you asked if I had a job suitable for you?'

The breath caught in my throat. 'Why — do you have something in mind?'

'Well, yes, but I'm not sure it would be the kind of thing you'd like.'

'Try me.' I held my breath.

'It's not easy on the telephone. Maybe we could meet? I happen to be in Leicester today. I could run out to the house if . . . '

'No,' I cut in. 'I was coming into town anyway.'

'Right. Do you know The Bell?'

'Yes. I know it.'

'Could we meet for coffee or a drink at, say around twelve o'clock?'

'I think I could manage that.'

'Good. I'll explain everything when I see you then.'

For a reason I refused to acknowledge I was glad I was having my hair done and when I looked into the mirror at *Armand's* with my hair newly cut and highlighted my confidence gained the necessary boost. In the cloakroom I saw that it was already a quarter to twelve. No time to lose. I hastily repaired my make-up then I went outside and hailed a cab to The Bell.

Adam Fenn was waiting for me in the lounge. He stood up when he saw me come in and I saw that he was wearing a light grey suit and blue shirt and tie.

'Hello again. I'm glad you could make it.' He pulled out a chair. 'Coffee? Or would you like a drink?'

'Coffee's fine, thank you.' As we waited I glanced at him. 'I was surprised to get your call this morning.'

He looked concerned. 'I hope you didn't think it an imposition. I wasn't sure whether you really were joking the other day. And you had been saying you were at a loose end.'

'I was serious actually,' I said. 'I don't know what made me blurt it out to you like that though, which is why I tried to back-pedal.'

He smiled. 'I see.'

The coffee arrived and I poured for us both. 'So, what is this job you have in mind?' I asked.

He spooned sugar into his cup and stirred thoughtfully. 'I need someone attractive and personable to help sell the pools,' he said.

I shook my head. 'I'm not a saleswoman.'

'No. I visualize this person as more of a rep'.' He leaned forward. 'How it happens at the moment is this. We usually get enquiries through the website which we follow up with brochures in the post — photographs, prices and descriptions etcetera.'

'Yes. That was how we did it.'

'But I've been thinking how much better it would be to provide the personal touch, a stylish lady such as yourself to take along the brochures in person and advise.'

'I don't know very much about swimming pools,' I told him doubtfully. 'I mean apart from using one.'

'That's all right. I'd give you all the training you'd need, clue you up on the technical side. The plan would be to visit the customers in their

99

homes, advise on sites, pool sizes — you know that we do several different models — explain the installation procedure, maintenance and things like that. We'll make a DVD for you to play for them and perhaps leave them to watch at their leisure.'

'Sounds like a very good idea.'

'There'd be a fair amount of driving, but I'd provide you with a vehicle.'

There was a tingling sensation in the pit of my stomach. I was definitely excited by the idea. 'I'd rather use my own car,' I said.

He raised an eyebrow. 'Which is . . . ?'

'A Mercedes convertible.'

He threw back his head and laughed. 'Better and better. What a boost for the company's image! I'd pay you a car allowance of course.'

'Well, naturally,' I said with a straight face. Suddenly we were both laughing.

Adam looked at me. 'So, are you interested?'

'I'm interested.'

He beamed delightedly. '*Great!* This calls for something stronger than coffee. How about a champagne cocktail?'

'I don't know. I'm driving.'

'Better still, join me for lunch.'

'Well . . . '

'Don't say you're going to turn your future employer down?' He gave me a mock stern look and I laughed. 'All right, you're on. But I warn you, I could eat a horse!'

8

KATIE

We couldn't really have chosen a worse time to start our hiring business at Fantaisie. Ascot was over and so were all the other fashionable summer functions. Imogene was a bit depressed about it at first but I suggested that we buy some cocktail and ball gowns to begin with. Advertising was important but Imogene was nervous about spending money.

'We should have a website,' I told her.

She stared at me. 'Have you seen what these website firms charge?'

'I bet I could find someone to make you one,' I said. 'There are lots of students living round my way and they're all familiar with computers. They'd be glad to earn some pocket money.'

Imogene looked doubtful. 'Well, see what you can do. They'd have to come here and do it to my precise specifications. I couldn't have any cock-ups.'

''Course not.' I'd already thought of someone actually. Danny Harris, my landlord's young son. He was studying computer programming at college and I knew he'd welcome the challenge. I was right. He came up to the King's Road one evening with me and built us a super website right there in the back office. Imogene was delighted.

Meanwhile, I managed to keep up my own

design and dressmaking business when I could find the time. There had been a flurry of summer weddings and I was getting quite a reputation for my wedding dresses. The problem was, would I be able to keep up with the work once the hiring business took off?

Once the website was up and running we started to get enquiries and our ball gowns began to go out. We weren't setting the world on fire but we soon recovered our initial outlay and began to make a profit. It wasn't a bad start but Imogene was still cautious. She was reluctant to buy in any other kind of stock for hiring until the spring.

'It would all just hang there, dead money,' she said. 'And I need to buy in new stock for the winter — to sell.'

I couldn't argue with her. We'd pulled off the bank loan which had enabled her to pay off her debts and she'd also re-mortgaged her house to buy new stock. The next twelve months were going to be crucial for Fantaisie — which meant my future as well as hers — and I had to admit that she had far more to lose than I did.

At home I was busy with a gown for the smartest wedding I'd dressed yet. I'd already made the two bridesmaid's dresses, blue silk with a voile overlay, and the bridal gown was what I considered to be the best I'd designed yet. It was a close fitting style, made in ivory-watered silk with long sleeves in cobweb-fine lace. Falling from the waist at the back was a waterfall train with two cream roses nestling at the waistline. It was going to look wonderful as she walked down the aisle and I was so proud of it. The bride, Carole, who was reed slim and very pretty, looked beautiful in it but on the evening when she should have been having her final fitting she arrived looking upset.

I took one look at her tearstained face and my heart sank as I guessed what she was about to tell me. 'Carole. What's wrong?'

'I'm sorry, the wedding's off,' she said. And burst into tears.

I made coffee and sat her down with a box of tissues and bit by bit the whole story came out.

'Ian just walked out,' she told me. 'He says he can't go through with it — that he's made a mistake.'

'Are you sure it's not just wedding nerves?' I asked. She shook her head.

'He says I'll thank him when I've had time to think about it. *Thank him!* Can you believe it? He's left me to cancel the wedding and send back all the presents — cancel the church and break the news to everyone. It's a *nightmare!*' She reached for another tissue. 'He's such a coward, doing it like this, leaving me to face everyone and pick up all the pieces.'

I was sympathetic of course but I couldn't help wondering what was going to happen about the dresses I'd made. The material had cost me a bomb and I'd spent hours working on them, at weekends and evenings when I should have been in bed, asleep. She stopped blowing her nose and looked at me with red-rimmed eyes.

'I'm so sorry about the dresses, Katie,' she sniffled. 'They're so lovely and I know you've put a lot of time and effort into them. I'm sorry but as you must realize, I don't have any use for them now.'

I fought down my dismay and anger. I really couldn't afford to lose the money I'd paid for the materials. 'Is there a chance you could pay at least some of the cost?' I asked.

She bit her lip. 'Ian was going to pay for the dresses,' she said.

'Then I'll send him the bill.'

She shook her head. 'He's got a job in Saudi Arabia and he leaves early tomorrow morning.'

Under my breath I called him all the rats in Christendom. He wasn't just a rat and a coward, he was a crook as well.

'Your parents?' I asked hopefully.

'They're losing so much money as it is,' she said. 'The hotel we'd booked for the reception, the printing and the flowers we'd ordered. Some people have been considerate but others insist on instant payment.'

Maybe I should too, I thought, but one look at Carole's devastated face stopped me from saying so.

I took a deep breath. 'Look, don't worry about it,' I said. 'I'm sure something will turn up, either for you or for me. Just you go and cope with all you have to do and we'll sort something out about the dresses later.'

She looked relieved. 'Oh, Katie, thank you so much. You know I'll always recommend you to my friends.'

'Thanks.' *That's going to help a lot*, I added under my breath.

Next day at work I tried hard not to let my depression show, but Imogene knew me too well not to notice. Halfway through the morning she said, 'You're not yourself this morning, Katie. Is something wrong?'

'It's just a bit of a set-back,' I told her. 'One of my customers has let me down — through no fault of her own.'

'In what way?'

'I made her wedding dress, bridesmaids' dresses too, but she turned up last night with the news that the wedding's off.'

Imogene looked appalled. 'Don't tell me she's left you holding the baby — or in this case the dresses?'

I nodded. 'Afraid so. The fiancé has left her in the lurch, gone abroad to work, and her mum and dad are up to their eyes in debt, paying for all the trimmings.'

'It's not right that you should lose out though.' She was silent for a moment then she said, 'Last week on your half day I had someone in asking if we sold wedding dresses. I had to say no of course. What a pity I didn't know about your set-back then.'

I felt my spirits rise. 'You didn't happen to get her phone number, did you?'

'No.' Imogene looked thoughtful. 'But I think I know how I could find it. She was recommended by a regular customer, Sylvia Hanson.' She looked at me. 'She might have found a suitable dress by now of course and . . . ' She hesitated. 'Maybe I ought to see this dress of yours before I try and get in touch with her.'

105

'In case it's a complete dog, you mean?'

She grimaced. 'No! But to be fair I haven't actually seen any of your work first hand, have I? I really should take a look first. Surely you agree?'

I did agree but I couldn't help being a bit put out too. 'I'll bring it in tomorrow,' I said. 'There are two bridesmaids' dresses too. Do you think she might want those?'

'Bring them in and we'll see.'

I glanced at her. 'I'll have to get a cab,' I said. 'I couldn't bring three delicate dresses like that on the tube.'

'Yes, yes, whatever,' she said irritably. 'I'll pay the fare of course.'

I arrived at the shop the following morning with the three dresses shrouded in their polythene covers and unveiled them for Imogene. I could see at once that she was impressed but she wasn't going to enthuse too much.

'Mmm, not bad,' she said, her head on one side. 'Not bad at all. I quite like the train and the lace sleeves are pretty.' She looked at me. 'I did manage to get hold of that woman's phone number last evening by the way.'

'And?'

'She hasn't found a dress yet.'

'So, are you going to ring her?' I asked, holding my breath. 'Have I passed the test?'

She smiled. 'I think I'll let you ring her,' she said. 'The number's on the desk in the office. Do it now if you like.'

I looked at her. 'Just one thing, do I tell her I made the dresses or would you rather we kept that to ourselves?'

'Let her see them first,' Imogene said. 'After that it's up to you.' She touched my arm as I passed her on my way to the office. 'Well done, Katie. The dresses are beautiful.'

The customer's name was Hilary Mason and she wanted the dress for her daughter, Isobel who'd arrived home from her job abroad engaged and in a hurry to get married before her leave was up. With no time to get a dress made she was considering buying one off the peg as a last resort. Mrs Mason arrived that afternoon with Isobel in tow. All morning I'd been having kittens, imagining that the girl would turn out to be four foot six and fifteen stone, but when she arrived I was able to relax. She was easily as slim as Carole, though maybe an inch or so shorter. She fell in love with the dress on sight and when she emerged from the changing room her mother gasped with delight.

'Oh, darling, it's perfect! Better than anything else we've seen.'

Kneeling down I began to pin up the hem. 'It needs shortening a little but that's not a problem. When is the wedding?'

'Next Saturday.'

'I'll see that it's ready for you,' I said, standing up. 'I don't know if you're interested but we also have two bridesmaid dresses . . . '

'I'm not having any bridesmaids,' Isobel said.

Her mother looked thoughtful. 'Izzy, what about poor Sarah?' she said. 'I know she was hoping you'd ask her and she is your only sister. Surely just one bridesmaid . . . ' She looked at me. 'May we see?'

107

I took out one of the blue dresses and Mrs Hanson purred with pleasure. 'That shade of delphinium blue would suit Sarah so well,' she said. 'And it's just her size too. What do you say, Izzy? You'll make Sarah's day if you let her do it.'

Isobel sighed. 'Oh, all right if you're so set on it.' She looked at me. 'We'll bring her in to try it on in the morning if that's all right.' She was looking inside the neck of the wedding dress. 'I notice there's no label,' she said as I took the dress from her and put it back on its hanger. 'Who is the designer?'

I glanced at Imogene who gave me an encouraging nod. 'Me, actually,' I said.

Both Isobel and her mother stared at me. Isobel recovered first. 'You designed and made it?'

'Yes. I've done quite a few, for private customers.'

Mrs Hanson looked at Imogene. 'You have a very talented assistant,' she said.

Imogene shook her head. 'Partner,' she corrected. 'Katie is my business partner.'

Two out of three dresses was fantastic but hearing myself described for the first time by Imogene as her 'business partner' really made my day.

Mrs Hanson asked the price and I held my breath. Imogene knew what making the dresses had cost me and the price I had planned to charge Carole, but the price she named took my breath away. Mrs Hanson nodded.

'Very reasonable,' she said. 'Will the alteration be extra?'

When Isobel and her mother had left Imogene looked at me. 'Right,' she said. 'I'll give you what you were going to charge your customer for the three dresses and the balance can go into the business. Agreed?'

I agreed. 'And what do you think about our advertising a bridal gown design service?' I suggested.

9

SOPHIE

I have to admit, somewhat grudgingly that the builders have made wonderful headway with the house. In a matter of weeks the bathroom and kitchen were finished and gleaming and Greenings was looking almost as I'd visualized it. But I still wasn't happy about the loan Rex had squeezed out of my parents in order to do it.

For the first few days after my trip to see Katie and Fran, Rex and I hardly spoke and finally I decided that I needed to speak to my parents face to face. I saw no reason why I should tell Rex about my intended visit. He hadn't told me he was about to ask for a loan, so why should I? There were only another two weeks left of the school holidays so no time to waste. I rang to ask for a convenient time and day. My mother answered the telephone.

'Sophie! Of course you can come and see us. You don't have to ask. We're usually here.'

'I thought tomorrow afternoon,' I said. 'Will that be all right?'

'Of course, darling. Dad and I will look forward to seeing you.'

I put the receiver down with a grimace. *Of course darling! Dad and I will look forward to seeing you.* How could she still be kidding herself that we'd ever been a normal family?

The village where they'd bought their dream retirement house was about ten miles from Hamsleigh. The village was called Little Penfold. It had pretty thatched cottages, a medieval church and a village green complete with duck pond. The house was modern, but built of the local stone, in keeping with the rest of the village. When I drove in through the gates my dad was mowing the front lawn. He switched off the mower and came to meet me.

'Hi, Sophie. Nice to see you, at last.'

'We've been very busy with the house,' I told him.

'I know, we heard all about it from Rex. Sounds like quite a project.'

I slammed the car door. 'That's what I'm here to talk about,' I said.

He pulled a face. 'Oh dear, sounds slightly ominous.'

'Shall we go inside?' I asked. 'Or do you want to finish the lawn first.'

'No, it can wait.'

Inside the hall it was cool. A large leaded window on the landing let in the sunlight, illuminating the mock Jacobean staircase and the collection of reproduction antiques my parents had collected for their new home. Mum came down the stairs to meet me, a big smile on her face. She wore a floaty summer dress, her hair newly coloured a rich auburn.

'Darling! What a treat,' she said, air-kissing me on both cheeks. 'Do come through to the conservatory. Mrs Brown had a baking session this morning so you're in luck.'

'I can't stay long,' I put in. 'I just wanted to clear something up.'

For the first time Mum noticed Dad's appearance. '*Geoff!* Go and change if you're going to have tea with us. You're absolutely filthy.'

He made his way obediently upstairs and Mum led the way through to the conservatory. 'Do have a seat,' she said. 'When your father comes back I'll go and put the kettle on.'

'Look, Mum, I'm not stopping, so don't bother to go to any trouble. It's about this loan that Rex arranged with you.'

She flushed. 'Oh. I think perhaps we should wait for your father.'

'If you say so,' I said impatiently. 'He needn't really have bothered changing.'

The conversation limped along for a few minutes, then Dad arrived looking fresher in a clean shirt and slacks.

'Will I do?' he asked Mum.

She shook her head. 'Oh, Geoffrey, please! Anyone would think you were hen-pecked.'

He took a seat and they both looked at me expectantly.

'It's about the loan,' I began.

'Before you go on,' Dad put in. 'There is absolutely no need to pay it back until you're completely sure you're ready.'

'I don't know what Rex told you about our financial state. I had no idea he was going to ask you for a loan,' I said. 'He did it without consulting me. The first thing I knew about it was when the builders he'd hired began work. It was a shock. And not a pleasant one.'

'Oh, for heaven's sake, why?' Mum asked.

'Because the whole idea was for us to stand on our own feet. We were supposed to be doing all the restoration work ourselves.'

'But why should you when we're happy to help? It would have taken you years to get the place as you wanted it.'

'It was important to us — well, *me* — to do it ourselves,' I said. 'Rex is capable and qualified to do the technical stuff and I thought he agreed with me about being independent. Clearly he didn't.'

'I think he was finding it all a bit much with his work and everything,' Dad said, prompting a warning look from Mum. 'Anyway, this way it'll be done a lot sooner than you hoped,' he finished cheerily. 'That's good, isn't it?'

I looked from one to the other. 'I suppose so, in one way,' I told them. 'Because now as soon as it's finished we can put the house up for sale and pay you back.'

They exchanged glances. 'Sell your dream house! Why should you do that?' Mum asked.

'Because now the whole thing is ruined. I've finished the decoration and the builders should be through in a couple of weeks' time. I suggest we pay you back plus the current bank interest as soon as a sale goes through.' I stood up and picked up my bag and jacket.

Mum jumped to her feet, her cheeks flushed. 'Why are you being like this, Sophie? All we're trying to do is help you. That's what families do, isn't it?'

113

'Normal families, yes,' I said. 'But we've never been a normal family, have we? Your way of solving every problem is to throw money at it. That's how you brought me up — throw enough luxuries at her and she can't complain that we're never there for her. That was your maxim. Well I'm afraid it doesn't work any more. You'll get your money back with interest if we have to live in cardboard boxes to do it.' I headed for the door. 'That's all I wanted to say so I'll go now. Goodbye.'

Mum followed me through to the hall, her high heels clacking on the polished floor. 'Really, Sophie, you're behaving like a spoilt child,' she said. 'You were brought up with the best that money could buy. You wanted for nothing, yet now you're treating your father and me as if we neglected you.'

At the front door I turned to her. 'There's more than one way to neglect a child. Where was the love, the bedtime stories, the hugs and trips to the park that all the other kids took for granted?'

'We were building a business,' she argued. 'To make a good future, a good life.'

'All I wanted was a warm and loving relationship with my mum and dad!' There was a huge lump in my throat now and I felt the tears welling up. 'The things I saw other children getting as a matter of course. That's all I wanted.'

'*You think we didn't want that too?*' Her face was drained of colour now. She looked pinched and drawn, older than her age. 'You're right of

114

course. We never did have any time to spare. But we could have taken the easy way out and sent you to boarding school. Have you ever asked yourself why we didn't?'

'I don't know. Guilt, perhaps? Why don't you just admit that having me was a disaster — one big mistake?'

'That's not true, Sophie. We'd have liked more children, but the business took off. Do you think we don't regret those years when we were too busy, too exhausted every night after work to enjoy our own child. Do you think we don't yearn for the years we can never get back? That's why we jumped at this chance to make it up to you in some small way now.'

I took a step backwards. 'I — I've got to go.'

She took a step towards me. 'Sophie! Don't go like this. Why are you so bitter? It can't have been so very terrible.' She shook her head. 'Sometimes I feel I don't know you any more.'

I turned in the act of opening the car door. 'That's just it,' I told her. 'You don't. You never even bothered to try.' I got into the car and began to reverse out of the drive. When I looked she was still standing there on the drive. She seemed to have shrunk, the fake auburn hair looked garish in the afternoon sunlight, a contrast to her white face. I swallowed hard and drove away.

★　★　★

When I got home Rex came to meet me in the hall.

'Why did you do it?' he demanded. 'Why did

115

you have to be so bloody cruel?'

I pushed past him. 'I don't know what you're talking about.'

'Your mother rang me,' he went on. 'After you'd left. She was absolutely distraught.'

'I might have known she'd go bleating to you the minute I'd left.'

'And well she might. It seems you chucked their money back in their faces.'

I laughed. 'If only I had any to chuck! I did tell them they'd get it all back, with interest, as soon as we could sell the house.'

He shook his head. 'Sometimes I wonder about you, Sophie,' he said. 'I couldn't hurt my folks the way you've hurt yours this afternoon. All I can say is, I hope it's made you happy.'

I turned halfway up the stairs. 'If you hadn't gone crawling to them with your begging bowl this would never have happened,' I told him. 'You knew I wanted Greenings to be our project. And before you say anything, yes, I know you were finding it hard but you didn't even discuss it with me. You just jumped in with both feet. Well now we're going to have to sell the house because of what you did. And don't pretend you're not relieved,' I added as a parting shot.

★ ★ ★

The following day, in a defiant mood I drove into Leicester to hit the shops. If I was going to change my image I had to do it before the new term began. First I went to the hairdresser's where I'd already made an appointment for a cut and blow-dry. The girl slipped the protective cape round my shoulders and looked at me through the mirror, picking up a strand of my waist-length hair.

'Have you thought this through?' she asked. 'Do you really want it all off?'

I nodded. 'It's ridiculous at my age, hair this long. I'd like a short, simple, easy to manage style.' I smiled at her. 'And don't worry. I'm not going to burst into tears at the first snip.'

When she'd finished I looked into the mirror and could hardly believe my eyes. I'd completely forgotten that my hair had a slight natural wave. Relieved of its weight it now had bounce and lift. The new style framed my face and the little half fringe flattered the shape of my eyes.

'You won't need any colour or highlights,' the girl said. 'Not many people have this lovely rich chestnut colour naturally.' She looked at me, her head on one side. 'If I might make a suggestion, a richer lipstick shade would look good on you.'

I bought the new lipstick, a deep coral shade, paid the bill and left the salon with a spring in my step, ready to look for a change in dress style.

I bought a stylish suit and a couple of slim skirts in a length that came just above my knees. Next I chose several pretty tops to wear with them. I bought plain court shoes to wear instead of the gypsy sandals I'd slopped around in for years and to replace the massive sack-like ethnic bag I carried around with me I picked out a smart organiser handbag. No more rummaging in the depths of that monster for keys, wallet etc. I glanced in the direction of the dresses.

Something pretty and feminine for informal evening occasions perhaps? Then I totted up in my head what I had already spent and decided to leave it for the time being. I was just about to step on to the escalator on my way to the coffee shop when I spotted it. A suede jacket in a lovely caramel shade. I walked across and fingered the butter-soft skin.

'Would you like to try it on?' a voice at my elbow asked. 'The colour is just right for you.' I didn't need asking twice.

Turning this way and that in front of the mirror I knew that the jacket might have been made for me. It could hardly have been more different from my old image but it suited me in a way I would never have thought possible. The style and colour were just right, but more than that; it summed up who I wanted to be — the new assertive, independent me. I had to have it.

On the floor below as I drank my coffee I debated with myself what to do. Should I introduce the new me gently or should I hit Rex with it right between the eyes? I made up my mind, finished my coffee and went off to the Ladies with my collection of bags. Luckily it was empty and I swiftly changed into one of the new skirts and tops, plus the suede jacket and shoes, pushed my old clothes into the store's bags and went off to the car park.

* * *

When I got out of the car the builders were just packing up the van ready to leave for the day.

Bob looked at me and gave a long, low whistle.

'Wow, Mrs T. I wouldn't have known you. You look a proper stunner.'

'Thank you.' I reached into the back of the car for the bag containing my old clothes and turned to see Rex standing in the doorway. The expression on his face was unreadable.

The builders' van trundled away down the drive and I walked towards Rex. 'I'll put the car away in a minute,' I said. 'I'm dying for a cup of tea.'

He didn't move out of the way but continued to stare at me. 'What the hell have you done to yourself?' His voice was rough with anger and I saw the tell-tale colour creeping up his neck.

'Done to myself!' I laughed. 'Anyone would think I'd come home covered in tattoos and piercings!'

'You might as well have.' He moved aside and I walked past him into the hall.

'Just what are you trying to prove, Sophie?' he said behind me. 'What are you trying to do — merge into the wallpaper?'

'Thanks very much!' I turned to him. 'Surely even you have to admit that I'm too old for the Bohemian art student look. I've turned thirty. I'm a professional artist and a teacher. I need a more sophisticated look now.'

'Is that what this is then?' He held out his hands mockingly. 'The new, improved, *sophisticated* Sophie Turner!'

'Yes, if you like.'

'What first attracted me to you was your individuality,' he said, following me through to the kitchen. 'You were a rebel. You flouted the rules. You had your own voice. To me you were someone special, Sophie.'

I rounded on him. 'Oh for God's sake, Rex. I'm still the same person. Just because I've had my hair cut and I've decided to dress my age, doesn't mean I'm any different inside.'

'You're wrong. You've been different for some time.' Suddenly all the anger went out of him and he sat down at the kitchen table. 'All that fire and enthusiasm you used to have — it's all turned to bitterness and it doesn't suit you, Sophie.'

'You don't even see that I'm exhausted most of the time.' I threw down the bags of shopping and sat down opposite him. 'You don't even care that I've worked like a dog all through the summer holidays, decorating this house while you did next to nothing. Then after all I've put into it you humiliate me by asking my parents for the money to do your share of it.'

'Oh, for Christ's sake, put another record on, can't you!'

'It's over, Rex.' I leaned forward. 'The money gets paid back as soon as possible. Shall I tell you something, Rex? The reason you were attracted to me was because I was different, a girl with well-off parents who went against all the things *you'd* been brought up to respect. You wanted to kick out at all that conventional respectability and you thought I was the one to help you do it. Well, you were wrong. I'd have given anything for the childhood you had even though you like to pretend it was poverty stricken. And for your information, all that student rebelliousness was just a way of trying to shock my parents into noticing me.'

He sprang up. 'Oh, *poor little rich girl!* For God's sake, Sophie, you don't know you're born. Why don't you grow up and face the fact that your folks did their best for you. Stop punishing them because they didn't put you on a pedestal and fawn all over you!' He stood looking down at me. 'You know, I don't think I can take much more of this,' he said, his voice frighteningly calm. 'I think I'll pack a bag and move in with a mate for a few days. I think we both need time and space to think things through.'

My heart gave a lurch. 'Just because I've had my hair cut and bought a few new clothes?'

'You know it's not just that.' In the doorway he turned to look at me. 'It was just the match that lit the fuse.

'Fuse?'

'Yes. It finally proved just how much you've changed. I don't know who you are any more, Sophie. I don't like this new you and I'm not even all that sure that I want to.'

★ ★ ★

Rex didn't come home. I waited a week, then ten days and nothing. I was determined not to ring him. After all, he was the one who'd walked out, but as the days and nights went by I missed him more and more. Was our marriage over? Could a trivial thing like cutting my hair and changing my look have made him want to leave? How

121

shallow was that? But if I was strictly honest with myself I knew deep down that it was more, much more than just that.

Looking in my diary I saw that the date Fran, Katie and I had arranged for our next meeting was in a few days' time, just before I went back to school. In a sudden panic I toyed with the idea of cancelling the meeting. But then I changed my mind. It would be good to see them both, a little respite to cheer me up before starting the new term. Since we'd bought Greenings most of my friends had dropped out of my life. Also I wanted to see how they would react to my new image. Rex's response had given my confidence a battering and I badly needed reassurance. I'd have to keep quiet about our temporary split of course. (Given that it was temporary.) Anyway I knew there was a strong possibility that I'd cry if they showed me any sympathy. How humiliating would that be?

We'd picked a Thursday because it was Katie's half day and arranged to meet at Napolitano, the Italian restaurant where we'd met last time. I was there first, wearing a slim beige skirt and apricot top, and of course the suede jacket. I sat at a corner table with a gin and tonic, watching the door. I didn't have to wait long. They both arrived together. I steeled myself, waiting with bated breath for their reaction to my new look.

10

Fran had picked Katie up at Fantaisie on her way to their lunch date and they arrived at the restaurant together. Katie scanned the tables for Sophie.

'Looks as if she isn't here yet,' she said. 'Maybe her train was late.'

But Fran was smiling. 'She is here. Look, over there at the corner table.'

'Where?' Katie frowned. 'I can't see her — unless — oh my God! Is that really Soph?'

Fran nudged her. 'I don't think that's quite the reaction she expects,' she whispered.

'But she looks so — so *different!*'

'That's probably the idea. Look, she's seen us, wave! Come on. Let's join her.'

Fran took the chair opposite Sophie. 'Well, well, look at *you!* We didn't recognize you at first.'

Katie sat down in silence and, noticing her quietness Sophie turned to her. 'You look stunned, Katie.'

Recovering quickly, Katie laughed. 'Well, I am — a bit. What made you decide on such a drastic change?'

Sophie shrugged. 'I wasn't aware that it was all that drastic,' she said. 'I'm still me. It just suddenly occurred to me that I was too old for the whole arty thing.'

'Oh, I loved that gorgeous ethnic look. It

suited you beautifully. Not many people could get away with it. I always used to admire your individual style.'

'Well I think you look fantastic,' Fran said, kicking Katie under the table. 'I love your hair. And that jacket is to die for.'

Sophie smiled, relaxing a little. 'I know, I couldn't resist it.' She slipped it off and hung it on the back of her chair. 'Right, who's for a gin and tonic?' She beckoned to a waiter. 'Let's see what's on the menu. I don't know about you but I'm starving!'

They each ordered and during the meal Katie talked about the new exclusive wedding dress hire service they were planning at Fantaisie and how hard she was finding life, what with the travelling and her designing work out of hours.

'How about you?' Sophie turned to Fran. 'You must be missing Harry. I expect the house feels empty without him.'

Fran took a sip of her drink. 'I miss him of course,' she said. 'But I've been offered a job and I'm giving it some serious consideration.'

The other two looked at her with interest. 'What kind of job?' Sophie asked.

'Selling swimming pools.'

They looked at her speechlessly for a moment then Katie said, 'Wow! So, what would you have to do?'

'Drive out to the potential customers' homes, look at the site and advise them on which of the firm's models would suit them best. Look at the possible location and then play them a demonstration DVD.'

'Sounds like fun,' Katie remarked. 'So how did you come to find it?'

'We bought a pool from this firm earlier this year. The boss came out to check if everything was satisfactory the other day. We chatted and he offered me the job.'

'So what qualifications do you need for that?' Katie asked.

'None really. There'd be full training and the salary is generous too. I've promised to give him my answer at the end of this week.'

'What does your husband think about it?' Sophie asked.

Fran's smile slipped slightly. 'Well, I haven't actually told him about it yet.'

Katie pulled a face. 'Are you afraid he won't approve?'

'He wouldn't let me go back to work for him,' Fran said defensively. 'So he can hardly say much, can he?'

'S'pose not. If you ask me, husbands are all very well until they start telling you what to do,' Katie said. 'Ouch!' She winced under her breath as Sophie kicked her ankle.

'So . . . ' Eager to change the subject Fran looked at Sophie. 'Back to the grind next week, eh? I wonder what your colleagues will think of the new image.'

'It doesn't matter what they think,' Sophie said. 'It's here for keeps now so if they don't like it they can do the other thing.'

Sensing the tension in her friend Fran reached across the table to touch her hand. 'They'll love it. I guarantee it!' She picked up her handbag.

'I'm going to freshen up before we choose our dessert. Anyone coming?'

Katie shook her head. 'I'll look at the menu while you're gone. I don't eat desserts very often and I'm going to make the most of it.'

'I'll come with you.' Sophie got up and followed Fran.

The restaurant was quiet and the Ladies was empty. Fran went into one of the cubicles and when she came out she was disturbed to find Sophie standing in front of the mirror dabbing tears from her cheeks with a tissue. She slipped an arm round her shoulders.

'Sophie, what is it?'

With a great effort to compose herself Sophie managed a smile. 'Oh dear, I didn't want to do this,' she said. 'Especially in front of Katie. She wouldn't understand.'

'What wouldn't she understand?'

'It's Rex. He's left me.'

'*Oh no!* Oh, my poor Sophie. Was it the strain of restoring the house? We weren't doing the work ourselves but I know how stressful it can be.'

'That was partly the problem. It was important to me that we did it all ourselves. Rex knew that. First he employed a firm of builders to finish the work without discussing it with me and then I found out that he'd asked my parents for financial help behind my back.'

'I see. Is that so bad?'

'It wouldn't be except that they were only too keen to *give* us the money. Rex had already committed us to taking it, employing the

126

builders and everything. So I insisted that we take it only on condition that it is paid back the minute the house is finished and we've sold it.'

'You're going to *sell* it? Doesn't that rather defeat the object?'

Sophie shook her head angrily. 'I didn't want money from them anyway. I don't want *anything* from them. They've never been like real parents to me and I wanted to prove to them that money doesn't buy you love and respect.'

Fran was shocked. 'I never realized you felt that strongly. When we were kids I always envied you all those luxuries you had. They gave you everything.'

'Except the one thing I wanted — a proper family life like everyone else had.' Sophie looked at her friend. 'If you'd only known how much I envied you. Every day after school your mum was there waiting — to take you shopping or to the park. I'd have given anything for that.'

Fran stared at her. Sophie had envied *her!* If she only knew how stifling it was. 'So, is Rex in agreement with selling the house?' she asked.

Sophie shrugged. 'He thinks I'm being unreasonable. We had an awful row when I found out what he'd done. But the thing that finally tipped him over the edge was *this*, believe it or not.' She pointed to her reflection in the mirror. 'Me having a make-over. Changing the way I look seemed to be the final straw for him. He accused me of trying to prove something. He said a lot of other things, stuff I'd rather not think about but it boils down to the fact that in his eyes I'm no longer the person he married.'

'And he just walked out?'

'Yes,' Sophie sighed.

'When was this?'

'Almost a fortnight ago. I've heard nothing since, no phone call, no e-mail, not even as much as a brief text. Nothing.'

Fran tried to make light of it. 'He's probably just making a point. Have you tried to ring him?'

'His phone is permanently switched off. I've no idea where he is. It looks as if . . . ' Sophie swallowed hard. 'As if it's over.'

'Oh, surely not. He'll come to his senses. Look, surely you could pay your folks back in small instalments if you really feel you have to. Why sell your dream house?'

Sophie sniffed. 'It's been more like a nightmare over the past few months. Rex never really wanted it anyway.'

'Give it time,' Fran advised. 'Don't do anything rash. And keep ringing him. He can't keep his phone switched off indefinitely, can he?' She grinned at Sophie's reflection in the mirror. 'Cheer up, love. It'll all come right. You'll see. Hey, what about Katie then. She's designing wedding dresses for the elite now!'

Sophie smiled in spite her herself. 'I know. Same old Katie. I wonder why she always feels the need to embellish everything?'

'Maybe it all stems from feelings of inadequacy,' Fran speculated. 'I don't think she had a very happy childhood. She always tried to make things sound better than they were at school. Old habits die hard.'

'Poor little Katie,' Sophie said. 'She's such a

dear you can forgive her anything, can't you?'

Fran picked up her bag. 'Speaking of which, she's had time to learn that dessert menu by heart. We'd better get back.'

Each of them chose the richest dessert on the menu, assuring each other that they'd diet for the rest of the week. They drank a leisurely pot of coffee between them then Sophie looked at her watch and announced that she'd have to leave to catch her train.

'The builders are still working at Greenings,' she explained. 'And I'd like to be back before they leave for the day.'

When they'd said their goodbyes Fran looked at Katie. 'What are you going to do with the rest of your half day?'

'Work! I've got loads to do at home,' Katie said. 'If the wedding dress hire service really takes off I might even have to get someone in to help me. At the moment I'm working weekends and burning the midnight oil through the week.'

'You're making all the dresses yourself?'

'Yes. They're exclusive; that's the speciality. Designs no one else will have.'

'I hope your boss is paying you well,' Fran remarked.

'She's not my boss,' Katie corrected. 'I told you before — we're partners.'

'Mmm.' Fran looked thoughtful. 'I'm wondering if that was possibly a shrewd move on her part.'

'What do you mean?'

'Think about it. What would she have to pay a designer to provide her with exclusive dresses to hire out — not to mention what the actual making would cost?'

Katie bridled. 'Well I'm happy with it,' she said. 'Fantaisie is an upmarket outlet for me. I couldn't have a better showcase for my work.'

Fran smiled. 'That's true.' She looked at her watch. 'So, you don't fancy a film or something?'

'Better not.' Katie shook her head. 'By the way what was the matter with Sophie? She looked a bit down — 'specially when you came back from the loo.'

'Oh, I think the house renovation is getting her down a bit,' Fran said lightly. 'She hasn't really had a break these holidays and she's tired.'

'Tell me about it!' Katie stood up. 'I can't remember the last time I had a break. I'd have thought Soph's mum and dad would have helped her out. After all, they always seemed to be loaded. She never wanted for anything as a kid, did she?'

Fran shrugged. 'Well, who knows? I expect she'd rather be independent.'

Outside the restaurant they said goodbye, promising to keep in touch. Fran looked at her watch. It was three o'clock. Better make her way across to St Pancras to catch the train home. She had started to walk towards the Underground station when her mobile began to ring in her handbag. Moving into a doorway she took out the phone and saw, to her surprise, that the call was from Adam Fenn.

'Hello, Mr Fenn.'

'Mrs Grayson. Hi! I wondered whether you'd had any more thoughts about the job?'

Her heart gave a jerk. 'Well, I've thought about it a lot.'

'Yes, and . . . ?'

'I like the idea very much.'

'You seemed quite keen when we last spoke. Am I to take it that you're going to accept the offer?'

'Well, I . . . '

'Is there a problem?'

'No. It's just . . . '

'Look, I'm in London today, interviewing prospective staff, but maybe I could pop over to see you, tomorrow perhaps?'

'I'm in London today too.'

'You *are*? How lucky is that? If you're free why not meet me for a cup of tea and we could have a further chat — see if we can iron out any snags.'

'Yes, all right. Where do you suggest?'

'Where are you at this moment?'

'I'm in Kensington High Street. I've just had lunch with some friends at the Napolitano.'

'Couldn't be better. I'm ten minutes away. Hang on there and I'll come and pick you up.'

Fran ended the call and replaced the phone in her bag. For some reason she found that she was trembling. She badly wanted the job but how could she make a decision when she hadn't even broached the subject with Charles yet? And just what was she letting herself in for?

11

FRANCES

While I waited for Adam I thought about
Sophie. All those years ago I'd thought she was
so lucky to have her own space with no one
hassling her all the time; no over-protective
mother forever in her face, on to her every move.
And all the time that was all she actually wanted.
I was sure that if she'd had my situation she'd
have changed her mind. But then you never
know with people, do you?

Adam was as good as his word. I'd only been
waiting fifteen minutes when his car drew up at
the kerb and he leaned across to open the
passenger door. I got in and as he pulled away
from the kerb he shot me an appreciative glance.

'You're looking very glamorous today.'

To my embarrassment I felt myself blushing.
'Thank you,' I said. 'I suppose it makes a change
from jeans and a T-shirt.'

He laughed. 'Or a bikini.'

Again my cheeks warmed. 'Well, I wasn't
expecting visitors that day.'

'Oh, please don't apologize.'

When he turned into Arlington Street and
pulled up outside the Ritz I looked at him. 'Wow!
I wasn't expecting anything as grand as this.'

He smiled 'I thought we'd do it in style. I've
had quite a tiresome day and I wasn't expecting

a treat at the end of it so I intend to make the most of it.'

Seated at the table in comfortable and luxurious surroundings I looked at the menu; every kind of tea imaginable and sandwiches with exotic fillings were on offer, not to mention mouth-watering cakes. I looked up at Adam. 'I've just eaten a very good lunch,' I told him.

He shook his head. 'Don't tell me you're not hungry. A healthy young woman like you! Who could resist all these delights?'

I laughed. 'When I break the bathroom scales tomorrow morning I shall blame you.'

'I'll risk it.' He beckoned the waiter. 'We'll have a pot of Earl Grey and a selection of everything,' he said with a wicked grin in my direction.

'So, was your lunch some kind of celebration?' Adam asked as we waited for our tea.

'No, just a meeting of three old friends,' I told him. 'We were at school together and we meet now and again to catch up.'

'I see. It's always nice to get together with people you know really well.'

'I wouldn't say that we do,' I said thoughtfully. 'We met again a few months ago at a school reunion — after a long gap. I think we've all become quite different people since our school days.'

'I wonder, do we ever really change that much?'

'Perhaps not,' I said. 'It could be that we never really knew each other in the first place.'

He gave me a sharp look. 'That's a very

133

profound statement.'

'I discovered just today that while I was envying one of these friends back then, she'd been envying me my life,' I told him. 'The odd thing is that as it turns out, neither of us really had anything to envy at all. In reality nothing was as we imagined it was.'

He nodded. 'The grass is always greener. Isn't it always the way? If I've learned one lesson from life it's never envy anyone because you never really know the truth about another person's life, however much you think you do. We none of us show all our cards to the world.'

'That's very true,' I said quietly. His words had struck a chord. I thought about my own life and wondered what Sophie would think if she knew the secret I'd kept from them all during that last term.

Our tea arrived and Adam's mood changed. 'We're getting far too serious,' he said. 'Now, you pour while I outline the terms of your new job.'

He'd got it all worked out to the last detail and he clearly wanted — and expected — me to take him up on his offer. When he'd finished speaking I looked at him.

'I'll put my cards on the table, Mr Fenn.'

He cut in, 'Adam, please.'

I nodded. 'Adam. The truth is I haven't had a chance to run this past my husband yet. I must ask what he thinks before I give you a definite answer.'

He looked surprised. 'Oh, I see. Forgive me but from what I've seen of you so far you seem very much in charge of your own life.'

'I hope I am. But out of courtesy . . . '

'I understand, of course.' He paused, glancing sideways at me. 'Would I be right in thinking that you're not too optimistic about his reaction?'

'To be honest, I don't think he really wants me to work at all,' I told him. 'He's a bit old fashioned — likes to visualize me joining the local bridge club or pushing a trolley round the hospital.'

He pulled a face. 'A dinosaur in other words.'

'Not really. Anyway, I promise I'll sound him out about it this evening.'

'I'd really like you to take this job, Fran,' he said. 'I have a feeling you're going to be an excellent asset to my business.'

'Thank you. It sounds interesting and challenging and I really want to take you up on your offer. And I promise that, all things being equal, I will.'

'You'll ring me?'

'Tomorrow. I won't keep you hanging about.'

'That's very considerate.'

★　★　★

On the train on the way home I thought about Adam's offer and the job he had in mind for me. It sounded quite exciting and the salary he had offered was extremely generous, especially as he had hinted at commission and bonuses. All that remained was obtaining Charles's approval, but I wasn't optimistic about that, seeing it as a definite stumbling block.

I was in the kitchen making his favourite meal — steak and kidney pie — when Charles arrived

135

home. I was pleased to see that he was in a good mood. He threw his briefcase on to the worktop and put his arms around my waist.

'I can't tell you how good it is to come home to a wife cooking your favourite meal,' he said, dropping a kiss on the top of my head. 'I always feel sorry for all those poor guys having to get the dinner on and wait around for their wives to get in.'

My heart sank a bit but I refused to let myself think in anything less than a positive way. I served the pie and followed it with a raspberry cheesecake, sneakily bought from M&S on my way home. Stacking the dishes in the dishwasher afterwards I made coffee and carried the tray through to where Charles was already relaxing in the conservatory with his newspaper. He looked up as I came in.

'I got Lauren to put an ad in the local paper for a cleaning woman a couple of days ago,' he said. 'Has anyone applied yet?'

I looked up. 'Lauren?'

'My PA.'

'Oh, is that her name? You didn't tell me you were going to put an ad in.'

'But we really need someone to take over the housework, don't we?'

'To be honest I've been glad of the housework to occupy myself since Harry went off to school.'

He shook his head. 'Really darling! Surely you can find something more edifying to do than housework. So you've had no replies?'

'Not as far as I know. I had no idea the ad was in.'

He shrugged. 'Oh, well, never mind.' He went back to his paper.

Handing him his coffee I decided that there couldn't be a better time to take the bull by the horns.

'Speaking of jobs, I was offered one myself the other day,' I said as casually as I could, sitting down opposite him.

He glanced up. 'A job? What kind of job?'

'As a rep for Tropicalle Pools.'

He grunted. 'Huh! Very funny.'

'No, seriously. It's quite a prestigious job. I'd travel around, assess the sites, play the prospective buyers a CD and . . . '

He sat up. 'What on *earth* are you talking about?'

'This job. There'd be full training and . . . '

'Are you telling me that you actually *applied* for a job selling swimming pools?'

'No. I was offered it.'

'By whom?'

'By the boss, Adam Fenn. He called to make sure that we were happy with our pool and we got talking. It was the day that Harry started his new school and . . . '

'Who is this Adam Fenn?' he cut in. 'I'd like to have a word with him. Clearly he thought he was on to a good thing. Bloody cheek!'

'What do you mean?'

'He saw you as a lonely, bored housewife at a loose end and thought you'd be ripe for the picking. What a nerve. Would he let *his* wife hawk his wares from door to door?'

'It's not like that at all. The salary is very good.

And there'd be commission and bonuses.'

'I bet!' He glared at me. 'You'd have to sell the pools first. Anyway what makes you think you could do a job like that?'

'I worked for you efficiently, didn't I?'

He shrugged. 'I didn't expect you to drive around the country peddling stuff.'

'I told you; it's not at all like that.'

'I sincerely hope you told him what he could do with his ridiculous job offer.'

'No. I'd like to take it, Charles.'

He stared at me. 'You must be joking!'

'I'm not joking. It sounds fascinating and challenging. I said I'd let him have a decision in the morning and I mean to say yes.'

'Over my dead body! I'm not having my wife traipsing from door to door like a gypsy. Anyway, you wouldn't last a week. Do you really want to humiliate yourself as well as me?'

'You are the one who described me as a lonely, bored housewife.'

'Correction! I said *he* saw you as that. Don't let yourself be taken in by this conman, Fran.'

'He's not a conman. It's an interesting job and I intend to take it.'

For a moment he stared at me, then he played his trump card. 'What about when Harry is home for the holidays? I suppose he'll have to amuse himself and make his own meals, will he?' He stood up and threw down the newspaper he'd been reading. 'I'm going up to the study. I've had a particularly rough day and I didn't expect to have to listen to a load of junk when I got home.' In the doorway he turned. 'Take the

138

wretched job if you're so set on it — if it's more important to you than your own son. I can't think why you made such a fuss about him going away to school. You obviously couldn't wait to be free of him!'

When he'd gone I sat for a long time with a huge lump in my throat. How could he think that of me? I had to admit that I hadn't thought about the holidays but now that I did I could see that it might be a problem. Charles hated the thought of me working for Adam, or working at all. That much was more than clear. What would life be like if I stuck to my guns? Charles could make life extremely unpleasant when he didn't get his own way. Taking things all round, was it really worth it? Reluctantly I had to admit that it wasn't, even though I despised myself for letting Charles win, yet again.

I didn't sleep much that night and I was in the kitchen making breakfast when Charles came down the next morning. He seemed to have forgotten about our row the previous evening, remarking on the weather and complimenting me on the full English breakfast I'd cooked, mainly to give myself something to take my mind off my problem. As he rose to leave he put his hands on my shoulders and pulled me to him.

'That was a delicious breakfast. What would I do without you, darling?' He kissed me soundly. 'Even if you are a bit of a silly girl sometimes.' He kissed the tip of my nose and picked up his briefcase. 'Maybe you'll get some replies to the cleaning woman ad today. That'll leave you free to go out and find something to occupy yourself.

You're not doing anything today, are you?' I shook my head. 'That's a good girl.' He touched my cheek and chuckled to himself. 'Selling swimming pools indeed! Whatever next?'

With a heavy heart I watched from the window as his car drove off down the drive. I'd held down the responsible job of PA to Charles — the managing director of a successful electronics firm — and carried it out efficiently. He knew that, yet now he saw me as a fluffy little housewife and mother circa 1950. He seriously expected me to be satisfied with running the house and cooking his meals, marking time till the end of each term when Harry would be home. In a couple of years Harry would have lost interest in me as a person. He'd probably see me as his father saw me — the little woman in the background, quietly providing the everyday needs of her men folk and asking for nothing in return. How could I allow myself to sink into that kind of life?

I went upstairs, showered and dressed. Soon I would have to ring Adam and tell him I wouldn't be taking the job. I dreaded it. I wasn't likely to get an interesting offer like that again any time soon. I was halfway down the stairs when the phone rang. My knees shook. Was it Adam ringing for my decision?

In the hall I picked up the receiver. 'Hello.'

To my relief a woman's voice answered — a voice I didn't recognize. 'Oh, is that Mrs Grayson?'

'It is. Are you ringing in answer to the advertisement in the *Herald*?'

'Er, that's right.'

'Would you like to come round for an interview?'

'Yes. I'll come later this morning if that's all right with you.'

'Yes, of course. It's Crayshore Manor, on the edge of Melford village. Do you know it?'

'I'll find it. Would eleven o'clock be convenient?'

'Fine. And your name?'

'Mrs Jenkins.'

'Right, Mrs Jenkins. I'll see you later then.'

I rang off and stood — my hand still on the receiver — trying to pluck up he courage to ring Adam. Making up my mind I picked it up again and punched in his number. His secretary replied.

'Tropicalle Pools.'

'May I speak to Mr. Fenn please?'

'I'm sorry, he had to go out to see a client. Can I give him a message?'

'No, I'll ring him later.'

'Can he ring you back? I'm not sure when he'll be in.'

'No. I'll leave it for now,' I said.

'Shall I tell him who was ringing?'

'It's Mrs Grayson,' I told her, 'Mrs Frances Grayson.' I replaced the receiver with a sense of frustration. All I wanted now was to get it over with. It would have been so easy to leave a message with his secretary that I couldn't take the job, but I couldn't do it. I owed Adam more than that.

It was dead on eleven o'clock when the front

141

door bell rang. I opened the door to find a woman in her fifties standing on the step. She wore a shabby brown coat and her long greying hair was caught back into a ponytail from which thin, wispy strands were escaping.

I held the door open for her. 'Please come in, Mrs Jenkins. Come through to the kitchen. I was just going to make some coffee. Would you like a cup?'

In the kitchen I went to the sink to fill the kettle. Looking round, I saw that she was still standing in the doorway. 'Won't you have a seat?' I offered.

'Thanks, don't mind if I do.' She came into the room. 'Look, I won't beat about the bush,' she said. 'I'm not after any cleaning job. I'm not Mrs Jenkins. I'm just plain Sheila Philips and I'm here on a personal matter.'

'Oh!' I was taken aback. 'What do you want then?' The expression on her face and her hesitation made me look at her more closely. 'I'm sorry, have we met before? Do I know you?'

She smiled wryly. 'We have met before, yes, but I wouldn't expect you to remember.'

'When was this, where . . . ?'

'It was thirty-one years ago. You were the baby girl I gave up for adoption.'

My heart missed a beat and just for a moment I wondered if I had heard her right. 'You're saying that you are my . . . ?'

'That's right. I'm your birth mother.'

'But, how did you know where to find me?' I asked at last, my voice a cross between a squeak and a whisper.

'It wasn't difficult,' she said. She calmly took a seat at the kitchen table and looked at me. 'Did you say something about coffee? I've come quite a long way.'

I plugged in the kettle and looked at her. 'Look, forgive me for asking, but how can I be sure you're who you say you are?'

She shrugged. 'How many people know you're adopted?'

'Not many,' I conceded. 'Only my husband and parents. Oh and Dad's sister, Aunt Mavis . . . '

'Exactly, Mavis Garner. She was my best friend at school. I was pregnant and about to have an abortion when her brother and his wife found out they couldn't have kids. They were only too thrilled to take you off my hands.'

I stared at this woman sitting at my kitchen table coolly drinking coffee and talking about me as though I was a bundle of unwanted rags. I'd often wondered about my birth mother, even fantasized about finding and meeting her someday, but this was very far from how I'd imagined it would be. 'How very lucky for you,' I said drily.

She bridled. 'I can't see that you've got any room to talk,' she said. 'I went to see Mavis a few weeks ago because I got it into my head that I'd like to know how you'd turned out. She was telling me what an ungrateful little bitch you turned out to be and about how she helped out all them years ago with your little teenage secret.'

I gasped. 'Secret?'

She laughed. 'No need to look like that. Like mother, like daughter. That's what they say, isn't it? Up the duff at sixteen and just as glad to get shot of it as I was by all accounts, so don't pretend no different to me. I've been there, remember. Seen it all and got the bleedin' T-shirt as they say!'

My heart was beating fast now. 'I don't know why you're here,' I said shakily. 'But I'd like you to go now. I don't think we have anything more to say to one another.'

'Oh, don't you? Well I don't agree.' She looked around her. 'I think you owe me more than a cup of coffee sat at the kitchen table like some skivvy, don't you?'

'I don't think I owe you anything.'

She raised her eyebrows. 'Oh — that right, is it?' She looked around her. 'You've done all right for yourself. Eye to the main chance I bet when you decided to sleep with the boss! I heard all about how you wrecked his marriage.'

'I did nothing of the kind.'

'No? Sorry, my mistake. Got a little boy, I hear. I expect hubby knows all about your other kid, cos of course you're too decent and moral to keep a thing like that from him, aren't you?'

I walked to the door and opened it, my insides quaking. 'Please go,' I said. 'I've heard enough.'

She didn't move. 'Oh come on now. No need to get all uppity. Look, I'll put my cards on the table. I'm down on my luck. I lost my job and the Council are threatening to chuck me out of my flat because of the arrears on the rent. I need a bit of help. I know Mavis would've helped me

144

out but she's only got her pension, bless her.' She glanced around her. 'But you now, you're well set up. You'd never miss a few quid.'

'If you're asking me for money you're wasting your time. I haven't got any.'

She gave a short bark of laughter. 'Excuse me, dear! I wasn't born yesterday.' She paused. 'Your hubby'd be really surprised to hear about what you got up to before he met you, I bet.'

So that was it. She was here to blackmail me. 'He already knows,' I bluffed.

'That's funny. Mavis seems to think different, said her sister-in-law told her that when your boy was born you were scared stiff something might be said about him not being your first.'

I came slowly back into the kitchen and sat down opposite her. 'All I have is a small allowance,' I said.

'I'm not greedy,' she said with a smirk. 'An allowance eh? What a good idea — sounds fine to me. Shall we say a grand a month?'

'What?' I stared at her.

'Oh come on, I bet you'd be willing to pay a housekeeper that.'

'It was you who rang this morning, wasn't it?'

She shrugged. 'Had to make sure you was in, didn't I?'

'It's out of the question,' I said. 'My husband would soon ask where the money was going.'

'That'd be your problem.'

'You do know that blackmail is a criminal offence, don't you? I've only to ring the police . . .'

'Ooh! Then the fat *would* be in the fire,

145

wouldn't it? Everything would have to come out. No, I don't think you'll do that.' She smiled. 'You wouldn't want to risk losing all this — and your precious boy into the bargain, would you? From what I hear this hubby of yours is a very proud man, likes to put on a good show. He wouldn't want you causing him to lose face, would he?' She sat back in her chair and half closed her eyes. 'I'm just trying to imagine how an article in the paper would look. *Boss of Grayson Electronics duped by lying wife.*'

My heart turned to ice. 'I couldn't possibly manage a thousand,' I muttered.

'Half then for starters,' she said quickly. 'Five hundred and I'll make sure your secret is safe, for the time being.'

I swallowed hard. 'You'd better give me your address.'

She chuckled. 'Oh no you don't! I'm not that wet behind the ears. You can meet me with the cash each month at Paddington station, in the café. Say eleven o'clock the first Monday in every month.' She produced a diary from her handbag and opened it, marking the page. 'That's a week next Monday for the first payment. Oh and by the way, make it cash, no cheques.' She stood up and drew her coat around her. 'Mind you don't forget.' She pushed past me into the hall. 'G'bye then sweetheart. Thanks for the coffee.'

After she'd gone I sat for a long time at the kitchen table, too stunned to think straight. How could this be happening? It felt so surreal. And how on earth was I going to pay her five hundred

146

pounds every month without Charles finding out? It was true that he gave me an allowance but it was only for small things. If I wanted to buy anything expensive he gave me his credit card — as long as he approved. It was going to be really hard finding five hundred every month. There was only one answer.

Slowly, on trembling legs I got up and went into the hall. Lifting the receiver I dialled Adam's number. His secretary put me through at once. He sounded pleased to hear from me.

'Frances! I'm so sorry I was out earlier. It was an emergency. Do you have good news for me?'

'I swallowed hard. 'I've decided to take the job, Adam,' I said. 'There's just one snag.'

'What's that?'

'The school holidays. I can't be away from home when Harry is here.'

'Of course you can't. I'd already thought of that,' he said. 'Don't worry. We'll work something out. I can't tell you how delighted I am, Frances. Can you come up to the office as soon as possible? I'll get my secretary to draw up a contract for you to sign and we'll have a celebratory lunch.'

'That would be nice. Thank you, Adam.' I put the phone down with a sigh, He'd sounded so pleased.

Now all I had to do was to break the news to Charles.

12

KATIE

In some ways I wish I'd never suggested starting up a wedding gown design service to Imogene. Ever since our ad went in (we paid a fortune to put it in one of the major Sunday supplements but it paid off) we've been inundated with requests and worked off our feet. At least when I say 'we' I really mean ME. After working at Fantaisie all day I've been working hard all the rest of the hours God sends at home, doing sketches for the clients' approval and then working on the dress itself, not to mention fittings and alterations. I'll swear Imogene thinks it all happens by magic. She objects when I yawn at work and constantly pulls me up for looking fagged out.

'Have you pressed your dress lately, Katie? It looks as if you've slept in it! Why don't you wear a bit more make-up? You look like Marley's ghost this morning.'

When I asked her who the hell 'Marley' is when she's at home she accused me of being sarcastic as well. Seems I can't win! I'll be glad when we're proper legal partners. At the moment I still feel like the hired help most of the time.

★ ★ ★

148

I really enjoyed the last date with the girls, although Sophie wasn't looking very well. She looked tired and seemed to have something on her mind and I couldn't help wondering if the so-called change of image had anything to do with it. The new haircut and clothes looked great but somehow she didn't look like the Sophie I'd always admired so much. I suspect she told Fran what it was all about when they went off to the Ladies together after lunch but Fran didn't tell me anything after Sophie had left. I must admit that I felt a bit hurt. I hope they're not going to start leaving me out. I know I'm not really in their league — never have been. I'm sure they didn't believe me when I told them about my partnership with Imogene or my success with my designing. Serves me right for being such a fibber at school, I suppose. I admit that I do still tend to big things up a bit but I do like to think I've grown up since school and whatever anyone says about me I've always been a loyal friend. Perhaps we'll have another lunch date soon. I hope so because I really do value having friends like Fran and Sophie. Maybe next time I should take the initiative and ring them.

I was thinking all this one Monday lunchtime when Imogene had gone off on a buying trip. I was on my own for the day and as we were fairly quiet I was snatching a quick sandwich in the office. When I heard the boutique door chimes I peered out and saw to my surprise that a man stood in the shop — quite a dishy man at that. He was around forty, with thick dark hair, silvering at the temples like in all the best romantic novels. He wore a well-cut grey suit and a crisp white shirt. Father of the prospective bride? I speculated. Stepping forward, I smiled.

'Good afternoon, sir. Can I help you?'

He turned and smiled, his brown eyes lighting up in a thousand watt smile that quite knocked me back on my heels.

'Oh, good afternoon. You wouldn't happen to be Katie MacEvoy would you?'

'Yes, I am,' I said, surprised.

'Forgive me for dropping in on you like this,' he went on. 'But I was at a wedding recently and, being in the rag trade myself I couldn't help admiring the bride's dress. It was really beautiful but the cut wasn't familiar to me. I was intrigued because I pride myself on being able to recognize the signature of most of the popular couturiers so I asked the bride's mother, Mrs Hanson, who the designer was. She gave me your name and told me where I could find you. You're very talented.'

'Oh!' I blushed. 'Thank you.'

He glanced round. 'I was surprised to hear that you were working here as an assistant. That can't be right, surely?'

'No, actually I'm a partner,' I told him. 'Imogene, Miss Shaw, is out all day today.'

He nodded. 'I see. So do you design all the wedding dresses?'

'Yes. I make them too,' I told him.

'That must be an awful lot of work.'

'Well, put it this way, I don't get a lot of spare time.'

'I can imagine.'

'Yes.' The conversation seemed to peter out at that point and I cleared my throat. 'So, is there something I can show you, Mr — er . . . ?'

'Drew.'

'Is it wedding dresses you're looking for, Mr Drew?'

'Just Drew.' He was smiling again. 'It's what all my friends call me. I'll be straight with you, Katie.' He raised an eyebrow. 'May I call you Katie?'

'Yes, I suppose so.'

'I'm not looking for dresses today. I'm more interested in you. I happen to think you have a great future and, if you don't mind my saying so I think your boss — sorry, *partner*, is exploiting you.'

'Oh no,' I said quickly. 'In fact, if it hadn't been for her I wouldn't be selling my designs at all. I was just a humble dressmaker before.'

'Far from humble, Katie, trust me,' he said. 'Look, come and have a bite of lunch with me — and bring some of your design sketches. I'd like to talk to you.'

'I can't, I'm afraid. I'm here on my own today. Anyway, I don't take a lunch break. I usually just snatch a sandwich.'

'But you must get some time off, a half day?'

I nodded. 'Yes, Thursdays — which is when I have to go home and catch up on my work.'

'Well, how about just this once you take time out on your half day to have lunch with me?' He looked at my doubtful expression. 'No strings, Katie, just a talk. I really feel you should be made aware of what you're losing out on.'

'I'm quite happy as I am,' I told him. 'I'm not the ambitious type.'

'No harm in hearing what I have to say though, is there?' he looked at me. 'No sinister intentions, I promise. We'll lunch in a public restaurant.' He grinned mischievously. 'Within screaming distance of a policeman!'

I blushed. 'Oh! I'm not . . . ' I stopped, aware that he was pulling my leg. The smile assaulted me again and I felt myself caving in. He really was dishy and I had to admit that I was intrigued and flattered by what he said. 'OK then — Thursday.'

'Do you have a mobile?'

'Yes.'

'Give me your number and I'll text you where to meet me.'

'You could always pick me up here,' I pointed out.

'Better not,' he said. 'Don't want your partner to think you're being poached, do we?'

'It's not exactly out of the question that I might have a lunch date,' I said.

He chuckled. 'Far from it. Nevertheless . . . '

After he'd gone I thought a lot about what he'd said and also implied. He'd been interested enough in my work to come and seek me out. Was I really good enough to compete with professional designers? I doubted it but it'd be interesting to find out. As for Imogene — I didn't really see why I should tell her. It was only lunch and a chat after all. She didn't tell me everything she did in her free time. And it wasn't as if I was thinking of letting this man headhunt me, was it? (I couldn't help a little thrill running up my spine at the thought of little old me being head hunted.) Fran and Sophie were *never* going to swallow this one!

The week went by fairly uneventfully and I'd almost forgotten about the glamorous Drew when I received a text from him on Wednesday afternoon. He'd booked a table for two at a rather smart restaurant on the Strand and asked me to meet him there at one-thirty in the bar. It set me off in a panic of wondering what to wear. I decided on my newest buy. I'd had my eye on the outfit for ages and Imogene let me have it at cost price in our last end-of-season sale and so far I'd never worn it. It was a well cut wool suit by one of my favourite designers. I loved the colour, a subtle shade of green which complemented my red hair. When I took it to work with me on the Thursday to change into, Imogene raised an eyebrow.

'Mmm! Got a date?'

'Something like that,' I said cagily. I'm no good at secrets and I hoped she wouldn't press me for details. She didn't, but she couldn't help making one of her barbed remarks.

'Well, I wish you'd take as much trouble over your everyday appearance,' she said, looking at my newly washed and tamed hair. She walked away, grinning to herself as though the mere idea of me having a lunch date I needed to dress up for was highly amusing. A few minutes later she remarked that she hoped it wouldn't stop me finishing the dress I was putting the finishing touches to. I assured her it wouldn't.

Drew was already waiting for me in the restaurant bar when I arrived. He saw me in the mirror above the bar and swung round on his stool to smile a welcome.

'Katie! You're looking lovely. What will you have?'

'Just an orange juice please.'

'Sure you wouldn't like a vodka in there to stop it being lonely?'

I shook my head. 'I've got a lot of work to go home to. I don't want to fall asleep over it.'

He ordered my drink and sat looking at me until I felt my colour rising. Had I overdone the make-up?

'Your hair is the most wonderful colour,' he said at last. 'Titian.'

'That's a new name for it.'

'What do you call it?' he asked.

I laughed. 'It was always 'carrots' at school. Or 'corkscrews' because it's so frizzy.'

'You should let it flow freely,' he said, bending forward to pull out the combs I'd held it back with. He sat back to admire the effect. 'It's amazing.'

'It's too curly,' I corrected. 'It was a bit damp when I set out this morning. That always tightens it up.'

He took a sip of his drink without taking his eyes off me. 'You're the same over your looks as you are about your talent — self deprecating.'

'I know my limitations.'

'I beg to differ, you clearly haven't the slightest idea what you could aspire to.'

A waiter came to tell him our table was ready

and he stood up and held out his hand. 'Let's go and eat. We can talk later.'

The meal was delicious but I hardly tasted any of it. I had a strange feeling in the pit of my stomach. Did he really mean what he said? And what would happen next?

'What does your boyfriend think of your work, Katie?' he asked over the dessert. I shook my head.

'Haven't got one.'

He looked at me, his head on one side. 'I find it very hard to believe that some lucky guy hasn't snapped you up. Although having said that, someone who is as dedicated to her work as you must find hardly any time for romance.'

'That's true,' I agreed. 'And anyway, I never go anywhere I'd be likely to meet guys.'

'So you've only yourself to please? Footloose and fancy free. Well that can't be bad, can it?' He pushed his empty plate away and signalled to the waiter that we were ready for coffee. 'Katie, did you bring some sketches for me?'

I opened my bag and pulled out a handful of sketches, torn from the pages of my sketchbook. He looked at them thoughtfully. 'If I asked you very nicely would you let me take these to show to a fashion house I sometimes work with?'

My heart skipped a beat. 'Why?' I asked. 'I mean, what for?'

'With a view to their commissioning some of your work in the future.'

I shook my head. 'I have trouble keeping up with the workload I've got now.'

He raised his eyebrows. 'You don't intend to

stay at Fantaisie for ever, do you? This would be the next step in your career.'

I bit my lip. 'But what about Imogene? She gave me this opportunity in the first place.'

'And she's had all your hard work, loyalty and devotion back. I think you've more than repaid any debt you owe her, Katie. Just think, one day you could have your own label. You could be famous. Surely that's your aim?'

My head was spinning and I hadn't had so much as half a glass of wine. 'I haven't really thought that far ahead,' I said. 'I don't know.'

He shook his head exasperatedly. 'But you *must* know. When you were growing up — how did you see yourself as an adult; what did you dream about?'

I shook my head. 'There was no room for dreams when I was a kid. Only the hope that I would somehow survive and earn a living,' I told him. 'I'm a poor kid from Ireland. I lost both my parents when I was still at school and I grew up with a brother and sister-in-law who only saw me as a nuisance. I left school with hardly any qualifications.' I looked him straight in the eye. 'I've always been a nobody, Drew. I've never had any illusions about it.'

'*No!*' He thumped the table so hard that diners at the next table looked round. 'You're bright and beautiful and talented, Katie. You could be anything you wanted to be. Up there with the best of them — Versace, Dior, Westwood. All you need is confidence. Believe me. Believe in *yourself.*'

His words shook me to the core. No one had

ever told me I was beautiful before. Everyone I'd ever known had implied if not actually *said* that I was plain and ordinary. I looked up to find him waiting for my answer.

'Well? What do you say?'

'I'll have to think about it,' I said.

He smiled suddenly. 'So, what shall we do with the rest of the day?'

'I told you, I have to go home and work.'

He looked at his watch. 'We've got time to catch a matinée. Have you seen *Phantom of the Opera?*'

I shook my head. 'No, but I told you. I have to . . . ' I got no further. He got up abruptly and held out his hand to me. 'If you want to go and freshen up I'll wait for you in reception,' he said. 'I've already bought the tickets so don't even *think* of making any more excuses because I'm not taking no for an answer.'

The show was enthralling. I'd never been inside a West End theatre before and I soon forgot all about work and the dress I should be finishing in the sheer magic and excitement of it all. When the curtain went up after the interval on the Masquerade scene I gasped with enchantment at the vibrant spectacle of all the characters in their amazing, colourful costumes standing on the great staircase. Drew reached out and took my hand, giving it a squeeze.

'Fancy designing for the theatre?' he whispered. 'Remember what I said; you could do it, Katie. Anything is possible if you just believe.'

It wasn't until long after I got home that I realized that he still had my sketches.

13

SOPHIE

It's the end of October. Soon it'll be half term and I still haven't been able to talk to Rex. I've tried to ring him and sent him text after text but he never gets back to me. The last time I tried to ring he'd obviously got himself a new phone — and number, so the link has finally gone and I'm slowly coming to terms with the idea that our marriage is over.

He'll have to get in touch eventually of course. Half of Greenings is his and once it's sold he'll have some money to collect. Not all that much, it's true. We only put down the minimum deposit and once the debt to my parents is paid back there won't be much to share out. Though now that the builders have finished and the house is sound and saleable it should be worth a lot more than we paid for it. I have to admit that it does look wonderful. Just the dream home I visualized. The only downside is that I'm rattling around in it sad and alone.

At the beginning of term my colleagues at school were surprised by my new look. I had one or two snide remarks from two of the bitchier female teachers and the cheeky young sports master remarked with a wink that it was great to see my legs at last. But I was too preoccupied with bigger problems to get annoyed and they all soon found something else to gossip about. Fran, bless her, was so kind to me when she found me in tears that day at the restaurant. She rang me a couple of times after our lunch date to ask if there was any news, but lately I haven't heard from her. Everyone has their own life and problems to worry about, so why should anyone care about me? Anyway I expect she's looking forward to seeing her son at half term.

The new intake of kids has been worse than usual this year. Hardly any of them have the slightest interest in art. It doesn't matter how innovative I try to make it for them the lessons usually end in disruption and somehow I just don't seem to have the energy to deal with it. On one particularly bad day someone started throwing paint around and before I could take control of the situation it had developed into chaos. As luck would have it John Harrison, the head, happened to walk past as things were reaching crisis point. To my embarrassment he walked in and read them the riot act. As he passed me on his way out he asked me quietly to look in to his office for 'a chat' after school.

I've always liked and respected John Harrison since he became headmaster three years ago. He's a talented teacher in his forties with a great track record for pulling round failing schools and he's done wonders since he came here. I've always found his treatment of staff and children fair and kindly, though his patience isn't endless and he can be extremely tough if he has to. As I made my exhausted way upstairs to his office after the bell had gone, I had a horrible feeling that this was going to be one of those occasions.

I knocked and he called out to enter. As I opened the door he looked up. To my relief he was smiling. 'Ah, Sophie, come in and sit down.' He put the file he was working on to one side and gave me his full attention. 'So, that commotion in the studio this afternoon, what was that all about? I've never known you to lose control of a class before.'

'It's this year's new intake,' I said wearily, sinking on to a chair. 'They just don't like art and I can't get them interested. It doesn't seem to matter what I try and do.'

'That's not like you. You're usually so inventive. Surely there must be something you could find that would grab their imagination.'

'They don't seem to have any.' I shook my head. 'They think that art is for infants. I tried sculpture last week but they insisted on calling it plasticine. When I give them complete freedom to draw what they like they draw crude, obscene pictures, and as for painting — well, you saw for yourself what they do with paint.'

He looked at me for a moment. 'Surely it can't be all of them — the whole class?'

'There are two or three ring leaders. They take great pleasure in winding the others up.'

'Then single them out.' He leaned forward. 'You've had first year problems before, Sophie, and you've coped admirably So what's different about this term?' To my horror I could feel tears pricking the corners of my eyes. He noticed at once. 'Problems at home?' he asked softly. 'Want to talk about it? I'm sure you know that anything

160

you say inside this room goes no further.'

I blinked angrily at the threatening tears. 'It's no excuse. I shouldn't be bringing my domestic issues into school.'

'Sometimes it's unavoidable.' He took a box of tissues out of the drawer and passed them silently across the desk.

I took a deep breath. 'Rex has left me.' Saying it out loud to my boss was like admitting defeat and failure. It made me feel utterly desolate, but I swallowed hard at the lump in my throat, determined not to avail myself of the tissues. 'It's a long story,' I went on. 'And a lot of it is my fault.' I looked up at him. 'But *not all!*'

He smiled. 'That's more like the Sophie Turner I know.' He looked at his watch. 'Look, it's too early for the pub but Mary's Tearoom down the road will be open. How about a cup of tea and an off-the-record chat?'

'Aren't you expected at home?'

He shook his head.

'But you must have work to do. It's not fair for me to take up your time with my dreary moaning.'

'If a member of my staff has a problem then it's mine too,' he said as he got up and reached for his coat. 'As I think we've proved this afternoon.'

★ ★ ★

Mary's Tearoom was decorated in the Olde English style. The ceiling had mock beams and there were blue and white checked table cloths

161

and willow pattern china. When we arrived it was almost empty and we took a table near the fireplace with its blazing electric log fire. John ordered a pot of tea and two slices of Mary's home made carrot cake. I shook my head at him.

'I'm not hungry. You'll probably have to eat mine.'

'Nonsense. You look as though you could do with a good meal. It's my guess you've been neglecting yourself.'

'Do I look as bad as that?'

He grinned. 'You know what I mean. Seriously, you've lost weight. I'd guess that you feel that cooking for one is a bit pointless.' He cocked an eyebrow at me. 'Am I right?'

'You seem to know a lot about it.'

'I do as a matter of fact. Between ourselves, Hillary has taken the boys and gone back to live with her parents in Yorkshire.'

'Oh my God, John. I'd no idea. I'm so sorry.'

He shrugged. 'Me too. But we're here to talk about you, so fire away.'

I shook my head. 'I feel awful now, burdening you with my domestic troubles when you've got far worse yourself.'

The waitress brought our tea and John picked up the pot. He looked at me. 'Milk and sugar?'

'Just milk, thanks.' I watched him pour. 'I don't know where to begin.'

He passed me my cup. 'The beginning is usually favourite.'

The tea was hot and very welcome and for a moment we were silent. At last I put my empty cup back on its saucer and looked at him. 'We

162

bought a house,' I began. 'A very old, very run down house. It was me who wanted it. The idea — my idea — was to renovate it ourselves. It was meant to be fun. I saw it as my dream house.'

He raised an eyebrow. 'And Rex's, his too?'

'He wasn't so keen, but he agreed.'

'Because he loved you.'

I smiled wryly. '*Loved* being the operative word — past tense. Renovating the house has been a nightmare. We've never had so many rows. Rex was working freelance you see, from home. The idea was for him to do a lot of the plumbing and carpentering work, fit it in around his own work. But he never seemed to get round to it, whereas I worked every minute I could, evenings and holidays, on the decorating.'

'And naturally you started to feel resentful.'

'You could say that. In the end he went behind my back, cap in hand to my parents and asked them for money to pay a builder to do the work.'

'So, was that a problem?'

I sighed. 'It's complicated. They insisted on *giving* us the money.'

'Lucky you!'

'*No!*' he looked shocked by my vehemence as I punched the table, making the cups rattle. 'Sorry, but you don't understand. I've never got on with my parents. When I was a child I hardly saw them. They were always too busy with their business to be bothered with a demanding child. Their idea of parenting was to throw money at me. They couldn't see that it was their attention I needed. Now that I'm an adult they seem to think they can still buy me. They want me to be

163

forever in their debt.'

'Maybe they are just trying to make it up to you,' he said. 'Hence the gift.'

I shook my head. 'It's too late for that. When I got my first job I promised myself that I'd stand on my own feet from that day on. I vowed to take nothing more from them. I don't want their money if that's all they've got to give, which is why I was so angry with Rex for asking them for help without consulting me.'

'They're still your parents, Sophie,' he said softly. 'Don't let your pride spoil your relationship with them.'

'There's never really *been* a relationship.' I shook my shoulders impatiently. 'The truth is I went to see them after the business with the cash and I made it clear that I didn't want any more to do with them. Anyway, it's the relationship between me and Rex that's at stake now. And all because of . . . '

'Your stubbornness,' he cut in.

I stared at him. '*He's* the one not answering his phone,' I pointed out. 'He's the one who has cut off all contact.'

'What about the house? You're still living there, I take it.'

'Yes. It's finished,' I told him. 'It's just as I always dreamed it would be. But when Rex told me he'd accepted money from my parents I told him that Greenings would have to go on the market so that my parents can have their money back.'

He sighed, 'Oh, Sophie, *Sophie!* Can't you see what a mess you're making of everything? Can't you see how many people you're making unhappy?'

'And what about *me?*' I demanded. 'What about my happiness? Doesn't that count?'

He reached across the table to pat my hand. 'Sophie, forgive me for saying this but you sound just like a spoilt child,' he said. 'That same little girl your parents showered with gifts because they were too busy working to spend as much time with you as they'd have liked. Who do you think they did it for?' I stared at him. 'For *you*, of course. You were — you *are* their family. Who else do we work our socks off for?'

Suddenly I got an inkling of what he was getting at. 'Is that why Hillary left?' I asked quietly.

He sighed. 'Sometimes it's hard to get the priorities right, to balance career and family. It seems that — like your folks — I failed.' He looked up at me, smiling wryly. 'I'm a fine one to give you advice, aren't I? But I will say this: Get in touch with Rex, Sophie. Do it before it's too late. Don't let things drift on.'

I lifted my shoulders. 'I told you. I have been trying,' I reminded him. 'But now that he's changed his phone I've no way of finding out where he is.'

'Well, when you do you're going to have to put your pride in your pocket, aren't you? It's either that or wipe the slate clean, and I've a feeling that you desperately want things to be back as they were.' When I didn't reply he refilled our teacups and pushed mine towards me.

'Forgive me for asking, but this change of style

165

you've adopted, is it . . . ?'

'I was getting too old for the art student look,' I cut in impatiently. 'That's all it is. But oddly enough that was what tipped the scales with Rex. He thought I was trying to prove something.'

'Like what?' He frowned.

'I don't really know. Maybe he thought I was trying to shake off the person he'd married, turn myself into someone new.'

'And were you?'

'No! I told you.' I stopped suddenly, asking myself if perhaps there was a deeper, subconscious reason for changing the way I looked. I glanced up at him. 'Who knows? Maybe he saw something I didn't. I'm so mixed up I can't think straight any more.'

For a few minutes neither of us spoke then he asked, 'Are you still doing those child portraits, Sophie?'

I was surprised. I wasn't aware that he knew about my extra-curricula work. 'Yes, I suppose so.' I glanced at him. 'I've only ever done them in my spare time,' I said defensively. 'I've never let it interfere with my teaching.'

He smiled. 'I know that, Sophie. I wasn't objecting. I asked because I wondered if you'd do some work for me.' He spooned sugar into his cup and stirred. 'Hillary says I can have the boys in the school holidays and at half term. As that's all I'm likely to see of them I'd love to have a couple of portraits to keep me company when they're not there.' He smiled at me. 'Would you consider taking us on?'

'You want me to do it this half term?'

'Will you be free?'

'Do you need to ask? I've been dreading half term as a matter of fact. Rattling round in that house alone with nothing to do. But surely they'll be looking forward to better things to do than spend time posing for portraits. You'll have outings planned.'

'I'm sure they wouldn't mind the odd half hour.'

'How old are they?'

'Ian's seven and David is nine.'

A week was a very short time for two portraits and I hesitated, then I had a sudden idea. 'I could do them in pastel. It's a great medium for children and it's quick — far less sitting than you need for oils. I think you'd like the effect. A couple of half hour sessions would do and I'll bring my camera and take photographs to work on at home.'

'Fine.' He smiled. 'Sounds like a plan. You know more about the technical stuff than I do so I'll leave it up to you.' He beckoned the waitress for the bill. 'We'll talk about times and so on later.' He paid the waitress and stood up. 'Oh, just one thing: I want you to charge whatever your other clients charge, right? No 'mates' rates. Right?'

I grinned at him. 'Right, if you insist.'

★ ★ ★

John still lived in the Harrisons' family home, a pleasant detached house in a tree-lined avenue not far from school. When I went round for my

167

first session with his young sons on the Monday of half term week they were a little shy and apprehensive. Understandably the idea of sitting still for a whole thirty minutes while some strange female drew them was not appealing to two small boys. But once I began talking to them and showing them the pastels, the special paper and the brushes and tools I would use, we soon became friends. They were surprised when I told them they didn't have to sit still all the time. I set to work, making quick sketches of them while they told me about their new school and all the things they liked to do. I wanted to get to know all their expressions so that I could capture something of their personalities. In half an hour I had enough material to make a start at home and I took photographs to refer to later so that I could get their colouring correct. They seemed surprised when I began to pack up my camera and pencils.

'Is that all?' Ian asked. He sounded almost disappointed.

'Yes. That's all I need for now. Anyway, your dad tells me that you're going out for a day at the zoo, so I mustn't take up too much of your time,' I told them.

He turned to his father. 'Dad, can Sophie come to the zoo with us?'

Acutely embarrassed, I shook my head. 'No, Ian, I can't. Not today. I've got a lot of work to do and besides, your dad wants you all to himself. The three of you will have much more fun on your own.' I shot an apologetic look at John.

'Maybe another day,' he said to his son. As he showed me to the front door he said. 'You are perfectly welcome to join us, you know. Actually the boys seem to have taken a shine to you.'

But I shook my head. 'Thanks John, but I do have a lot to do.' I held up my case. 'I'm looking forward to going home to work on the portraits. Ian and David are wonderful subjects. It'll take my mind off — well, you know.'

'Well, we won't be setting off for another hour so if you change your mind . . . '

'It's sweet of you to invite me but I'll pass this time. I'd like another sitting though, maybe later in the week, so that I can check everything.'

'Of course. Just ring and let me know when.'

Back at Greenings I worked all day on the portraits. I'd never known such easy subjects as Ian and David. Their little faces seemed to spring out of the paper for me with hardly any effort all. Working at what I loved to do best, I lost myself in the sheer pleasure of it and I decided that I must invest in some new advertising to get more commissions. I'd let them drop off lately but once the house was sold and I was on my own again I'd need some extra income as well as something to take my mind off what I saw as my failure.

I was working upstairs in the little studio I'd created for myself at the back of the house looking out on the rambling garden. Autumn had created a whole new landscape as the trees had turned from a canopy of green to a glorious profusion of crimson, gold and russet. I sighed with nostalgia. Things should have been so different. Now that

169

the house was finished we should have been enjoying it together.

I'd just finished for the day and was thinking about going downstairs to make myself a meal when my phone rang. Picking it up, I saw that the call was from Katie.

'Hi!' I said. 'Nice to hear from you. Everything all right?'

'More than all right.' She sounded excited. 'I've got some exciting news, but I'll wait till I see you to tell you about it. Look, I expect you're on half term at the moment and I wondered if we could have one of our lovely lunch meetings.'

'That would be nice,' I said. 'But won't Fran be busy with her son at home from his new school?'

'I rang her and as it happens her husband is taking Harry to some big IT exhibition on Thursday at Earls Court so she's happy for us all to meet if you're up for it.'

'OK then. Usual time and place?'

'You bet,' she said. 'Looking forward to it no end. Can't wait to tell you my news!'

Walking through to the kitchen I realized suddenly that this had been my first happy day for months. I thought about my talk with John. He'd managed somehow to put a few things into perspective for me. Could he have been right about my parents and their motives for working so hard? Had I been unduly harsh with them over the money gift? I know Mum had been really upset at some of the things I'd said. Maybe I should apologize. On impulse I went through to the hall and picked up the phone, dialling their number. After a few rings I heard the receiver being lifted.

'Hi, Maggie and Geoff Bambers' house.'

I froze, recognizing Rex's voice. So that's where he was! Sucking up to my parents again. No doubt putting his side of things and getting their sympathy! Without speaking I slammed the receiver down hard.

'Damn you to hell!' I said aloud, shaking with rage. 'If that's the way you want to play — *fine!*'

14

Katie could hardly wait for her two friends to arrive at Napolitano — so much so that she was early. She chose a table where they would see her the moment they arrived, ordered herself a gin and tonic and settled down to wait.

Since her lunch with Drew she'd been waiting for news and a couple of days ago he'd been in touch again, this time by phone. The call had come when she was on the bus on her way home and, seeing his name come up, she'd answered it eagerly.

'Hi, Drew?'

'Katie. Good to hear your voice. I was wondering what you were doing on Thursday. I know it's your half day.'

Her heart missed a beat. 'Well not a lot really. I'm meeting a couple of friends for lunch, but apart from that . . . '

'OK, so what about dinner? As a matter of fact I've got some news that I think will interest you.'

'Oh! What's that?'

She could hear him smiling at the other end. 'Ah now, you're just going to have to wait and see. Dinner then?'

'Yes. That sounds nice. Where shall I meet you?'

'Give me your address and I'll come and pick you up. Can't have my protégée walking around the streets alone after dark now can I?'

She gave him the address, hoping he wouldn't think she lived in a slum. She had no idea where he lived but by the look of his clothes and general manner it had to be somewhere posh. And what did he mean by protégée? she asked herself, mystified.

Fran arrived first. Katie saw her as soon as she walked through the door. She thought she looked tense. Last time it had been Sophie who was preoccupied. Fran spotted her and waved, quickly adjusting her expression.

'Hi!' she said, taking the chair next to Katie. 'I thought I might be early. I travelled up to town with Harry and Charles on their way to this exhibition at Earls Court.'

'How are they?' Katie asked. 'How does Harry like his new sc hool?'

'Oh, they're fine,' Fran said dismissively.

Katie noticed that she left the enquiry about Harry's new school unanswered and wondered if it might be significant, but before she could pursue the question Sophie appeared and came across to the table smiling.

'Hi there you two. I'm not late, am I?' She took off her jacket and sat down. Seeing that the three had assembled, the waiter came across with menus and for a few minutes they were absorbed in making their choices. When they had ordered Sophie looked at Katie.

'So, what's this fantastic news?'

Katie took a deep breath, her cheeks turning pink with pleasure as she relayed her recent meeting with Drew and the events that followed.

'Now he says he's got some exciting news!'

She giggled. 'I can't wait!'

Fran and Sophie exchanged glances. 'I'd be a bit careful if I were you,' Sophie warned. 'He could be some kind of con-merchant. Have you checked out his credentials?'

Katie's face fell. 'What do you mean?'

'Is he known at any of these fashion houses he says he's working for? Surely you've checked up on him.'

Katie flushed a deep crimson. 'No. I trust him. He knew the name of one of our customers and that's good enough for me. He likes my designs, says I have a big future ahead of me. And he thinks Imogene is exploiting me.' She didn't mention that she had no idea what Drew's surname was and so couldn't check him out even if she wanted to.

Reading Katie's defensiveness Fran touched her arm. 'You have to be vigilant in business, Katie. Sophie is only thinking of you. There's such a thing as industrial espionage. He could be planning to steal your designs and pass them off as his own.'

'Drew would never do that. I'm sure he wouldn't,' Katie said.

The waiter brought their main course and they applied themselves to their food. Katie ate with her head downcast. She had looked forward so much to telling Fran and Sophie her fabulous news, thinking they'd be pleased for her but all they'd done so far was pour cold water on it. Could it be that they didn't believe her, or were they jealous? Surely not? How mean of them to begrudge her this one little bit of excitement.

But she swallowed her resentment. Last time they met Sophie had seemed preoccupied. Maybe her life wasn't as rosy as it seemed. She looked up.

'How are you, Sophie? Last time we met you seemed a bit under the weather.'

Sophie smiled wryly. 'Was I? Rex and I have been having a few problems. It's all to do with the house. It's costing far more than we expected it to. But apart from that I'm fine,' she said. 'My headmaster asked me to do pastel portraits of his two young sons. I've been working on them during this half-term week. I've got one more sitting with them tomorrow before they go back to their mother.'

Fran looked at her. 'Go back? Have he and his wife split up?'

Sophie nodded. 'Unfortunately, yes. Par for the course these days, isn't it? At least Rex and I don't have any kids, thank goodness.'

Katie picked up on the remark immediately. So that was why she'd looked so depressed last time. 'Are your problems that serious then?'

Sophie nodded. 'I'm afraid they are. Rex walked out and he's been incommunicado ever since. I wouldn't be surprised if the next time I hear from him it's through his solicitor.'

'Oh dear!' Fran turned to look at her. Outwardly Sophie's tone was flippant but she guessed that the light, offhand attitude was covering a deep hurt. 'I'm so sorry, love,' she said softly.

Sophie shrugged. 'It's OK. I've come to terms with it now.'

175

'What about the house?'

'On the market,' Sophie said briefly. 'Can't afford to live there on my own. Besides there's a massive loan to pay back.' She sighed. 'Not one of my better ideas, I have to say.' She looked at Fran. 'What about you, anything new on your horizon? What about the job you were offered. Have you decided to take it?'

Fran nodded. 'Yes. I start training after Harry goes back to school next week. I'm going to the office after lunch to arrange the final details.'

'Good for you. Was Charles all right about it?'

Fran paused just a beat too long before smiling brightly. 'Fine,' she said. There was a pause then she looked up at the other two. 'No, not fine actually. Something horrendous has happened.' She looked at her friends, trying to assess how they would take what she was about to tell them. 'I have a confession to make to you both. Neither of you ever knew about it, but I got pregnant in my last term at school.'

Sophie looked shocked. '*Fran!* I never even guessed. Why didn't you say anything?'

'I was too ashamed. The boy I thought loved me didn't want to know. I tried to keep it from my parents too, and I did for months. When they found out the balloon went up. They were even more horrified than I'd imagined.' She sighed. 'You knew of course that I was adopted?'

'Yes. I remember,' Katie said. 'I always felt it was a bond between us.'

'So how did your adoptive parents take your pregnancy?' Sophie asked.

'As you'd expect. It was made clear to me that

there was no question of my keeping the baby unless I wanted to be a single mother and alone at sixteen. They bundled me off to Dorset to Dad's sister, insisting that the baby was to be given up for adoption as soon as she was born. Only on those terms was I to be allowed home after which it was all to be forgotten, never to be spoken of again.' She bit her lip. 'I need hardly add that Charles has never had the slightest idea.'

Katie looked from one to the other, wondering where Fran's dramatic revelation was leading. 'Are you saying that your daughter has turned up?' she asked.

Fran shook her head. 'No. She'd still be too young. It was actually my birth mother who suddenly turned up.' She smiled wryly. 'All adopted people fantasize about their birth mother. Some people resent the woman who gave them away, and some — like me, especially after I went through it myself — see her as a sad victim of fate.'

'And yours?' Sophie prompted.

'Well, she's certainly no victim. It turns out she was a friend of my adopted father's sister which is how she knows all about my baby.'

'So what was her reason for coming to find you?'

'Putting it bluntly, to blackmail me,' Fran said. 'She's down on her luck and she thinks I'm rolling in money and that I owe some of it to her. She's threatening to tell Charles about my teenage pregnancy.'

Sophie gasped. 'You'll go to the police of course.'

177

Fran shook her head. 'How can I? It would all have to come out if I reported her. I'd lose everything including Harry. My life would be shattered. I'm going to have to pay her somehow. She refuses to believe that I have no money of my own, which is why I have to take the job.'

'Oh, Fran! Maybe if you confessed to Charles he'd take it reasonably. After all, he loves you. You're his wife and the mother of his son.'

Fran shook her head. 'You don't know him. He'd never forgive me for lying to him, besides, my — this woman is threatening to go to the papers. Losing face is Charles's worst nightmare.'

'Then he must be a very shallow man if you don't mind me saying so.' Sophie covered Fran's trembling hand with her own. 'And you didn't lie; you just didn't tell him. So when you told him you were taking the job, what did he say?'

Fran's eyes filled with tears. 'Don't even ask! I've had the most horrendous week. I can't begin to tell you . . . '

Katie looked from one to the other. It seemed that her friends didn't have the charmed life she'd imagined. What she'd heard over lunch today made her feel for the first time in her life that she was the lucky one. Not that her news had aroused the interest she'd hoped for. In fact it had gone off like a damp squib. She looked at her watch and was shocked to see how late it was. She was going to have to go or she wouldn't have time to wash her hair before meeting Drew. She looked at Fran apologetically.

'I'm really sorry love, but I'm afraid I'm going

to have to go.' She laid a hand on her friend's arm. 'I wish I could help in some way. I hate to leave you right now but I've got this urgent appointment and I can't be late.' She opened her bag to put her share of the meal on the table. 'Look, Fran, Soph, you know where I am if you want to talk — any time,' she added.

Sophie looked up. 'Oh, Katie, you're not meeting this Drew person, are you?'

'No,' Katie lied. 'It's a really important appointment though. I can't be late.' She stood up and gathered her bag and coat together. 'I do hope everything works out for you both.'

'For you too, Katie. Good luck.'

'Maybe we'll meet again soon.'

'Yes, we really must. Have a nice evening.'

'And remember what we said about being careful about this Drew of yours,' Sophie warned again.

They watched Katie whisk out through the restaurant door then looked at each other.

'Do you think we upset her?' Fran asked.

Sophie shook her head. 'She can be so naive. I had to warn her. I hope this Drew guy isn't stringing her along.'

'Me too. Poor little Katie.' Fran smiled wryly. 'I'm afraid we rather pricked her balloon. I wish I hadn't gone on about my own problems now.'

'So do I. I suppose we could have shown more enthusiasm. It must have made us look like a couple of pessimists pouring cold water over her plans.'

Fran looked at her. 'Is there really a serious problem between you and Rex?'

179

Sophie sighed. 'I'm afraid so. The trouble started when he went to my parents for a loan, behind my back.'

'I'm sure they were only too happy to help you out.'

'Oh, they were, but I wasn't. I wanted this to be our project — achieved without any help from anyone, least of all them. I reacted by insisting on putting the house on the market to pay them back.'

'Oh, Sophie!' Fran looked incredulous. 'That must have been so hurtful.'

Sophie bit her lip. 'I realize that now. At the time all I could think of was my own hurt.'

'And now?'

'I don't know.'

15

FRANCES

I felt so much better for getting some of my worries off my chest to Sophie over lunch. Now it was time to face Adam. Ostensibly my meeting with him was to make the final arrangements for my training but I also had a huge favour to ask him and the thought of it was already making me nervous.

I'd been looking forward to Harry's half-term so much and so far it had been a disaster. Charles had driven over to collect him while I waited eagerly at home, preparing Harry's favourite meal. But he'd seemed oddly subdued when he arrived home. All the questions I asked him were responded to with a one syllable answer. I put it down to tiredness after the journey but later after he'd gone up to have his bath I went up to collect his dirty clothes for the wash. Upstairs I put my head round the bathroom door only to be greeted by an indignant yell.

'*Mum!* I'm in the bath.'

I laughed. 'I know that. I only want your clothes to put in the wash.'

'I'm nine years old. I get bathed on my own now!'

There was something in his voice, a shrillness that was more than just embarrassment.

'It's all right, Harry. I am your mum,' I

reminded him. I pushed the door open and began to walk into the bathroom only to be met with a wet sponge hitting me in the face.

'*Go away!*'

Shocked, I withdrew quickly but not before I'd seen the bruises on his chest and shoulders. The sight shook me but I decided to play it down for now and wait until he was in bed.

He was sitting up reading a book when I knocked on his door. 'Is it safe to come in? I've brought you some cocoa.'

'Thanks, come in.' He blushed. 'Sorry Mum but I've sort of got used to doing stuff on my own,' he said.

I happened to know that the boys at school took communal showers but I let it go. I put the mug down on the bedside table and sat down on the edge of his bed. 'You haven't said much about school,' I said. 'You're happy there, aren't you? He nodded, his eyes still on his book. 'Made many friends?' Again he nodded. 'Teachers nice?'

He put the book down. 'Mum, I'm a bit tired, so . . .'

'I saw them, Harry,' I said. 'I couldn't help it. How did you get them?'

'Get what?' he mumbled, hiding his face in the mug of cocoa.

'You know what — the bruises.'

He shrugged, unable to meet my eyes. 'You know how rough rugby is. Everyone's got bruises.'

'Not like the ones you've got. What happened, Harry?'

'*Nothing!*'

'Did a teacher do it? Because if that's the case . . . '

'No. Give it a rest, Mum!'

I waited a moment, making it clear that I wasn't going away. He put his book aside and lay down. 'I want to go to sleep now.'

I tucked the covers round him and bent to kiss him but he turned his head away. 'Harry, what's wrong?' I asked. 'I'm not going anywhere until I get a proper answer.'

'*I told you. It's nothing!*' As he turned to me I saw the tears welling up in his eyes. 'Go away, Mum. Stop interrogating me!'

'Are you being bullied?' I asked quietly.

The tears got the better of him and he hid his head under the duvet. 'Honestly, it's nothing,' he repeated. 'Anyway, I promised Dad . . . '

I pulled the duvet back. 'You promised Dad what?'

'That I wouldn't tell you. He says it happens to everyone their first year. I've got to toughen up — grin and bear it.'

Inside I was seething but I managed to sound calm as I asked, 'Who did it, and why?'

'Older boys. It's what they do, because you're a kid. They make you do stuff and if you don't do it right they . . . '

'Hit you?'

He didn't need to answer my question. Determined not to be emotional, I tucked him up and switched off the bedside light. 'Go to sleep now and try not to worry about it,' I said, dropping a kiss on the top of his head. 'Night-night. See you in the morning.'

Downstairs Charles was sitting in the conservatory reading his paper, a whisky and soda on the table beside him. I sat down opposite.

'Did you know that Harry was being bullied at school?'

He glanced up. 'I'd hardly call it anything so melodramatic. A bit of joshing and being ordered about is par for the course in the first year,' he said casually.

'I'd hardly call intense bruising of the chest and shoulders *joshing*,' I said. 'Have you seen the state of him? He's black and blue!'

He looked at me over the top of the paper. 'He's a young boy. I expect he bruises easily. Anyway I told him not to go bleating to you about it. I knew you'd overreact just like you do over everything.

'He didn't *bleat* as you put it. I happened to walk into the bathroom when he was in the bath and he was very reluctant to tell me how he got the bruises. I notice that these young thugs are careful not to inflict any *visible* damage. What I've just seen on Harry's body is what the police would probably see as actual bodily harm. It should be stopped, Charles.'

'Oh, for heaven's sake stop emoting, Fran.' He sighed. 'It happens to everyone, believe me. It always has and it never did me any harm. Stop stressing about it and let the boy learn to toughen up.'

I stared at him. 'I can't believe you're taking this so casually. We're not living in Victorian England.'

He threw down his paper. 'Would you rather

he took a thrashing from a gang of drugged up council estate yobs?'

I knew this was another sideways swipe at the fact that his upbringing was more upper class than mine. I chose to ignore it. 'Does the headmaster know this goes on?'

'Probably,' he said with a shrug. 'I daresay it happened to him too when he was a first year. You've always spoiled the boy, Fran. That's why I wanted him to go away to school. If you had your way you'd have him grow up a namby-pamby mummy's boy.'

'Need I remind you that he is still only nine years old?'

'Exactly. Nine, not five. High time for him to start growing up,' he said. 'And while we're on the subject, there'll be no visits to zoos and theme parks this half term. I've taken some time off and I've made a list of things for us to do together, as father and son.'

'So I'm to be excluded?'

He shrugged. 'You're welcome to come along too if you think you'd be interested.' He picked up his paper again, a sign that the argument was at an end.

I took a deep breath. 'While we're talking, Charles, there's something I have to tell you.' I'd rehearsed this conversation in my head over and over during the past few days and I'd decided to use the word 'tell' rather than 'ask'.

He folded his newspaper and sighed exagger-atedly. 'What is it *now?*'

'The job I told you about — the one with the pool company. I've decided to take it.' Before he

185

could react I ploughed on, 'I've come to an arrangement with them about the holidays and half terms. I start training next week after Harry has gone back to school.' I sat back, immensely relieved to have actually said it at last. When I looked up his face was flushed, his eyes glittering with anger.

'You'll do nothing of the sort,' he said, 'I told you — I won't have it.'

'And you're going to stop me *how?* Lock me in the house, chain me to the railings? It's a perfectly respectable job, Charles. There is absolutely no reason why I shouldn't accept the offer and I've decided to take it. As I said before, we've moved on from the Victorian age.' Inside my stomach was churning. I knew I would never have been brave enough to stand up to him like this if it were not for sheer necessity. I just had to find the money to pay Sheila Philips somehow.

I hardly saw anything of Harry after that. Charles took him to football matches, to the Motor Show and the IT exhibition he was personally involved in. Each day he had arranged something totally male-orientated to take him to; and in spite of what he'd said, it was made clear to me that I wasn't expected to tag along. Today was Thursday. Just two more days before Harry returned to school and, presumably, the torture inflicted by the older boys. I'd hardly seen him, except during our evening meal and at bed time. Today I travelled up to London with them both for my lunch date with the girls and that was the most time I'd spent with my son all week.

On the subject of my job Charles had been

ominously silent. Presumably he was waiting until Harry had gone back to school to think up some way of getting back at me. I pushed it to the back of my mind. Whatever happened I was taking the job Adam had offered me. I had no choice; it was as simple as that.

After I'd said goodbye to Sophie outside the restaurant I went straight to Adam's office where he had a contract ready for me to sign. My hand shook as I took the pen he handed me. I was burning bridges. There would be no turning back now.

He looked at me. 'Are you all right, Frances?'

I nodded, trying to laugh off my nervousness. 'It's not every day I sign a contract.'

'You are sure about the job?'

I looked up at him. 'Yes, of course — but . . . '

'*But!* That's an ominous word. You have reservations?'

I shook my head. 'Not reservations.' I glanced round. 'A massive favour to ask actually.'

Reading my thoughts, he stood up. 'Come on, we'll go and have a drink, find a quiet corner where you can ask away.' He smiled, holding out my coat for me. 'Don't look so worried, Frances. It can't be that bad.'

'*Can't it?*' I said under my breath.

He took me to a club he belonged to in St James's Place where we found a quiet corner in a large upstairs room overlooking a leafy garden. Settling me in a large leather chair by the window he ordered a pot of tea then sat down opposite me.

'OK. Fire away.'

'You're going to think this is a terrible cheek.'

'Suppose you let me be the judge of that.'

I took a deep breath. 'I need to borrow five hundred pounds.'

To his credit, he didn't bat an eyelid. 'You mean you'd like an advance against your first month's salary?'

'Yes — I suppose so — please.' I looked at him. 'Adam, I know it's an awful cheek. After all, you hardly know me. I feel I owe you an explanation.'

'You don't need to explain anything to me.'

'Yes, I do.' I raised my hand. 'Please, let me. The money — it's not for me.'

I stopped talking as the waiter appeared with our tea. Adam silently poured me a cup. Passing it to me, he said quietly, 'Take your time, Frances. I can see that you have something you need to get off your chest, but remember, you really don't need to do this. You can have the advance without question.'

I took a sip of my tea. 'I can't tell you how grateful I am.' I put the cup back on its saucer. 'I'll be brief. It sounds bizarre and melodramatic but I'm being blackmailed over a serious mistake I made a long time ago,' I took a deep breath and began, 'I . . . '

He cut in. 'No, Frances. You don't have to tell me. You say you're being blackmailed. There is only one answer to that and it's *not* handing money over.'

'I know, but this mistake I made — Charles doesn't know.'

'And this person is threatening to tell him?' I

nodded. 'That's despicable. You know what you should do.'

'Ideally, yes, but I can't lose my son. If Charles knew he'd never let me see Harry again.'

He winced. 'Surely it can't be that bad.'

'He'd consider it was.'

'So, I take it that it happened before you married him.'

'Yes, when I was sixteen.'

'*Sixteen!*' For a moment I thought he was going to laugh. 'You made a mistake when you were sixteen! Join the club!' When he saw that he wasn't reassuring me he went on, 'Frances, seriously. It can't have been that bad.'

'It was.' I couldn't look at him.

'And this woman has kept her mouth shut about it all these years?'

'She only found out recently. It's complicated.'

'So how much is she demanding from you?'

'She wanted a thousand a month but she finally agreed on five hundred. I've made one payment out of what I had in the bank.' I opened my bag and took out my personal bank statement. 'You see — I have nothing left and the next payment is due next week.'

He glanced at the statement. 'Your husband keeps you this short?'

'I have to account for every penny I spend. So you see . . . '

'Does this blackmailer have a reason for doing this to you or is it sheer vindictiveness?'

'She says she's down on her luck, on the point of being made homeless.'

'And you believe that?'

I shrugged. 'I don't have much choice, do I?'

'I'm not happy about this, Frances,' he said. 'I don't mean the advance; you're more than welcome to that. It's the situation. You realize she won't be satisfied with five hundred for long?'

I nodded. 'That's why I need this job, Adam.'

'You're *going* to *be working to pay a blackmailer?*'

'What else can I do?'

'Why don't you just tell your husband everything? After all, you were little more than a child when this thing happened.'

'He wouldn't see it that way. And even if I did she'd have her revenge. She's already threatened to go to the press.'

He smiled wryly. 'He's hardly a celebrity, is he? Just a moderately successful businessman. I doubt if the press would be very interested.'

'She's talking about the trade papers and, believe me, it would have a huge impact.'

'I still think it's worth calling her bluff.'

'I'd have to think carefully about that. Meanwhile she'll be expecting more money — in five days' time.'

He looked at me thoughtfully. 'Frances, are you really sure you want this job? You're not accepting my offer for the best of reasons.'

'I know it must look as though I'm making a convenience of you,' I said. 'But even before this happened I wanted to accept your offer. I promise you I'll put everything I have into it.'

'I'm sure you mean that.'

'I do; I promise I'm not wasting your time, Adam. I wouldn't do that.'

'Right then, we'll get started on your training next week. And as for this wretched woman, let me think about it. I'll find a way to put a stop to her devious little game.'

Travelling home on the train I felt relieved. I'd unburdened myself to Sophie and Adam had agreed to giving me an advance on my salary. My future looked a little brighter — until I remembered that Harry was returning to school in two days' time, back to school and his bullies and there wasn't a thing I could do to help him. I could hardly bear the thought.

16

KATIE

After I left the girls I went and bought myself a new dress for my dinner date with Drew. It cost a bomb but it was gorgeous and I reckoned that I owed it to myself, and him — especially if we had something to celebrate. I also invested in some straigheners for my hair, then went home and experimented with them. The effect was quite dramatic.

While I was getting ready I thought about what the girls had said at lunch. It had been a big shock, hearing about Fran's teenage pregnancy and her birth mother turning up like that, but I told myself that it couldn't be as bad as she'd painted it. Everything would work out in the end. She'd always been so lucky. As for Sophie, she'd always been used to having things her own way. Maybe it was time for the tables to turn. 'I wouldn't mind betting,' I told myself as I took a final look in the mirror. 'That next time we meet everything will be fine again.'

Drew arrived dead on time and I showed him round my flat, which didn't take long. One bedroom with a tiny en-suite shower, a cupboard sized kitchen and my living room which doubled as a work space. He admired the computerized sewing machine I'm buying on the never-never and he took some time looking at my work in progress on the drawing board I'd set up in the window.

'You mean you live in here too?' he said, shaking his head. 'I can't imagine how cramped you must feel. Where do you relax?'

I laughed. 'I don't have time to relax so that doesn't really bother me,' I told him. 'And as for 'cramped' I've never lived any other way.'

He put his hands on my shoulders and looked into my eyes in a way that I found a bit disturbing. 'You're worth so much more than this, Katie. And I'm going to see that you get it. Get your coat. We're going to hit the town.'

I gasped when I saw his car. The long champagne coloured Mercedes stood at the kerb and had already attracted a group of local kids. As we emerged from the flat I saw one of them reach forward, a rusty nail clutched in his grubby little fist. I yelled at him.

'Oi! Clear off, you little buggers, before I call the police!' They scattered immediately.

Drew grinned at me. 'Wow! The voice of authority.'

I blushed. 'Sorry, but when you live in an area like this you have to show your muscles sometimes otherwise you'd get walked all over.'

He slipped an arm round my shoulders, the broad grin still on his face. 'I'm glad to hear it, Katie. It's dog-eat-dog in our business so I'm relieved that you know how to be feisty.'

At the restaurant the maître d' took our coats and ushered us to our table. Drew immediately ordered a bottle of champagne. I looked at him. 'I didn't know you were pushing the boat out.'

'I certainly am.' He smiled. 'And with good reason. My confidence in your work was well justified. I showed the designs you gave me to the owner of one of the houses I work with. She was impressed and there'll be a job waiting for you with her if you're interested.'

My heart missed a beat. 'A job — doing what?'

He laughed. 'Designing, of course. All the top design houses have a team of junior designers working for them. Your work would bear the house label of course but it's a step on the ladder towards creating a label of your own.'

I digested this. 'I see. What designer would this be?'

'Rosie Sams.'

I gasped. 'Oh, Drew! I've loved Rosie Sams's designs for ages,' I said.

He nodded. 'Your style is perfect for her, which is why I showed your drawings to her first.' He looked at me, his head on one side. 'So, are you ready to take that first step to fame? I can fix it for you.'

'Shouldn't I see if I get through the interview first?'

'No. I told you, it's a done deal. All you need to do is drop by and have a word with Rosie about when you start.'

I shook my head. 'I can't see how I'd fit in the time to work for anyone else at the moment.'

'Katie, you don't understand. If you took the job at Rosie Sams you'd have to give up your present job. You'd be working full time at her studio and your work would belong exclusively to the Sams label.'

I stared at him. 'But Imogene and I have only just got the hire business off the ground,' I told him. 'I'm a partner, in the hire side of the business that is. The plan is to open another outlet near to me later if we do well. I'll be running that on my own and . . . '

'Have you put money into the business?' he interrupted.

'No, but my contributions are the designs and the ideas.'

'Which are yours and yours alone. It means that as she doesn't have to agree to buy you out you can leave whenever you like.'

I felt as though all the breath had been knocked out of me. 'I couldn't let Imogene down like that.'

'She'll still have the business, won't she?'

'I suppose . . . '

'Not to mention the stock that you've already supplied?'

'Well, yes . . . '

'Any legal contract between you?'

'We haven't got around to that yet,' I admitted.

'Then you're home and dry.' He spread his hands. 'Nothing to stop you. Just take the plunge; give in your notice and take the first step to fame!'

But I couldn't help feeing guilty. 'It would be an awful shock for her, just when business has started to pick up.'

'No sentiment in business, Katie. This is your future we're talking about.' He reached across the table to take my hand. 'After all, it's thanks to you that she didn't go under, isn't it?' He looked at me, one well-shaped eyebrow raised. 'Don't tell me opening up a hire service in the East End is the height of your ambition.'

'Well, no, but . . . '

'Well, the offer is there. Just take some time out to think about it.' The waiter brought the champagne and uncorked it with a loud pop. Drew looked at me as he passed me the first bubbling glass. 'But don't spend too much valuable time thinking about it, my darling. There are dozens of other highly qualified, talented young hopefuls out there dreaming of a chance like this.' He held up his glass to me. 'Here's to a dazzling career for Katie MacEvoy. May she fizz and sparkle like this champagne.'

I touched my glass to his. His offer was irresistibly tempting and I couldn't help feeling excited as I took my first sip of champagne and gasped as the bubbles danced down my nose.

But what would Imogene's reaction be? My heart plummeted at the prospect of breaking the news to her.

17

SOPHIE

I travelled home thoughtfully from my lunch date with the girls. Fran's revelation about her teenage pregnancy had shocked me. How could she have kept it secret, especially from Katie and me? The three of us were so close back then. Poor Fran. She must have been frantic with worry. We may have been close school friends but I'm beginning to realize that we didn't really know much about one another at all.

I was grateful that she hadn't asked me to go into details about my split with Rex. There was very little to report anyhow. Ever since he'd answered the telephone at my parents' house I'd stopped trying to get in touch with him, or them. They were obviously in agreement about me. That much was clear. They all think I'm spoilt and selfish. But if that's what I am, my parents have to take the blame for it. As for my marriage, all that remained now, I told myself bleakly, was to wait for the divorce papers to drop on to the mat. Clearly Rex had stopped loving me and maybe in some ways I deserved that.

Had I stopped loving him?

I've tried hard to come to terms stoically with our break-up but the truth, however much I might try to deny it, is that the more time that goes by, the more I miss him. I can't help remembering the time when we were first married, the fun and the love we shared. The way we'd laughed at the same stupid jokes and how we loved the same music and films; the secret code we shared when other people were present, certain looks and words that only he and I knew the meaning of.

I refuse to allow myself to dwell on things like that for too long now, telling myself that in time all that would have passed anyhow. We'd have become an old married couple, bored and jaded with nothing to say to each other any more. The trouble is that somehow I can never quite make myself believe it. It's when I wake in the small hours that the waste and futility washes over me in a tidal wave of regret. It's then that the truth stares me in the face, taunting and cruel. *Admit it, Sophie. All of this is your fault. You have only yourself to blame.*

★ ★ ★

I've had two viewings from the estate agents for Greenings since going back to school after the half-term break. One was from a young couple looking for a home in which to start their family. The girl was heavily pregnant and her husband was solicitous, taking her arm on the stairs and frequently asking her if she was all right. They loved the house.

'We really wanted to have moved well before the baby arrived,' the girl told me. 'But we've looked at so many houses and none of them has had the right *feel*. They didn't feel like home if you know what I mean.'

I knew exactly what she meant. Even in what was then a close-to-derelict state I'd known that Greenings was just what I wanted the moment I walked through the door.

'How can you bear to sell when you've put so much into it?' the young man asked me. 'You must have worked so hard.'

'One of those things,' I said lightly. 'My husband and I have split up and moved on. The house is too big for me alone.'

They exchanged pitying looks. 'I'm so sorry,' the girl said, touching my arm gently.

Her husband cleared his throat. 'The price is a bit more than we wanted to pay,' he said. 'Would you consider accepting a little less?'

'I suggest you put in an offer to the agent,' I said. 'And we'll go from there.'

When I showed them out and closed the door behind them I had a huge lump in my throat. The girl had seen all the things I'd seen in the house. The way the light slanted through the landing window, making patterns on the hall floor, the cosiness of the big living-kitchen, and the elegant beauty of the Georgian staircase. I remembered the day we first saw it. I'd had so many plans, so many dreams of us living together in a perfect home we'd created out of chaos.

I told myself not to be sentimental. It was just a building after all; a heap of bricks and mortar. But it had been something wonderful that I'd seen Rex and I creating together and now there was only me. How could it all have gone so wrong? Why couldn't Rex have seen that to me the house had stood for warmth and security — a real home, wrapping itself around us like a big fleecy blanket. Now it was just a dream from which I'd had a sharp awakening and the thought of starting again on my own somewhere cold and impersonal made my heart sink.

The second couple were older and childless — a smart city couple who, I gathered, would hardly live in the house at all, except at weekends. We stood in the kitchen, my favourite room in the house and the one I liked best to show off. The woman looked around, wrinkling her elegant nose.

'Of course all of this would have to go,' she said with a sweep of her arm. 'I'd have to up-date. I couldn't possibly live with these oak cupboards and that ghastly dresser. I see it in pale wood and stainless steel — with an island in the centre instead of that table.' She flung out a hand towards my chintz settee under the window and sniggered. 'Who ever actually *sits* in the kitchen?' she said with a tinkling laugh that sounded like breaking glass. 'I might even have that window bricked up and have halogen lighting instead.'

'I doubt if you'd be allowed to do that,' I said briskly. 'The house is grade two listed.'

'Oh, what a *bore!*' She looked at her husband who was peering out of the window. 'What do you think, Damion?'

He pulled a face. 'Have you seen that garden? I don't fancy spending all my weekends mowing grass and pulling up weeds.'

She followed his gaze and sighed. 'God, yes! I

200

see what you mean. But maybe we could have it all block paved,' she suggested. 'And chop down some of the trees.'

'Again, I think you might have a problem there,' I told her. 'Most of the trees are quite old and have preservation orders on them.'

She bridled. 'You mean you're not allowed to do what you like on your own property?'

'Not all the time, no. Not with a house of this age.'

Her husband smiled at her. 'I told you that moving to the country has its downside.'

They left soon after and I knew with relief that I wouldn't be hearing from them again. Two days later the agent rang me with an offer from the first couple. The phone was ringing as I got in from school. It was a ludicrously low offer and I turned it down at once.

'They're very keen,' the agent told me. 'They really love the house and they want to move in quickly because of their situation.' He paused. 'And they're renting at the moment so there's no chain.'

'I'm still not selling Greenings for that price,' I told him. 'We spent a fortune and worked our fingers to the bone renovating.' I almost added that it had cost us our marriage as well, but reminded myself that the fault for that lay elsewhere.

'So what would you be prepared to take?' the agent was saying.

I sighed. If I really had to part with Greenings I'd prefer it to be to the young couple and their coming baby. I knew they would love it as much as I had. The thing was, was I really ready to let it go yet? 'Leave it with me,' I said. 'If they come up with a better offer I'll consider it, but it will have to be quite a lot better.'

That evening I drove round to John Harrison's house with the boys' portraits which I had now mounted and framed. He was some time answering my ring at the bell and when he appeared he was wearing a blue striped apron and looking flustered. He looked relieved to see me.

'Oh, Sophie, thank goodness it's only you.'

I laughed. 'I'm not sure whether that's a compliment or not!'

'Come in.' He held the door for me to enter the hallway. 'To tell you the truth I was trying to make an apple pie,' he said. 'But the pastry seems to have a life of its own.'

'Want me to take a look?'

'Would you?'

''Course.' I handed him the parcel. 'Just lead me to the kitchen.'

I could see at once that he'd tried to roll out the pastry while it was too crumbly. I scooped it all back into the bowl, added a few drips of water and kneaded it together. When he saw me roll out a smooth sheet he shook his head.

'You're a genius.'

I laughed. 'Why are you making a pie anyway? The supermarket's full of them.'

'I've invited a couple of friends over for supper,' he told me. 'And I don't want them thinking I'm totally helpless.'

'Then lie through your teeth,' I advised.

'Always works for me.'

He held up a bottle of sherry. 'Fancy a glass of this? I think you deserve one.'

'Just a small one then. I'm driving. But shall we get this pie into the oven first?'

When John produced a tin of apple pulp I opened it without saying anything. Clearly he wasn't about to overplay the Jamie Oliver impression. Five minutes later the pie was in the oven and we were sipping dry sherry at his kitchen table.

'I've had an idea,' he said suddenly. 'Why don't you join us for supper?'

I shook my head. 'I don't think that's a very good idea. For one thing you're my boss and for another you don't want to start tongues wagging, do you?'

He pursed his mouth regretfully. 'Mmm, I suppose you're right.'

'On the other hand I'm not leaving until you unwrap that.' I pointed to the parcel containing the portraits, still lying on the table.

'Oh my God, I'd forgotten! Is it the portraits?' He unwrapped the two framed pictures and looked at them for so long that I began to think he was disappointed, but when he looked up at me I saw that there were tears in his eyes.

'Oh, Sophie, you've captured them both perfectly. Thank you so much.'

I heaved a sigh of relief. 'I'm glad you like them.'

'I do. They're wonderful, not only a good likeness but you've caught something of their characters too. Although they look alike they're

203

quite different in temperament and you've caught that.'

'That's what I was aiming for,' I told him. 'I'm happy if you think it came off.'

'I do. Now, you must let me write you a cheque.'

'No, really, there's no hurry.' I stood up. 'You have supper guests coming and I mustn't hold you up any longer.'

But he had reached into the pocket of his jacket, hanging on the back of a chair, and was already writing out a cheque. He handed it to me. 'Here, and don't argue.'

I gasped when I looked at it. 'John! This is far too much,' I protested but he waved my arguments away.

'You don't know what it means to me to be able to see those two when I wake up in the mornings. It'll make up for . . . ' He swallowed hard and I reached out a hand to him.

'I know. John, I'm so sorry. Is there no hope of . . . ?'

'None at all,' he cut in. 'Hillary has met someone else. It seems serious.' He looked up at me, his face earnest. 'Sophie, don't let it happen to you. If there's any chance at all of patching things up with Rex then grasp it with both hands. You've no idea how painful it is being made to face the fact that the marriage you've invested so much in is over for good.'

'At least we don't have children,' I said.

'But you're still young enough to have them. And you do still love him, don't you?' When I didn't reply he went on. 'Don't deny it. I can tell you do. Don't let your pride or mistakes from the past stand in the way. Make a new start, and do it soon.'

I was astonished at his outburst. He was my boss — my headmaster. This was such personal stuff. As though he read my thoughts he shook his shoulders and turned away.

'Listen to me, talking to you like a Dutch uncle! What the hell do I know? It's none of my business anyway. But thanks so much for the portraits, Sophie. They mean a lot to me.'

I slipped my coat on and he came to the door with me. 'Thanks for the cheque, John,' I said. 'I still think it's too much.'

'It's not nearly enough,' he said.

'Have a nice evening with your friends.' I sniffed. 'John! The pie! Better take it out of the oven before it's burnt to a crisp.'

He rushed off and I walked down the drive towards the car thinking about what he'd said. If the prospective buyers came up with a reasonable offer I'd have to get in touch with Rex somehow soon, maybe it should be sooner rather than later.

Back at home I decided to text him. If he saw that the message was about the house surely he would answer. I sent a simple message: *Received offer on the house. Need to speak. S.* I waited. Half an hour later the phone in the hall rang.

'Sophie, it's me. Your text said you've had an offer on the house.'

'At last!' I snapped. 'I thought the prospect of money would get you going!' The words were out of my mouth before I had time to think, sharp and bitter. But once I'd started I couldn't stop myself. 'I've tried so many times to ring you but you were too busy sucking up to my folks to be bothered. Did you manage to get any more cash out of them?'

'Did you ring just to have a go at me, Sophie?' he said coldly. 'If so I'm going to hang up.'

'No, *don't!* Yes, I did have an offer,' I told him. 'They're a nice young couple with a baby on the way. They love the house as much as we — as much as *I* do, but they can't manage the asking price.'

'Well, as you've decided on that yourself without any input from me perhaps you would like to put me in the picture,' he said pithily.

'I didn't decide. It was the agent's valuation,' I said. 'Rex, we really need to talk properly. We can't agree anything about selling the house over the phone.'

He paused. 'Do you want me to come to the house?'

'It would be best.'

'When?'

'I'm here now.'

There was another long pause at the other end, then he said, 'As long as it's not going to develop into yet another row.'

'It won't.' I bit my lip. 'I'm sorry about just now.'

'OK then. In about an hour.'

He arrived before the hour was up. He looked strained and I thought he'd lost weight. He needed a haircut too. When I let him in he was brisk and to the point, refusing my offer of coffee or to come and sit down with me. Standing awkwardly in the hall he said, 'I can't stay long. What was this offer then?'

I told him, adding, 'I've turned it down but I'm pretty sure they'll offer more in a day or two.'

'So it's not a firm offer?'

His whole attitude was that I'd wasted his time, which irritated me. 'It was meant to be. Look, it's your house too, Rex,' I pointed out. 'The original offer was ludicrous but anyway I can't accept anything without your say-so.'

'You've already turned one offer down without consulting me.'

'I told you, it was way too low. And anyway you haven't been exactly easy to get in touch with, have you?'

'I suppose not,' he conceded. 'But now I'd like to put an end to the whole miserable business.'

'I see.' His words cut me like a knife. They sounded so final. I felt my eyes fill with tears. 'Whatever you want,' I said.

I saw his expression soften. 'I meant the house sale.'

'Right, so — what do you suggest?'

He shrugged. 'Accept something closer to the asking price?'

'Very helpful.'

'Well, what do you want me to say?'

'I expected you to take more of an interest,' I said. 'Maybe even try to be helpful. You've opted out of it all. I'm the one taking all the responsibility of selling and holding down a job as well.'

'And still living here in your precious house,' he countered. He ran his fingers through his hair exasperatedly and looked at me. 'Sorry.' He sighed. 'Did you say something about coffee? Maybe this needs thinking about in more depth.'

I wasn't sure whether he was talking about the house or us.

In the kitchen I made coffee and we sat at the table, two cups of coffee cooling in front of us. I was aware that we'd both dropped our defences now and were ready to talk realistically. We agreed on an acceptable price for the house price and I felt relieved.

'If I asked you where you were staying would you tell me?' I asked him.

'It's never been a secret.'

'Except that I never got the chance to ask.' I looked at him. 'Are you staying with my parents?'

He looked startled. 'Of course not! What gave you that idea?'

'I rang them once and you answered.'

'Oh, that. I just happened to be there. I dropped by to see them.'

'Why?'

'Why not? They are my in-laws.' He paused. 'As a matter of fact your father hasn't been too well. Your mother had rung to tell me and I thought I'd go and check up on them — see if there was anything they needed.'

I felt a pang of resentment. 'She didn't ring me.'

He raised an eyebrow. 'Are you surprised after the things you said the last time you saw them?'

'What's the matter, with Dad I mean?'

'He's better now. He had a few chest pains and the doctor said it could be angina. He's on some tablets.'

'I see. So, if you're not staying with them . . . '

'I'm always on the end of my phone,' he interrupted. 'I'll pick up in future. It was just that I didn't want any more arguments.'

I swallowed hard. What I was about to say was going to take some courage and loss of pride but I couldn't let him go without knowing.

'We can't go on like this. Where are we going, Rex?' I asked him. 'Do you want this to be permanent — a divorce?'

He shrugged. 'I'm not sure what either of us wants any more.' He looked at me directly for the first time. 'There doesn't seem to be much left for us to agree on, does there? All that's happened — since we bought the house and after — has made me realize how little we ever really knew each other. Everything about you when we met — the way you dressed, your views and everything we had in common — all that was just an act, wasn't it, to get back at your folks? I see that now. I never really got to know the real Sophie Bamber until we bought this house and your true colours came out.'

'You were the same,' I accused. 'Trying hard to be something you weren't at college, escaping from your working class roots, turning yourself into an artist.'

'I never turned myself into anything,' he argued. 'I was always an artist. And I still respect my parents and upbringing. I know they did their best for me and I'll always be grateful. I'm not the one with a chip on my shoulder. You are! Whether you like it or not, Sophie, you're your parents' daughter so why don't you start living up to it? They're good, hard working people who made a success of their lives. Their only fault was trying to give you a good life.'

'Oh, they've brain-washed you well, haven't they?' I sneered.

He stood up, shaking his head. 'I can see that you're never going to change, Sophie. Well, we've agreed on the house price so I'll leave it to you to let me know when it's sold.' He turned as I was letting him out of the front door. 'As for your question about divorce — maybe it's the only thing we have left to agree on.'

18

FRANCES

True to his word Adam handed me an envelope containing five hundred pounds on my first day at Tropicalle Pools and on the first Monday in November I took it along to Paddington Station and waited for my nemesis in the café. She arrived promptly and seized the brown envelope from me swiftly before anyone could see. She checked it and looked at me with a triumphant smile.

'I'm glad to see that you know which side your bread is buttered,' she said, snapping her handbag shut. 'Make sure you're here again on time next month or you'll regret it.'

As I watched her leave I asked myself how that creature could possibly be my biological mother. I shuddered, thanking God that I'd inherited none of her baser qualities.

My training didn't take long. Adam came out with me for the first few visits and by the time the month was through I was making my first visit alone. November was hardly the best time to be selling swimming pools, I told myself, but I was mistaken. There was a luxury model which was under cover and that was the first one I went out to sell. The buyers wanted it installed by Christmas and I had to ring Adam to make sure we could guarantee that. When he assured

211

me that we could I made my first sale and drove back to London feeling on top of the world. I was an independent woman again at last. I tried to forget the fact that I was paying a large percentage of my earnings to a blackmailer.

Harry still occupied my thoughts for most of the time and I was grateful to have my job to take my mind off what might be happening to him. On the morning that Charles took him back to school he had clung to me, his little face bravely controlled in a way that almost broke my heart.

'You will write, won't you?' I asked him.

He nodded. 'I can't say much though, Mum,' he answered, confirming my suspicions that the boys' letters were vetted before they were posted. Charles waved away my fears, describing me as a 'stifling mother', full of Dickensian imaginings. But I know my own child and I knew he was miserable.

Since I'd stood my ground with Charles over taking the job he'd been very cool with me and one evening, two weeks into the job he suddenly announced that he was selling my car. He told me just as we sat down to eat. Raising his head to look at me he said casually,

'Oh, by the way. I've decided that I can't justify the extravagance of running two cars.'

I stared at him. 'But you know I need the car for my job.'

'Then I suggest you buy your own,' he said. 'Either that or get this Fenn person to supply you with a company vehicle. It must be a tin-pot company he's running if he can't stretch to that anyway.'

The following morning I had to go to Adam with this latest bombshell.

'You must be wishing you'd never offered me this job,' I said.

He looked up with a thoroughly unfazed expression. 'I was thinking of buying a company car anyway,' he said. 'To keep in reserve. I hope I might need more as the business expands. Tell him I'll buy it from him.'

When I told Charles I thought he was going to have apoplexy. 'It's not for sale,' he snapped. 'Not to him anyway.'

'So you're selling it out of spite,' I said. 'I don't know why you're behaving like this, Charles, but it won't make any difference. I need to earn my own money. I need to have something to occupy my mind too, especially with Harry going through hell at that dreadful school.'

His response was to get up and leave the room without another word.

* * *

One morning I found that my latest assignment was in Surrey with a Ms Woodley. It didn't take long to drive out to Virginia Water and I arrived soon after eleven o'clock. Harway House was a mock Tudor villa, set back from the road and surrounded by trees. As I made my way up the drive I reflected that it must be very private and idyllic in summer when the trees were in full leaf. Now the drive was a carpet of fallen leaves that crunched under the wheels of the new company car that Adam had supplied me with.

My ring at the bell was answered by a woman I took to be the housekeeper and she ushered me into a large conservatory at the back of the house, saying that she would inform 'Madam' that I had arrived.

I recognized Celia Grayson, Charles's ex-wife the moment she walked in and I saw from her face that she recognized me too. She was carrying the firm's brochure and introductory letter and she stopped in her tracks when she saw me. Her eyebrows rose in a cynical half smile.

'Well, *well!* I thought the name was coincidental, but it's hardly unusual, is it — Grayson. Personally I never liked it, which is why I reverted to my maiden name. I must say that Charles's little bit on the side was the last person I expected to see.'

Her words took my breath away. 'Charles and I are married,' I told her, keeping my voice as level as I could. 'And I've never been anyone's 'bit on the side'.'

She shrugged. 'It's immaterial now, isn't it?'

This was going to be uncomfortable but I'd done nothing wrong and I was determined to keep cool. She was as elegant as I remembered her, her hair perfectly cut and styled and her skirt and cashmere sweater expensively understated. She indicated one of the conservatory's comfortable wicker armchairs.

'Do have a seat. So, Charles has you working for your living, does he?'

I forced a smile. 'No, I choose to work, especially now that our son is away at boarding

214

school,' I said. 'The time hangs heavily and I like to be occupied.'

'Well, good for you.' She paused. 'And your son is away at school.'

'Yes.'

'How old is he now?'

'Harry has just turned nine.'

She raised one eyebrow. 'Nine! How time flies.' She paused, pretending to look at the brochure. 'I expect you know that we haven't lost touch, Charles and I,' she said without looking up.

'You haven't — lost touch?'

'No? He hasn't told you?' She raised challenging eyes to mine. 'Oh yes, we often meet, for lunch or a drink.' She glanced around her. 'And as you can see he's been very generous with his settlement. He makes sure I still have the kind of life I've always been used to. But of course he will have told you all this.'

I wasn't sure what she was doing. Testing me? I decided not to play. 'He hasn't mentioned you,' I said.

I'd obviously touched a nerve. I saw her colour deepen. 'Did you really think he'd ever be able to let me go?' she said. 'Charles and I had a very passionate relationship. He always said he'd never find anyone who could arouse his passions as I could.'

'I'm not really interested in what's past.' I flipped open my order book and looked up at her. 'I'm only here to do my job. So, have you had a chance to decide which of our pools you'd like? Can I help or advise you on anything?'

Her nostril flared. 'I don't think there would ever be anything *you* could advise me on,' she said sharply, throwing the pools brochure on to the coffee table with a resounding slap. She stood up. 'And speaking of past and present, I wouldn't feel too smug and secure in your marriage if I were you. You might well have a shock coming. You've provided Charles with a son and that's all he ever wanted you for. Oh, and I don't think I'm interested in having a pool installed by this firm,' she said. 'So if that's all you're here for you can leave.'

She walked back into the house through the open patio doors and suddenly she was gone, leaving me to find my own way out. What was all that about? I asked myself as I got into the car.

It was as I was turning the car ready to leave that I noticed the other car that was parked round the corner of the house. It was a scarlet Mercedes convertible, the registration number of which was all too familiar to me. It was the car that had once been mine.

Back at the office I discovered that Celia had telephoned the moment I'd left and made a complaint about me. Apparently I'd been rude and arrogant, which was why she had decided not to buy a pool. Adam wanted to know what had happened.

'It was rather unfortunate,' I told him. 'Ms Woodley turned out to be my husband's ex-wife. I was perfectly civil to her but she was clearly unhappy to see me and I suppose this is her way of getting back at me.' I looked at him. 'I'm so sorry, Adam. You must be wondering how many

216

more problems I'm going to create for you.'

He shook his head. 'You're doing a great job, Frances. I've had very good feedback from satisfied customers. You've more than made up for this one cancellation. It was just an unfortunate coincidence. They happen.'

Driving home that evening I thought about Celia, the lavish lifestyle that Charles was clearly paying for and the fact that he'd given her my car. But I decided not to say anything — for now anyway. My main aim at the moment was to get Harry away from that archaic school. It wasn't going to be easy and I had no idea how I would do it, but I had to try.

★ ★ ★

It was the following week that I received a phone call from Sheila Philips. It was during the early evening while I was in the kitchen preparing a meal.

'Hello, Frances.' I recognized the voice at once and my blood froze. Charles could so easily have picked up the phone.

'What do you want?'

'I've been thinking,' she said. 'Five hundred isn't anywhere near meeting my needs. I think we'd better put it up next time — say seven fifty.'

'I told you, I can't give you any more,' I said, holding the receiver close to my mouth just in case Charles should overhear.

'Well I think you'd better find a way,' she said nastily. 'That is if you don't want me to spill the beans.'

My heart had been beating fast but suddenly the true realization of the situation hit me. 'You'll just have to do your worst then, won't you?' I said daringly. 'As long as you realize that once you have there'll be no more money.'

There was a silence at the other end and I knew in that moment that I'd got her. She wasn't very bright and she hadn't bargained for having her bluff called.

'Now look, if you know what's good for you . . . ' she began threateningly.

'Oh, but I do,' I interrupted. 'And I think a little visit to the police might be good for me; very good for me, but not so good for you.'

'And telling your old man the truth about your past would mess things up for you good and proper, and well you know it,' she said. 'But we'll leave it for now. Don't think you can fob me off forever though, will you.' She hung up before I could reply.

I replaced the receiver and stood for a moment, thinking. It couldn't go on. Her demands were going to go up and up. But what could I do? I couldn't call her bluff for ever. Suddenly I made up my mind. The first chance I got I would go down to Dorset and see Mavis Waters, my so-called aunt. She had a lot to answer for in this. She could even be in on it. Somehow or other I had to get to the bottom of it.

19

KATIE

I had a couple of weeks in which to get up the courage to give in my notice to Imogene. Even then I trembled at the thought of telling her face to face. Drew had arranged a meeting with Rosie Sams for a Thursday afternoon for me so that I wouldn't have to take any time off. He'd also suggested giving in my notice before I went for the interview as it was a foregone conclusion that I'd get the job. When I went in to work on the morning of the interview I took my letter of resignation and put it in Imogene's in-tray on her desk, hoping she wouldn't see it until after I had left. I felt really guilty about doing it that way. I'd never done anything as underhand before. I knew I'd have to face her on Friday morning but by then my meeting with Rosie Sams would have taken place and I'd have the prospect of a new job to give me confidence.

At twelve-thirty I left Fantaisie and rushed home to grab a bite to eat and change. At three sharp I was waiting in reception for my meeting with Rosie, my heart drumming and excitement making my stomach churn. At last the telephone on the receptionist's desk rang and she nodded across at me.

'Miss Sams will see you now.' She got up and walked across to open the door for me and I entered on trembling legs.

The office was like something out of a Hollywood film set, all 'Art Deco' and ankle deep carpet. Rosie Sams got up from behind her desk, a small petite figure, her dark hair cut in a shining bob. She wore a plain black suit and pristine white shirt.

'Katie MacEvoy,' she said holding out her hand for me to shake.

'How nice to meet you. Please have a seat.' Sitting down again she took my drawings from a folder and spread them out on the desk. 'These show a lot of promise. Well done,' she said. 'Andrew was insistent that I meet you.' She looked up. 'He tells me your ambition is to enter the fashion world one day and I can see that you have the necessary approach.'

Andrew? For a moment I was puzzled then I realized that she meant Drew. 'Yes,' I said. 'It's always been my dream and I could hardly believe it when Drew — er — Andrew said you were willing to give me a job.'

She frowned a little. 'Did he? I'm not sure that he gave you the right impression,' she said. 'You understand of course that I do have half a dozen junior designers working for me at the moment.' She looked at me. 'They have all studied fashion design at college and are already qualified. Even so they do not earn a fortune as you might think. However, working for me will help them on their way as they move up the ladder. Do you understand?'

I wasn't sure that I did. What was she trying to tell me? But I nodded anyway.

'And so you see I couldn't offer you an actual design place.'

My heart plummeted as the truth struck home. 'Oh! So, what . . . ?'

'However, you would be very useful in the workroom,' she went on. 'Helping with the making up, alterations, modifications and so on. And of course at our shows where you'd be invaluable doing running repairs and helping the models to make their quick changes.'

A dogsbody. That's how she saw me! I could have cried. In fact I felt my lower lip beginning to wobble and clamped my teeth over it, swallowing hard. 'So, would there be room for promotion?' I asked.

She smiled. 'Perhaps, if you were to work hard and get some qualifications.'

'I see.'

'You're disappointed?'

'A bit, yes. There's no way I could afford to go to college,' I said. 'I'm on my own and I have to work for my living.'

'Well, I'm sure you would gain invaluable experience with us here and I'm willing to give you a month's trial if you'd like to accept a job in the workroom.

I stood up. 'Thank you, Miss Sams but that isn't what I wanted at all,' I said as firmly as I could. 'But thank you for seeing me, and for your offer of a trial, but I'm afraid I have to say no.' Suddenly remembering my drawings I turned towards her desk. 'So obviously you'll have no more interest in these.' I gathered them up and stuffed them into my bag.

She looked a little taken aback. 'Of course. Well, thank you for coming in to see me, Katie.' She got up to shake my hand again. 'And good luck with whatever you decide to do in the future.'

Outside I stood on the pavement for several minutes, trying to steady the angry thumping of my heart. Drew had sent me here on a wild goose chase. He must have known what the real situation was. Did he really think I'd take a job in the workroom, running around like some kind of lady's maid after the way he'd buttered me up? He'd insisted I give in my notice first as well. Suddenly my heart almost stopped. *My notice!* The letter of resignation! It was still on Imogene's desk. Was there a chance, the *slightest* chance that she hadn't seen it yet? I almost ran to the Underground station and leapt on the first train to Kensington, hoping against hope that I'd be in time.

As I opened the door of the shop I could see that Imogene was engaged with a customer. She glanced at me in surprise and I indicated by mime that I'd left something in the office. Thanking my lucky stars that she was fully occupied I slipped into the office and closed the door. To my dismay I saw at once that the in-tray was empty then I remembered that Imogene had a bad habit of sometimes sweeping her post into the top drawer of her desk to put off dealing with it.

I opened the drawer and began to rummage among the contents. Suddenly I saw my handwriting and grabbed the envelope, but as I did so my fingers touched something hard underneath. I pulled it out and saw that it was a framed photograph lying face downward at the bottom of the drawer. Turning it over, I saw to my surprise that it was a wedding photograph of Imogene and her husband and I vaguely remembered that it had once stood in pride of place on the desk. Imogene looked radiant in it, clearly in love as she gazed up at the handsome man at her side. I stared down in disbelief at the image. It was *him* — Andrew — *Drew*. So it had all been a cruel con trick all the time! He'd been trying to poach me away from her so as to ruin our chances of success at Fantaisie and I'd fallen for it hook, line and sinker! How could I have been so naïve?

'Did you find what you were looking for?'

At the sound of Imogene's voice I quickly closed the drawer and pushed the resignation letter into my pocket. 'Yes,' I said. 'It was just a bill I'd forgotten to pay.'

She threw herself down on her chair. 'Put the kettle on, Katie, there's a love. I'm completely knackered.'

I took the kettle through to the kitchen at the back and filled it. When I came back she was pulling the day's post out of the drawer.

'I suppose I'd better deal with some of this before I go home,' she said. 'By the way, I've hired out two more of your wedding dresses this afternoon. At this rate we shall be needing to open that second branch before you know it.' She smiled up at me. 'Don't know what I'd have done without you, Katie MacEvoy,' she said. 'I'd have gone under without you. If you ask me you're a bloody angel in disguise!'

20

SOPHIE

Just as I'd expected, the first couple came back with a better offer. I got the call as I was on my way home from school one rainy evening in late November. It wasn't quite up to what Rex and I had agreed on so I explained to the agent that I'd have to get my husband's approval on it. I promised to get back to him as soon as I could and I called Rex that evening. This time he answered his phone almost immediately.

'Hello, Sophie. You've had news?'

'Yes, another offer from the same couple; a bit better this time.' I named it and added that in my opinion it was near enough. 'We're getting into winter now and the agent says the market will slacken off until spring so maybe we'd be well advised to go with this.'

'I agree,' he said. 'To tell you the truth I can't wait to get out of this hole I'm living in.'

I remembered his resentful remark about me still living in the comfort of Greenings. 'Where are you living, Rex?' I asked. 'You might as well tell me.'

'It's a grotty bedsit in a Leicester back street if you must know,' he replied. 'It wouldn't be so bad if I had to go out to an office each day. Working from home means I'm stuck inside these four walls twenty-four-seven and it's driving me barmy.'

I felt a pang of guilt. 'I'm sorry, Rex. But it was you who walked out.' When he made no reply I added, 'I expect you're planning to buy yourself a flat with your half.'

'I haven't got any plans!' he snapped. 'Have you?'

'We've got the formalities to get through first,' I reminded him. 'As we own this house jointly we'll both have to go to the solicitor's to sign the papers and so forth.'

'I suppose we will.'

'So, I'll let you know when and where, etcetera.'

'Thanks very much.'

'Rex.'

'Yes?'

'Look, I'm sorry — about us and everything, I mean.'

'Right. I'll hear from you later then. Got to go now, bye.'

I snapped my phone shut with a mixture of exasperation and despair. Clearly he wasn't going to give an inch.

★ ★ ★

I'd thought a lot about Fran since our last meeting when she'd told me about her teenage pregnancy. I kept meaning to ring her and Katie to arrange another meeting but what with the house sale and talking to Rex I hadn't got around to it. As I travelled home from school next afternoon it was high on my list of priorities and I decided to ring Fran as soon as I got home. Even if she wasn't free to meet up we'd be able to catch up on our news, but what was to follow wiped the intention completely from my mind.

I saw that the red light on the phone was flashing as I closed the front door behind me. There were two messages. The first was from the estate agent asking if the couple who were buying the house, Sarah and John Cooper could come round and discuss fixtures and fittings. The second was from my mother. She sounded fraught.

Sophie, I thought you should know that your father is in hospital. He had a severe heart attack last night and he is in intensive care. Ring me if you want to see him.

With my heart beating fast I lifted the receiver and dialled the number. When she didn't reply at once I assumed that she must be at the hospital and suddenly I remembered that I didn't have a mobile number for her. She hadn't mentioned which hospital Dad was in and I began to panic. They'd think I didn't care and . . .

'Hello.'

'*Mum!*' I was breathless with relief. 'I've just got in and found your message about Dad. How is he?'

'Oh, Sophie!' She sounded close to tears. 'I was with him all night but they sent me home to get some rest. He's on the critical list; breathing with a ventilator and heavily sedated.'

'It sounds serious.'

'It is. Oh, Sophie, I'm so worried. I don't know what I'll do if I lose him.'

'Mum, which hospital is he in?'

'You want to see him?'

I winced at the surprise in her voice. 'Of course I do. Look, wait there and I'll come and pick you up.'

I hastily rang the agent and explained that my father was ill and I'd get back to him about the Coopers' visit as soon as I could. Then I rang Rex. To my surprise his phone was switched off. So he must get out sometimes, I told myself wryly. Without waiting to change I ran back out to the car and headed off in the direction of Little Penfold.

Mum looked pale and drawn. She clearly hadn't slept. In the car she told me what had happened.

'It was last night. We were getting ready for bed. He'd been complaining all evening of indigestion and then just as I was getting into bed I heard him call out from the bathroom. When I got to him he was slumped on the floor clutching his chest.' She turned to me, her lips trembling. 'He was in absolute agony, Sophie. I'm afraid I panicked. I didn't know what to do so . . . ' She glanced at me. 'I rang Rex.' When I didn't reply she went on, 'He's been so wonderful, Sophie. He couldn't have done more if he'd been our own son. He took over as soon as I rang him, organizing an ambulance and everything and he came straight over.'

I swallowed hard, resisting the urge to ask why she hadn't rung me.

She touched my hand on the steering wheel. 'It was Rex who insisted that I ring you,' she said quietly. 'I wanted to but I was afraid you might refuse to come.'

Appalled, I glanced at her. 'Oh, Mum. I'm so sorry, sorry for all the horrible things I said.'

She patted my hand. 'No, darling. All forgotten now. Your dad is the main priority at the moment.'

When we arrived at the hospital Rex was already there and it soon became clear that he'd been at Dad's bedside since Mum had been sent home to rest. She glanced at him enquiringly but he shook his head.

'No change I'm afraid, but at least he's stable. They're talking about a bypass operation when he's fit enough.' He glanced at me and reached for my hand. I took it gratefully. The sight of my dad, his pale face distorted by the ventilator and wires attaching him to the life support machine shocked me. I felt shaken but I knew I had to be strong for Mum. She smiled at Rex.

'Thank you for staying with him. Why don't you go and get a cup of coffee now that we're here?'

He nodded. 'I won't be far away. Come and fetch me if you need me.'

We sat beside the bed side by side and after a few minutes Mum reached for my hand.

'Sophie, there's so much I need to say to you.'

I shook my head. 'Not now, Mum.'

'Yes, now,' she said firmly. 'There is so much you don't know. I know that you feel we failed you as parents.'

I winced, remembering things I'd flung at her the last time we met. 'No, you — you gave me everything.'

'Except the one thing you longed for — a

mum and dad to be with you, to play with you and bond properly. Most of the time we were absent.'

'It's all in the past now,' I insisted.

'But it spoiled your childhood, Sophie and we are responsible for that. You've grown up bitter and resentful. It will never just be in the past.' She squeezed my hand. 'Let me at least tell you how it was for us.'

'Not now, Mum. We're here for Dad.'

'And this is what he'd want me to do. When he wakes up I'd love to be able to tell him we're a family again, the family we always wanted to be.' She looked at me. 'I'll be completely honest with you, Sophie. We never intended to have children. You already know that both of us grew up without parents. Your dad never even knew his. He grew up in a children's home. Mine died before I was five and my grandmother brought me up.' She smiled wryly. 'Rather resentfully if the truth be told. It wasn't a happy childhood. Neither of us ever had any role models. There was never anyone to teach us how to be good parents.' She shook her head. 'I know that sounds like an excuse but it's true. When Dad and I met and married we made up our minds that we'd make a success of our lives in spite of the bad start we'd both had. I'd trained as a hairdresser and your dad was good at business. We opened our first salon and after two years, the second. We were on our way. It was hard work. We worked fifteen hours a day, every day and we decided to forego having a family and concentrate on the business.' She sighed. 'Then out of the blue you came along.'

'You didn't have to go through with the pregnancy,' I told her. 'Even back then.'

She looked shocked. 'I couldn't have had an abortion. I've always hated the very thought of it. It was a shock at first but we thought of it as fate, something that was meant to be. I worked in the salon right through to the end.'

'You must have been so resentful,' I put in, but she squeezed my hand again and smiled. 'No. Maybe in the beginning, a bit, yes. But as the time went by and I felt you move and kick inside me it began to be the most important thing in my life. And when you were born and your dad and I first held you and saw your dear little face we were both completely bowled over.' She looked into my eyes. 'We loved you so much, Sophie. Whatever you think, we always loved you. We always will.'

I couldn't speak but I returned the pressure of her hand in mine and after a moment or two she went on.

'I stayed at home with you until you were four and believe me, they were the happiest four years of my life. Then things began to go wrong with the business. We lost one of our salons through lack of trade. It was the late seventies and there was a recession going on. Another of the salons began to go downhill and at last we decided that there was nothing else for it but for me to go back to work — take over and manage the failing salon before it fell apart like the first one.' She peered into my eyes. 'I made the mistake of thinking that you didn't need me any more now

230

that you weren't a baby, that someone else could take my place.' She sighed. 'I was so wrong. But it wasn't just for our future that we worked so hard. It was for yours too. We desperately wanted to build it all back up for you, to give you the privileges that neither of us ever had.'

I swallowed hard at the lump in my throat. '*Things* didn't matter to me though, Mum. I'd rather have had a mum and dad who were there for me.'

'I know darling, but we had no choice. We'd created standards, a lifestyle that we couldn't bear to give up. We wanted the best for you. We tried to give you all the things that children like, to make up for not spending time with you. Friends had suggested sending you to boarding school but we couldn't bear to send you away. And we've never believed in private education so you went to the local comp. You did well and we were so proud of you. I always believed you were happy there.'

'I was.'

'But not at home — not with us?'

'All those luxuries — they weren't important to me,' I told her. 'They were just things. When other children talked about their parents — trips, picnics and days out at the seaside — I boasted about my TV and video recorder, my pretty bedroom and the clothes other girls would have given their eye teeth for. I quickly came to know that I only had to ask for something and it would be mine. I know I became a horrible spoilt brat.' I looked at her. 'And that's something that has stayed with me. It's why I wanted Greenings so much and why I resented Rex so much because he wasn't as keen as I was.'

'And it was why you were so resentful when we loaned Rex the money to finish it?' She nodded. 'I can see that now, but you know, Rex didn't come to us to ask for a loan,' she went on. 'He came to ask our advice. He said he was worried about you. You were doing far too much and he couldn't help as much as he'd have liked because he needed to work.' She smiled. 'He's a man, darling. He hated the idea that you were earning more than him. It was your dad who suggested giving you both the money to finish the house. Rex said he'd only accept it as a loan and we eventually agreed that it could be paid back without interest once you were on your feet again.'

'But he did it without consulting me.'

'Because he knew what you'd say. Dad and I were so upset when we realized how angry you were about it. And devastated to think it had caused a rift between you.' She looked at me. 'Rex says you've asked him for a divorce. Is that true?'

'I asked him if *he* wanted one.'

'And he said . . . ?'

'He said it was probably the only thing left for us to agree on.'

'I think you both know, deep down, that's not true. You really should talk to each other.'

'I know.'

She looked towards the bed. 'Seeing your dad like this makes me realize that nothing is as important as the people we love. I hope and pray that I don't lose him, Sophie. If you still love Rex don't let him go without a fight.'

I smiled in spite of myself. 'We've done all the fighting.'

She smiled with me. 'You know what I mean. Why don't you go and find him now. He'll be in the cafeteria downstairs.

I found him sitting over his second cup of coffee. He looked weary. I sat down beside him. 'Hi there.'

He looked up. 'Any change?'

I shook my head. Suddenly a huge lump filled my throat and the tears welled up and spilled over. 'Oh God, Rex, you don't think he'll die, do you?'

'No.' He reached out and took my hand. 'I spoke to the doctor last night and he said that the sedation is giving his heart time to rest and heal. Once they let him come round and he can breathe for himself they're going to do a bypass operation. They have a big success rate for those here.'

I looked up at him. 'Have you been here since last night?' He nodded. 'I don't know why you're so good to us,' I said.

'Geoff and Maggie are part of my family,' he said. 'I'd have done it for my own dad.'

'Thank you, Rex. Mum and I have had a long talk. A lot of things are clear to me now. I think we understand each other at last.'

He smiled. 'I'm glad.'

'I've been an utter cow, haven't I?'

'You were passionate about the house,' he said. 'It meant much more to you than bricks and mortar. And at the time I thought it meant more to you than I did. I didn't really understand at the time but I can see it now. Oddly enough it was your mum who made me see it.'

'Rex,' I whispered after a pause. 'Are we over? Do you really want a divorce?'

He leaned forward and took both of my hands in his. 'I've never wanted to lose you, Sophie. I love you. What disappointed me was that you didn't seem to see how much.'

'I love you too,' I whispered. 'And I've missed you so much.'

'I've missed you too, but . . . ' He paused, his head down and his next words chilled me to the heart. 'To be honest, Sophie, I'm not sure we can live together any more.'

I stared at him. 'Why not?'

He shrugged. 'All these past months I've felt you slipping away from me. I don't feel I know you any more. I wonder if I ever really did.'

'I've know I've been horribly mixed up,' I said. 'The resentment I had towards Mum and Dad grew out of all proportion when I was in my teens. For a while I suppose I let it dominate my whole life until it got the upper hand. But now, since Greenings, since you left . . . '

'That's just it, Sophie,' he put in. 'You've got to decide who and what you are and what you want.' He looked up, his eyes meeting mine. 'Most important of all, if it's really me. Until you do I really believe we need to be apart for a while.'

'You look so tired,' I said, touching his unshaven cheek. 'I've put you through a bad time, haven't I? I can't blame you for wanting some time out, but I want you to know that one thing will never change. I love you and whatever happens I always will.'

His fingers curled round mine and squeezed hard. 'Well, we'll see, eh?'

For a moment we were silent then I said, 'Look, why don't you take Mum home and stay the night there with her. You can both get some rest. I'll stay with Dad tonight.'

'You're sure?'

I nodded. 'It's what I want to do. I'd like to be there when he wakes up.'

When Rex and Mum had gone I sat by Dad's bed and wondered how I could have been so stupid, cutting myself off from parents who loved me, bigoted and blinkered, seeing only my own side of things.

★   ★   ★

I woke as a nurse tapped my shoulder.

'We're going to take your father off the machine now,' she said. 'And bring him round to see if he can breathe for himself. Why don't you go and get some breakfast?'

I glanced at Dad. 'I wanted to be here when he wakes up,' I said.

'You can come straight back,' she assured me.

Stiff with sleeping in a chair all night I stood up and flexed my neck and shoulders. I took the lift down to the canteen and ordered myself some toast and a pot of tea, but all the time my mind was back in the ward, wondering if Dad would wake up and breathe unaided. If anything happened to him I'd never forgive myself for letting him go without telling him how sorry I was. I drank the tea and ate the toast without tasting it, looking at my watch from time to time. As soon as I thought a suitable interval had passed I hurried back up to the ward. The curtains were drawn around his bed but a nurse emerged as I walked in. She smiled.

'There is a distinct improvement,' she said with a smile. 'The doctor has been to see him and all being well he's hoping to operate in a couple of days' time.'

Behind the curtains Dad was propped up in bed and awake. His face was pale and drawn but his eyes lit up when he saw me.

'Sophie! Hello, love.'

'Hello, Dad,' I went to him and took his hand. 'You gave us all a real scare. How do you feel?'

'In the pink!' He said with a wry attempt at a joke. 'I admit I've felt better but the quack tells me they're going to slice me up and put the old ticker back to rights in a couple of days.'

'So I hear.' I squeezed his hand. 'Just you get plenty of rest and let them get on with making you well again.'

He looked around. 'Your Mum?'

'She was here all day yesterday,' I told him. 'So was Rex. I made them both go home last night for some rest but I'll go and give them a ring in a minute.' I leaned forward. 'Dad, I'm so sorry — for everything.'

He shook his head. 'Don't let's talk about that. Your Mum and I, we made a bit of a hash of things — too busy trying to make a success of the business. Didn't mean we didn't love you though.'

'I know you did. Mum and I had a long talk last night.' I swallowed hard. 'You get some rest now. I'll go and ring Mum and tell her you're awake again. I bet she'll be straight over to see you.' I made to leave but he held on to my hand.

'Sophie.'

'Yes, Dad?'

'I just want you to know that even though it took a trip to the hospital to bring you back, it was worth it.'

'Oh, Dad.' A huge lump constricted my throat as I leaned forward to kiss his cheek. 'Don't say that.' I whispered. 'You make me feel so ashamed.'

'No need love.' He patted my hand. 'No need.'

Downstairs I walked outside to get some fresh air. Taking out my phone I dialled in the number. Rex answered.

'Hi. It's me. Dad's awake and breathing for himself. They seem to think he's going to be OK,' I told him. 'There's talk of doing the bypass in a couple of days' time.'

'That's great news. Have you spoken to him?'

'Yes. He still looks poorly but he's in good spirits.'

'I'll bring your mother over as soon as we've had breakfast.'

I looked at my watch. 'And I'll have to go home for a shower and a change before school.'

'Sophie.'

'Yes?'

'It's Saturday.'

I smiled wryly. 'So it is.'

21

'It seems ages since we last met,' Fran said. 'It's great to see you both again. I'm so glad you rang, Sophie, especially as you say your father has been ill. Are you sure it's OK for you to be here?'

Sophie nodded. 'He had his operation ten days ago now. He went home yesterday.'

'And it's been successful?' Katie asked.

'Absolutely, though he'll have to take things easily for a few months.'

The girls were sitting at their favourite table in Napolitano — a meeting that had been arranged by Sophie a few days earlier. This time the only day they could all manage was Sunday and the restaurant was unusually quiet.

'Have you and Rex managed to sort things out?' Katie asked.

Sophie looked at her friend. 'Not really. We're speaking again. Rex has been so kind and helpful since Dad was taken ill. But he seems to think that he and I still need more time apart.' She sighed. 'I can't blame him really. I realize now what a total bitch I've been.' She turned to Fran. 'What about your — problem?' She couldn't bring herself to use the word 'blackmail' in a public place.

Fran shook her head. 'I've tried bluffing but I can't shake her off. I've made up my mind to go down to Dorset next weekend and see my aunt.

She seems to hold the key to it all and I want some answers, though I can't say I'm looking forward to confronting her. I haven't seen her for years and she always disapproved of me.'

'So Charles still doesn't know about any of it?' Katie asked.

'No.'

'It must be hard, keeping a worry like that to yourself.'

'It is. Sometimes I feel I have no one to turn to.' Fran took a sip of her wine. 'That's not my only worry though. Harry is being bullied at school.'

'Oh, Fran, how awful,' Sophie said. 'Surely Charles won't tolerate that?'

Fran shrugged. 'He refuses to take it seriously — says it happens to all new boys and that I'm making a mountain out of a molehill. I wish there were some way I could get rid of all my problems but my hands are tied.'

'Oh, Fran, I'm so sorry. I wish I could think of a way we could help.'

'There's nothing anyone can do about any of it, I'm afraid.'

'There's one way we could help,' Katie said suddenly. 'If Sophie's up for it we could come down to Dorset with you. I'm not suggesting that we all confront your aunt but we could be there to support you.' She looked at Sophie. 'Do you agree?'

'I do. I think it's a great idea. I don't like to think of you going on your own.'

Fran was touched. 'Oh, what a lovely offer, but I couldn't ask either of you to give up a Sunday for me.'

'You're not asking, we're offering,' Sophie put in. 'And I can't think of a better idea. Just say the word and we'll be there for you just like back in the old days. All for one and one for all!'

'You bet!' Katie reiterated.

'Fran and I could both do with some of your luck rubbing off on us, Katie,' Sophie said with a wry smile.

'I was just about to tell you about that,' Katie said with a sigh. 'You were right to warn me about the man I told you about and I wish I'd listened. He turned out to be my boss's ex-husband. He had an ulterior motive — to woo me away from Imogene and ruin our wedding hire service so that her business would go down the tubes.'

Sophie's mouth dropped open. 'What a rat! So there was no job for you after all, it was just a ruse?'

'Oh, there was a job all right,' Katie said. 'As a run-around and general dogsbody. Before I went for the interview I'd even written my resignation letter and left it on Imogene's desk. I even let Drew talk me into doing that and now I know why. Luckily I managed to get back to the shop after the disastrous interview and rescue it back before she'd had time to open it.'

When the waiter had departed with their orders Fran looked at Katie. 'So, did you tell Imogene what her ex had been up to?'

'God, no!' Katie took a long drink of her wine. 'Oh, I know I should have, and I will eventually but so far I haven't worked up enough nerve.' She shook her head. 'Aren't we gloomy today?

Hasn't anyone got any good news?'

Sophie forced a smile. 'My only good news is that Greenings is sold.'

Katie and Fran exchanged glances. 'That's *good* news?' Fran said. 'But you loved that house so much.'

'Too much,' Sophie countered. 'I got things out of proportion. Once contracts have been exchanged and I've moved out I hope that Rex and I might have the chance to start getting to know one another again.'

'All our hopes will be with you, Sophie,' Fran said, touching Sophie's hand lightly.

'They certainly will,' Katie confirmed. 'He must be mad if he doesn't see what a great girl you are.'

'I've been far from great over these past months,' Sophie admitted. 'I can't blame him for seeing a side of me he didn't like. What I have to do now is try to live it down.' She looked at Fran. 'At least we can join forces in trying to do something positive. Shall we make plans for this trip down to Dorset? How about next weekend?'

22

FRANCES

It was finally arranged that the three of us would travel down to Dorset in Sophie's car. I drove over to Greenings early on Sunday morning and left my car there. We'd arranged that Katie would take the train as far as Reading and we would pick her up at the station.

I'd planned to tell Charles that I was spending the day with Sophie but in the end I didn't have to tell him anything. He told me quite casually late on Saturday evening that he would be away for the day. He said he was going to see 'a client' in Surrey. I had my suspicions that the 'client' was Celia, his ex-wife, but as it fitted in neatly with my own plans I decided to let it go.

The moment I pulled into the driveway of Greenings I could see why Sophie had fallen in love with the place and when she opened the door to me and I stepped into the hall I could see just how much loving care had gone into its restoration.

'Oh, Sophie,' I said looking round. 'What a lovely house and what a good job you've made of it.'

She was hastily putting on her coat. Adjusting her scarf in the hall mirror, she looked round at me. 'It is beautiful, isn't it? But I've realized how out of proportion I'd allowed my priorities to get. People are more important than buildings, especially the people we love.' She smiled wryly. 'If you want to keep their love, that is. I've got an awful lot of making up to do both to Rex and my parents and it begins with letting go of this house.' She looked at her watch. 'We'd better go. It's almost a quarter past six and we don't want to keep Katie waiting.'

Her train was a few minutes late so we arrived with time to spare. When she stepped down from the train she was beaming.

'Hi, you two.' She grasped my arm. 'Whatever happens today you've got the two of us on your side,' she told me.

★   ★   ★

We made good time, arriving in Kingsmere — the village where Aunt Mavis lived — just before one o'clock. Seeing the place again after so many years brought back so many unhappy memories. I hadn't expected to be so overwhelmed. As she parked the car on the edge of the village green Sophie saw at once how affected I was. She tucked her arm through mine.

'Look, that pub over there looks nice. What do you say we have a bite of lunch before we do anything else? I don't know about you but I'm starving.'

Katie echoed her enthusiasm for food and I quickly agreed. Better to wait until later anyway, I told myself, pushing aside the idea that I was putting off the evil hour.

I'd made sure that Mavis still lived at her old

address by looking her up in the electoral roll. She'd never struck me as the kind of person who would want to move and sure enough there was her entry: Garner — Miss M.E. 24 Sunnyside Drive, Kingsmere, Dorset. The address at which I'd spent the most miserable and heart-wrenching months of my life.

The King's Head did us proud. We had roast beef and all the trimmings, followed by home made apple pie and cream, after which we all felt better and the prospect of tackling the formidable Aunt Mavis was a little less daunting. Following my directions, Sophie drove to Sunnyside Drive and parked at the end of the road. My heartbeat quickened as I got out of the car.

'Wish me luck,' I said as I bent down to close the door.

'Of course we do and we'll be waiting for you right here,' Sophie said.

'And don't rush,' Katie added. 'Take your time. You need to find out as much as you can, Sophie, and we don't mind how long we wait.'

As I walked down the road and opened the gate of number twenty-four, my knees were shaking. It was only as I rang the front door bell that it occurred to me that Mavis might be out. Should I have written, telephoned? I had thought of it but I didn't want her to be forewarned. I needed to see the expression on her face when I confronted her.

My stomach gave a lurch as I heard a fumbling at the lock and the door opened a few inches.

'Yes?'

She'd aged. I'd worked out that she would

now be over sixty. Her grey hair was still frizzed up in its customary tight perm but the years had taken their toll on her face, now pinched and wrinkled. But the eyes were the same, dark, and piercingly suspicious as they looked me up and down. I swallowed hard. 'It's me, Frances.'

'Frances who?' She opened the door a little wider and peered at me then I saw recognition on her face. 'Oh, *You!*' She sniffed. 'What do you want?'

'Can I come in? I need to speak to you. It's important.'

After a long moment's hesitation during which I thought she might be about to shut the door in my face she opened it wider. 'All right, come in if you must,' she said grudgingly.

The bungalow was just as I remembered it. I followed her through the narrow hallway to the sitting room, where she turned and looked at me challengingly. 'All right, Frances, say what you want and make it quick. I'm expecting company.'

'Your company wouldn't be Sheila Philips, would it?' I asked.

Her eyes narrowed. 'What do you know about Sheila?'

'It's more what she knows about me, isn't it?'

'I don't know what you mean.'

'Oh, I think you do. Don't tell me you don't know what she's been up to.'

'Sheila is an old friend of mine.'

'So I gathered. An old friend who let you take her unwanted baby for your brother and his wife to adopt; an old friend who is now blackmailing me for money to pay her rent!'

Her eyes flew open. '*You what?*'

'Don't pretend you don't know, Mavis. Sheila Philips arrived on my doorstep with the news that she is my birth mother. I can't say it filled me with joy to know that a woman as devious and amoral as she is gave birth to me.' She began to splutter that she didn't know what I was talking about but I ignored her and continued, 'You told her everything about me plus where she could find me. You told her who I'd married and passed on every bit of information you could about me so that she could come and demand money — make threats to ruin my life. What did I ever do to you to deserve that?'

To her credit she looked genuinely shocked. 'She might be a friend of mine but I can't be held responsible for what she does,' she said defensively. 'Anyway, you're no angel. You had an illegitimate child and broke my brother and sister-in-law's hearts. *And* you wrecked another woman's marriage!'

'That's not true.'

'Look how you abandoned my brother and his wife as soon as you found yourself a rich husband,' she went on. 'After disgracing them the way you did. It was disgusting; a fine way to pay them back. You owe me, Frances. If it hadn't been for me taking you in you'd have been sent to one of those mother and baby homes.'

'And that gives you the right to collude in blackmail, does it?' I asked her.

Her eyes slid away from mine. 'I told you,' she muttered. 'I can't be held responsible for another person's actions.'

'Yes you can. It was you who gave her all the ammunition she needed for her plan to ruin me — her own flesh and blood, her daughter. What kind of woman — '

'*She's not your mother.*'

The words stopped me in mid sentence and I felt my stomach lurch. I stared at her. '*Not* — then who is?'

'It's true that she brought you to me when she knew my brother and his wife wanted to adopt.' She shook her head. 'It was some young girl she knew. Sheila used to run a youth club in the village and this girl was in trouble. Sheila helped her out.' She shot me a defiant look. 'A bit like I helped you. They say history repeats itself, don't they?'

'So you thought it was time for me to pay for all that kindness.'

Mavis shrugged. 'She asked me about you and I told her nothing but the truth. How was I to know what she'd do?'

'And you think that pleading ignorance would hold up in court, do you?'

At the word 'court' her face dropped. 'What do you mean?'

'I mean that I've had enough,' I told her. 'Her price keeps going up and I can't meet her demands any longer. I'm going to have to go to the police, even if it means the end of my marriage.' I looked her directly in the eye. 'Blackmail is a very serious crime, Mavis. And whether you meant to be or not you are implicated in it.'

'I had nothing to do with it!' Her voice had the shrillness of fear in it now.

'You played right into her hands,' I reminded her. 'Without you, she couldn't have done a thing.'

I saw her Adam's apple wobble as she swallowed hard. 'What do you want me to do?'

'You're still in touch with her?' She nodded. 'Then warn her off. Tell her it's over, that if I see her one more time or get another telephone call I'll go to the police immediately.'

'She might think you're just bluffing.'

'If she thinks that tell her to try me. I mean every word of it, Mavis. And remember, you're in almost as much trouble as she is so it's in your interest to convince her.'

She nodded slowly. 'All right, I'll tell her.'

'Make sure you do.' I turned towards the door. 'No need to show me out. I'll find my own way.'

★ ★ ★

I almost fell into the car when I got to the end of the road. Sophie looked at me expectantly.

'Well?'

'It's over,' I told her. 'I think I put the fear of God into Mavis and she's going to warn the woman off. But the best thing of all is that she told me that the woman who's been making my life a living hell all these weeks isn't my birth mother after all.'

Sophie hugged me and Katie reached across from the back seat to put an arm round my neck, whereupon I burst into tears of sheer relief.

'I can't believe what I did in there,' I said as Sophie handed me a packet of tissues from her

248

bag. 'For the first time in my life I actually stood up for myself. And — and I think it worked. I think I've won!'

From the back seat Katie gave a whoop. 'Wow! Great news, Fran. We have to celebrate. Tell you what, we can't come to Dorset and go home without having had a cream tea, can we, even if it is the middle of winter? I think I saw an old fashioned tea room back in the village.'

* * *

When Sophie drove on to the drive I saw that the house was in darkness. I looked at her.

'Will you come in for a coffee?'

She shook her head. 'Thanks, but maybe another time. I'll get off home now if you don't mind, Fran.'

'I know, it's been a long day, hasn't it?' I leaned across to hug her. 'Thank you so much for taking me today and for all your support.'

'I'm just so glad everything worked out for you. It must be an enormous relief.'

'It is.' I gathered my coat and bag together. 'You will keep in touch, won't you? And I hope everything works out for you with Rex.'

'I'll ring you,' she promised. 'Bye, Fran and take care.'

I watched, waving as she turned the car and drove out through the gates, then I turned towards the house, fumbling in my bag for my keys. As soon as I let myself into the hall I knew that Charles was still out. The house had that unmistakably empty feel about it. I looked at my watch.

It was half past nine. He was certainly making a meal of his meeting with his mysterious 'client'.

As I passed the telephone I saw that the red answerphone light was flashing. Perhaps Charles had left a message. I pressed the button. To my surprise there were three messages recorded. I listened to the last one but it was not my husband's voice that echoed round the empty hall.

'This is Philip Masterson calling from St Eldred's school. Can you please telephone me as soon as you get this message? Thank you.'

My heart gave a lurch. Quickly checking I found that the other messages were from St Eldred's headmaster too, the first being recorded at six-thirty. I scrabbled frantically in my diary for the number and my fingers trembled as I punched in the digits. The phone was answered almost at once.

'St Eldred's. Masterson speaking.'

'Mr Masterson, it's Frances Grayson. I've been out all day and I've only just got your message. Is it Harry? Is he all right?'

'Mrs Grayson. I'm so glad you've rung at last. I've been trying all day and I didn't have a mobile number for either you or — '

'Please,' I interrupted. 'What's wrong?'

'I'm afraid that unfortunately Harry was involved in an accident this morning,' he said.

The words almost stopped the breath in my throat. 'An accident? What's happened to him, how bad is it?'

'It's not serious but we thought it best to have him checked over so he's in hospital.'

'So what kind of injury has he got? I'll come at

once if you let me know which hospital . . . ' I gabbled, my words tumbling over one another.

'Please don't be alarmed, Mrs Grayson. I'm sure Harry will be fine. He had a fall and the doctors thought he might have fractured his skull.'

'*What!* Oh my God!'

'But an X-ray shows that it is only a hairline fracture.'

'*Only?* How did it happen, Mr Masterson?'

There was a slight hesitation at the other end. 'I wasn't there at the time. From what I can gather there was some — er — horseplay at the top of the stairs. Harry slipped and lost his footing.'

'*Horseplay!* Is that what you call it? And Harry fell down the stairs and fractured his skull!' I swallowed hard in an attempt to slow the thudding of my heart. 'Mr Masterson, I don't know whether you are aware of it or not, or even if you care, but there is a serious bullying problem at St Eldred's.'

'Oh, hardly,' he said blandly. 'This school has a reputation for . . . '

'Just tell me which hospital he's in,' I interrupted. 'I need to be with my son.'

I scribbled down the address of the hospital then tried Charles's mobile number. His phone was switched off. I left a message on the voicemail for him to ring me and hastily scribbled a note in case he was on his way home, leaving it propped up on the hall table then I let myself out of the house and ran to get the car.

It took me an hour and a half to get to the

hospital and when I got to the children's ward it was after 'lights out'. Harry was fast asleep but I spoke to the ward sister and she told me that he would probably be discharged in the morning once the doctor had been round and was happy with his condition.

'Hairline fractures in children heal very quickly,' she told me reassuringly. 'Harry is concussed and he has a lump on his head and a black eye that will last a week or so but he's already making a good recovery.'

She found me a comfortable chair and a blanket and I sat by his bed for the rest of the night. I slept fitfully on and off and during my waking moments I made a number of decisions, the first of which was that Harry would return to St Eldred's over my dead body.

I woke at about five o'clock to find Harry awake and looking at me.

'Mum?'

'Hello darling. How are you feeling?'

He frowned. 'I wondered if you were really here or if I was dreaming. When they brought me here everything looked sort of funny.'

I got up to sit on the side of his bed. Switching the overhead light on, I could see now that the sister had been right. One eye was puffy and swollen, the skin red and already darkening to purple, and above his ear was a sizeable lump. I stroked his hair back from his forehead 'Mr Masterson said you'd had an accident. What happened?'

Again he looked puzzled. 'I can't remember it very well but they were trying to get me to slide down the banisters.'

'Who's 'they', Harry?'

He frowned. 'Some of the other boys; they called me a chicken and a wimp. I tried to climb on to the banisters but my foot slipped or something. I don't know what happened after that till I woke up in here.'

I pictured the staircase at St Eldred's and the tiled floor of the hall beneath and shuddered. If Harry had fallen over the banisters the other way he could have been killed. He was looking at me. 'Mum, do I have to go back to school? Can I come home with you?'

'Of course you can,' I said taking his hand. 'It's not long now till Christmas anyway so you won't miss much school.'

'Do I have to go back to St Eldred's after Christmas?'

'Not if you don't want to. But don't worry about that now.'

He brightened visibly 'When can we go home?'

'When the doctor has checked you over again later this morning.' I watched as he yawned. 'It's not quite morning yet, why don't you try to go back to sleep now?'

He allowed me to straighten the bedclothes and plump his pillow. 'You won't go away, will you?' he asked anxiously.

'No. I'll still be here when you wake up.'

He closed his eyes and in seconds he was asleep again. I drifted off soon after, relieved that he didn't seem too bad after all.

* * *

Later, while he was having his breakfast I took the opportunity to go downstairs and ring our landline at home. There was no reply. Charles's mobile was still switched off too, and when I switched my own mobile on there were no missed calls. As soon as it was nine o'clock I rang the office and asked to speak to him. His secretary told me he wasn't in yet.

'When he does arrive would you ask him to ring me on my mobile please?' I asked her. 'And tell him it's extremely urgent.' Then suddenly I had a thought. 'Could you tell me the name of the client he was with all day yesterday?'

There was a pause. 'I'm sorry Mrs Grayson, but I wasn't aware that he had an appointment yesterday,' she said at last.

'Well could you look in his diary, please?' Again a pause. Was the girl trying to pull the wool over my eyes? I pressed the point. 'As I said before it is extremely urgent that I speak to him as soon as possible.'

'Could you hold please?'

I waited impatiently for her to go through to Charles's office and locate his diary. At last she spoke. 'Mrs Grayson, there are no appointments in the diary for yesterday,' she said. 'None at all.'

Frustrated, I rang Adam and told him I wouldn't be in this morning, explaining the circumstances. He was sympathetic.

'Don't worry about a thing, Frances,' he said. 'I'll cover for all your appointments and I hope Harry is better soon.'

'Thank you.' I had a sudden thought. 'Adam, could you give me a number for Ms Celia Woodley.'

'The woman who complained about you, your husband's ex-wife?' He sounded surprised.

'Yes. It'll be in my work file but that's at home and I'm at the hospital now.'

'Why do you need it, Frances?'

'I can't locate Charles and I have a strong feeling that's where he is,' I told him.

'I see. Are you sure this is the right way to go?' he asked cautiously.

'I don't really have any choice, Adam. I have to find Charles to tell him about Harry. If he's with Celia then so be it. If not I'll have to think again. Don't worry, I'll go about it tactfully,' I added.

'Right, if you're sure.' He gave me the number which I jotted down. 'Let me know how things go, Frances. I hope you manage to get in touch with Charles. Harry must be asking to see his father.'

It suddenly occurred to me that not once had Harry actually asked for Charles.

'And don't worry about work,' Adam went on. 'Take as long as you need.'

I arrived back in the ward to find a young doctor was examining Harry. He glanced up as I arrived.

'Mrs Grayson?'

'Yes.'

'Can I have a word?' He turned to grin at Harry as he straightened the bedclothes. 'Right, young man, if you're very good we might let you go home later this morning.' He glanced at me and I followed him out into the corridor, anxious about what he was about to tell me. He looked very grave.

'Mrs Grayson, your son has a number of bruises on his body, some old and some quite new. Not all of them can be attributed to falling down the stairs. Can you throw any light on that?'

'He's been at boarding school since September,' I told him. 'I saw bruises when he came home at half-term. He wouldn't say much but I suspect bullying.'

'And yet you sent him back?'

'I didn't want to but my husband refused to take it seriously. He went to the same school when he was a boy. He made light of it, said it was a toughening up process.'

He looked shocked. 'It looks more like sadistic violence to me. I'd advise you to find him another school, one with a less Victorian attitude towards nine-year-old children.' He looked at me disapprovingly. 'Take him home and look after him, Mrs Grayson. By the look of him he's had three months of sheer hell.'

I watched as he strode off down the corridor, fuming that I had had to take the flack for what had happened while Charles was oblivious to it all.

Harry had another nap after breakfast and I went downstairs. Standing outside I dialled Celia Woodley's number. She answered at once in her usual imperious tone.

'Celia Woodley.'

I'd thought carefully about how to approach the situation and decided that the best approach was to be as devious as Charles. 'Good morning. Grayson Electronics. Mr Grayson's secretary speaking. Can I speak to him, please?'

She made no reply but a moment later Charles's voice replaced hers. He sounded uneasy. 'Laura? How did you get this number?'

'It's not Laura, Charles. It's Fran. Unfortunately I had to resort to subterfuge in order to get to speak to you.'

'Look, Fran, I can explain,' he blustered. 'I — '

'I'm not interested in your explanations, Charles,' I interrupted. 'I guessed where you were. Celia told me you and she had been seeing each other.'

'Celia did? Look, Fran — we have to talk.'

'I've been trying to reach you since last night to tell you that Harry was involved in more bullying at school yesterday,' I told him. 'This time it was serious. He's in hospital with a fractured skull.'

'Oh.' He sounded maddeningly unruffled. 'How is he?'

'It could have been a lot worse,' I told him. 'He was being forced to climb on the banisters and he's lucky not to have fallen forty feet on to a tiled floor.' There was silence at the other end of the line and I went on, 'I'm to be allowed to take him home today,' I told him. 'So if you're interested and you can bear to tear yourself away, Harry and I will be at home. Oh, and Charles; you're right. We do need to talk. We need to talk long and hard.'

257

23

KATIE

I found it hard to get up on Monday morning after the three of us had been down to Dorset, but as I rushed round getting ready for work I couldn't help smiling as I remembered what Fran had achieved with support from Sophie and myself. I was so glad that we went with her. Who'd have thought that meek and mild little Fran could have socked it to her nasty aunt like that? Surely that old bat who'd pretended to be her mother wouldn't have a leg to stand on now, and Fran's relief to find that she wasn't the daughter of a scheming old cow was a treat to see.

It was a freezing morning and I only just caught the bus by the skin of my teeth. It was only as I sat gazing out of the window at all the other hurrying commuters that I remembered that I'd vowed to take the bull by the horns today myself and sort out my own pressing problem. The difference was that I was going to have to do it all by myself. No one could help me out of the mess I'd made of things. It was all down to me and my stupid vanity. The sky looked even greyer when I reminded myself that by the end of this week I'd probably be unemployed, more than likely homeless too. I'd never be able to afford the rent of my larger flat

258

without a job and someone else had moved into my old one. I tried hard to be philosophical about it, telling myself that maybe it was no more than I deserved and I should learn a lesson from it.

As we were in the run-up to Christmas we were enjoying a run on evening and party wear, both selling and hiring out, and when I arrived at Fantaisie Imogene was already pulling the covers off the rails and preparing to open up for the day. We were busy all morning and even busier through the lunch hour which is the time when the office girls tend to pop in to see our latest stock.

As I said, I'd made up my mind to throw myself on Imogene's mercy today, to tell her about the tempting offer her ex had made me and how I'd been fool enough to fall for it. Imogene is not exactly famous for her tolerant forgiving nature and I fully expected fireworks and more likely than not, the sack, but I reckoned that she couldn't manage without me at least until Christmas and probably until after the January sale. She was a business woman after all so at least I was safe until then. On the other hand she could be pretty hellish to work with when she was miffed about something and the days ahead threatened to be difficult to say the least.

It was almost closing time before we had a minute to ourselves. As I tidied up, putting dresses back on hangers and slipping them on to the appropriate rails, Imogene looked at her watch and smiled at me wearily.

'Don't know about you but I'm knackered,' she said. 'Put the kettle on for a cuppa, there's a love. I didn't get a drink at lunch time and I'm spitting feathers.'

As I filled the kettle and switched it on, the butterflies in my stomach went into their version of the Highland fling. Reaching into the cupboard I pulled out the box of chocolate biscuits a regular customer had brought in for us last week and picked out all the wafers — Imogene's favourites.

'Tea up!' I called as I carried the tray through to the office.

She came through and sank down gratefully on her swivel chair, kicking off her shoes. 'Ah, that's better.' She looked at me. 'Thanks, Katie. Pull up a chair and have yours. We'll leave the door ajar then we'll hear if a customer comes in.' She picked up one of the wafers and nibbled it. 'Mmm, yummy!' She looked at me. 'So, tell me about your weekend.'

I knew I was only putting off the evil moment but I described my day out to Dorset with Sophie and Fran, leaving out the part about the blackmail as I reckoned that was Fran's private business. She smiled.

'Sounds like quite an eventful day.' She drank the last of her tea and began to slip her feet back into her shoes but I held up my hand.

'Imogene, hang on a minute. There's something I need to tell you.'

She stood up. 'Can't it wait till tomorrow? All I want is to get home to a warm bath and my supper.'

'It can't wait, Imogene,' I said. 'I have to get this off my chest and it's now or never.'

'Oh dear!' She looked at me and slowly sat down again. 'Sounds serious.'

'It is.' I cleared my throat and prepared to deliver the speech I'd been rehearsing for days. The trouble was, now that the moment had arrived it had completely gone out of my head. 'I've done something awful,' I began unceremoniously.

'OK, spit it out.' She sighed. 'You've been at the petty cash? Or am I going to get sued because you've pinched some top designer's creation?'

For an instant I was sidetracked. 'No! I'd never do that.'

'OK, so what is it?'

I took a deep breath. 'Some weeks ago this guy came into the shop while you were out. He said he'd seen a wedding dress designed by me and been really impressed. He'd gone to a lot of trouble to find out where to contact me.' I looked up to see how it was going down so far but Imogene's expression was just vaguely bored. I went on, 'He was attractive and, well, *nice* and he asked me out a few times, then he said he could get me a job with a top designer,' I cleared my throat. 'We got on well. He seemed to be really clued up about the world of fashion. I liked — I *trusted* him.'

'So some guy wined and dined you with the promise of a job.' She looked at me, one eyebrow raised cynically. 'And you're telling me you fell for it and went to bed with him?'

261

'Yes — no, at least not the bed bit. But that wasn't all. He got me an interview with Rosie Sams.' Her eyebrows shot up. She was well and truly hooked now and I hurried on, 'But there wasn't a job at all, at least not the kind of job he'd promised — not as a designer, only as some kind of runner and general dogsbody.' I swallowed hard. 'But I'd believed him, you see and before I went for the interview I left a letter of resignation on your desk. He — this guy — had insisted on that. I was going along with it, Imogene. I was going to let you down. I'm ashamed and I'm really sorry.'

Her eyes flashed. 'But what if there *had* been a job, Katie? What would have happened then?' I bit my lip and felt my face flushing. There was no answer to that. But to my surprise her expression suddenly softened. 'OK, so you were flattered. We've all been there and I'm no exception. What happened to the letter by the way?'

'I rushed back that afternoon and found it still unopened, so I tore it up.'

'Well, maybe you learned your lesson. Next time you'll be less trusting.'

I shook my head, wincing inwardly. *It wasn't over.* She hadn't heard the worst bit yet. 'N-no,' I stammered. 'There's more. It's *worse* than that.'

She frowned. 'How much worse can it get?'

'*Much* worse. While I was looking for my letter in the office that afternoon I found your wedding photo in the drawer and . . . ' I didn't need to go any further. She'd already guessed the rest. With

262

a groan she covered her face with both hands. Through her fingers she hissed the name. *'Andrew!'*

'Honestly, Imogene, I didn't have a clue. He told me his name was Drew.'

'The devious, conniving *bastard!*' She dropped her hands into her lap and looked up at the ceiling. 'He was determined to see me go bankrupt,' she said. 'And when he got wind of the new business you and I had embarked on he worked out this evil scheme to scupper the whole thing.'

'I promise you, Imogene, I had no idea who he was until I saw that photo in your desk drawer.'

She focused on me again, almost as though she'd forgotten I was there. 'I'm not blaming you, Katie. I know my ex-husband and I know how cunning he can be — and how persuasive. He didn't give a damn about humiliating you just as long as he could get back at me.' She shook her head. 'I'm not at all sure I couldn't sue him for this.' She looked at me thoughtfully for a long moment. 'Katie,' she said at last. 'Just how committed are you to Fantaisie? I know you're ambitious and I want you to be honest with me.'

I shook my head. 'I'm — er — not sure what you mean.'

'I mean how would you like to be a full partner?'

I swallowed hard. 'That sounds great but what would it really mean?'

She leaned forward. 'The lease of the shop is due for renewal. As I told you, Andrew's name is still on it. He and I are tied together and it's my guess that he planned to force me out of business so that he could take over and run his own business from here. What do you say we let him think he's succeeded?' She grinned gleefully, but I was no closer to understanding what she was getting at.

'I — don't quite see,' I mumbled.

'What if I were to drop out and *you* took on the lease?'

Suddenly the penny dropped. 'Oh, I see. But you said you and he were tied together.'

'Not if I let him think I'm going out of business. He'll run a mile from letting himself in for my unpaid debts.' She chuckled at the thought, but I wasn't laughing.

'But I don't have any money to put into the business,' I said quickly.

She shook her head. 'You wouldn't have to pay a penny.'

I looked at her doubtfully. 'Imogene, are you sure this is all legal and above board?'

'Yes. Naturally we'd have it all legally arranged.'

'Wouldn't it be easier to move to another shop?'

She shook her head. 'There's nothing else to let anywhere near here. We'd never get anything in as good a position as this. Besides, our customers are used to coming here.'

'I see. And you trust me enough to go ahead with this?' I asked. 'After what I almost did.'

'Yes, I do,' she said positively. 'Look, Katie, to be totally frank, I think you've learned now that getting a job with one of the big designer houses isn't on for you. Staying here and designing for us is your best bet, which you'll have to agree about when you've had time to think about it. You and I would be full partners, share the profits and the outgoings. But it would be your name on the lease. In other words we'd be throwing in our lots together. So . . . ' She looked at me, her head on one side. 'What do you say?'

'Would that mean I could throw you out any time I liked?' I asked cheekily.

She gave me a warning look. 'Don't push it, Katie.'

The butterflies that had played havoc with my stomach began to flutter again. 'Seriously, I like the idea very much,' I told her.

'No need to say right now. Obviously you want time to think about it,' Imogene said. 'Look, what are you doing for Christmas?'

I shrugged. 'Spending it alone as usual. Just me and my individual pudding and turkey burger.'

'Well I've booked myself into a spa,' she said. 'Nothing to beat a bit of pampering. Why don't you join me? Call it my Christmas present. You'd have plenty of time to mull over my proposition and if you want to go ahead we could start making plans.' She looked at me expectantly. 'Are we on?'

Smiling, I nodded. 'OK, we're on!'

24

SOPHIE

At school the Christmas preparations were gathering speed; the nativity play was being rehearsed and the older children were practicing daily for the carol concert which was to be performed along with the nativity play on the last day of term. In the middle of it all I had a call from the estate agent to say that the couple who had bought Greenings were anxious to move in before Christmas. Their baby was due at the beginning of February and they were keen to settle into their new home before then. We'd already exchanged contracts and there seemed to be no reason why the completion date couldn't be brought forward so I agreed. My only problem was where would I live until I'd found a new home? Did I start house hunting now? It wasn't really an option so near to Christmas. Did I look for a house or a small flat? That very much depended on whether Rex and I were going to get back together or not.

Since Dad came out of hospital I'd been visiting my parents every weekend. Sometimes Rex would drop in too, but so far neither of us had broached the subject of our separation. After what Rex had said that day at the hospital I hardly dared to bring the subject up again but now I knew I had to in some form or other.

At home I began on the packing. As Rex had left some of his stuff behind I knew I would have to contact him. Taking a break from the tedious task of sorting out what I needed immediately and what could go into storage I rang him.

'Rex, I'm going to have to move out of Greenings before Christmas and I wondered what you wanted me to do about the things you left behind.'

'Oh.' He sounded taken aback. 'I hadn't realized it'd be this soon.'

'The couple who have bought the house need to get settled in before their baby is born in February. I couldn't say no.'

'No, of course not.' He paused. 'Where will you be going, Sophie?'

'I haven't a clue at the moment,' I confessed. 'It couldn't really have come at a worse time. You know how frantic things get in the run up to Christmas at school.'

'Yes, I remember.' He cleared his throat. 'So, will you look for a flat?'

'I'd rather have a house, but it depends . . . '

'Well,' he interrupted. 'If you see something and you want me to look it over for you, you know where I am.'

He sounded like some casual acquaintance offering to do me a favour and my heart plummeted. 'Thanks,' I said. 'I'll bear it in mind. Meantime, what shall I do with your things?'

'Oh, just chuck everything into a box and leave it in the garage. I'll drive over and pick it up in a couple of days.'

'Right. If that's what you want.'

As I hung up the phone I swallowed hard at the lump in my throat. It all sounded like a foregone conclusion. Clearly he already saw our marriage as over.

At school the next morning there was another bombshell. At assembly John Harrison announced that he would be leaving at the end of term. He gave no reason so at break I went to his office with the excuse that I needed to put in an order for new art materials.

'You're going to be missed, John,' I ventured as he made a note of what I needed for next term. He looked up.

'You must be wondering where and why I'm going.'

I shook my head. 'It's none of my business. I just wondered why you're going so suddenly.'

He took a deep breath. 'The powers that be have kindly agreed to waive the statutory term's notice,' he said. 'I've had the offer of a headship up in Yorkshire and I thought it would be nice to be closer to the boys.'

'Oh, that's wonderful.'

He smiled. 'But you're wondering why the rush.'

'No. It's . . . '

'None of your business?' He smiled. 'So you said, but it *is* in a way, Sophie. I've already confided in you how things were between Hillary and me and I'm grateful for the support you gave me. You're an intuitive person, so it's not surprising that you're curious. This job has come about because the current headmaster has been taken ill and can't carry on, but apart from that I've heard on the grapevine that Hillary's new relationship is over.'

'Oh, so you're hoping . . . '

'I'm determined to do everything I can to get my family back together again.' He leaned forward. 'I've never stopped loving Hillary and you know how much the boys mean to me. Everything that went wrong was my fault and I won't let it happen again.'

The determination and hope in his eyes tugged at my heart. I smiled. 'Good for you, John. I wish you the best of luck — with everything.' I stood up and offered him my hand.

He took it. 'What about you, Sophie?' he asked. 'Has your situation improved?'

I sighed. 'I'm having to move out of the house before Christmas,' I told him. 'It's just not easy at this time of year.'

'I take it you'll be staying with your parents.'

I shook my head. 'It's a bit too far away to commute, especially at this time of year. And I probably won't start looking for somewhere permanent till after the holiday.' I shrugged. 'Meantime, bedsit-land, here I come.'

He frowned. 'Doesn't sound like a bundle of fun. What about Rex?'

'Rex has offered to give me the benefit of his advice, nothing more.'

'I see. I'm so sorry, Sophie.'

To my horror I felt the tears gathering in my eyes. 'It's all my fault,' I said briskly. 'No one to blame but myself.' I made the pretence of looking at my watch. 'I must go now. Good luck, John.'

That evening as I was preparing to go home,

Maggie Jackson, John's secretary, stopped me in the car park.

'Mrs Turner. I heard that you were moving out of your house and needed somewhere to move into quickly.'

'That's right. Do you know of somewhere?'

She nodded. 'As it happens the ground floor flat where I live will be vacant for three months. Mrs Lowe, the elderly lady who lives there is going abroad for the winter and she's keen to let it temporarily. She really wants someone to take care of the place while she's away so she won't be charging a high rent.'

My spirits rose. 'It sounds ideal.'

'I'll give you the address and phone number and you can pop round and see her if you're interested.'

I went round the same evening, having first telephoned Mrs Lowe to see if it was convenient. She turned out to be a very sweet old lady suffering badly from arthritis. Leaning heavily on a stick, she ushered me into a tastefully furnished sitting room.

'Do sit down, my dear. I'd almost given up hope of finding someone to look after the place,' she said. 'Not many people want temporary accommodation. I thought I might have to cancel my trip to Madeira and I was so looking forward to it. My poor joints do suffer so in the cold, damp winters we get here and of course I couldn't desert my poor dear Albert.'

My heart sank. Was there an elderly brother or husband to care for as well as the flat? 'Albert?' I enquired.

She laughed. 'Albert is my cat. I'll introduce you to him in a minute and we'll see if you and he will get along.' She peered at me anxiously. 'You do like cats, don't you dear?'

Relieved, I laughed. 'Yes,' I said. 'As long as they behave themselves.'

'Oh, I assure you that Albert is very well brought up,' she told me. 'I've had him since he was six weeks old. He's no trouble — goes in and out through the cat flap in the back door when he needs to so no nasty litter tray to clean. He likes his two meals a day, but he spends most of his time asleep in his basket in the kitchen. He's like me, getting on a bit now.'

She showed me round. As well as the spacious sitting room there was a small neat kitchen, a bathroom and a large bedroom. Everywhere was clean and well kept and I saw that it would suit me very well. After the tour of inspection, Mrs Lowe insisted on putting the kettle on for a cup of tea and Albert's large head popped through the cat flap when he heard the biscuit tin rattle. Mrs Lowe laughed.

'He's is very partial to a custard cream,' she said.

Albert turned out to be an enormous tabby with huge green eyes and as soon as I sat down he leapt on to my lap and curled up, purring loudly. Mrs Lowe laughed. 'There, he approves of you,' she said reassuringly. 'I'll be sure to leave you an adequate supply of his favourite food in the pantry so you won't have to worry about that.'

Over a pot of Earl Grey tea we discussed the

rent, which was ridiculously low. I protested but Mrs Lowe was adamant.

'I'm just so grateful to get a nice young professional woman to look after the place for me,' she said. 'What I've suggested will be perfectly adequate.'

Back at home and after some consideration I rang Rex. 'I thought you might be interested to know that I've found temporary accommodation,' I told him. 'It's a nice ground floor flat in the next road to school and the rent is miniscule.'

'That's a piece of luck,' he said. 'Are you sure there are no snags?'

'The only one as far as I can see is that I have to take on a cat as well as the flat. The owner is off to warmer climes for the winter and she was anxious to get a tenant who liked cats.' I laughed. 'Or it might be more accurate to say, someone her cat liked. Luckily I seem to have passed the test.'

'Well, good luck with that.' There was a pause then he said. 'Are you all right, Sophie?'

'Yes. I'm fine.'

'Only it seems a bit much, you having all the packing and upheaval to cope with on your own. Is there anything I can do to help?'

'No thanks, it's almost done anyway.' The words were out before I could stop to think and I immediately bit my tongue, longing to take them back. Was that his way of angling for a meeting? Did he want to talk things through?

'Oh well, just thought I'd offer,' he said quickly. 'See you then, Sophie. And good luck, with the move and the carol concert and everything.'

'Do you want to come?' I asked quickly, anxious to hang on to him a bit longer. 'Can I get you a ticket?'

He laughed. 'No thanks. Not really my thing. But thanks for asking.'

I put the phone down, kicking myself for not grasping the opportunity when I had it. Goodness only knew when I'd see him again.

I spent the weekend at Mum and Dad's, grateful to get away from the curtainless windows and stacked boxes. Greenings didn't feel like home any more. It was as though it had cast me off and lay dormant, waiting for its new owners to move in and warm it back to life again. I told Mum and Dad about the flat I'd been lucky enough to find and they were pleased for me but disappointed that I hadn't considered staying with them as an option. I explained that the possibility of bad weather could make the long drive into school every day difficult. 'Mrs Lowe wants to leave next weekend,' I told them. 'So I'll have to move in then because of the cat.' They laughed at my description of Albert.

'Sounds as though you'll be an expert in feline husbandry come the spring,' Dad joked.

I joined Mum in the kitchen later as she was making us all a bedtime drink.

'Has Rex been to see you lately?' I asked.

She glanced at me swiftly. 'Not for a while, no. Any particular reason for asking?'

I shrugged. 'I just wondered what he was doing for Christmas.'

Mum poured milk into a saucepan. 'He did

say something about going up north to spend it with his folks.'

'Oh. That's good then. He doesn't see them very often.'

She turned to me. 'You're so stubborn, the pair of you,' she said exasperatedly. 'Why can't you be sensible and start trying to work something out.'

'I don't think he wants to, Mum,' I said. 'I've given him several opportunities to suggest a meeting but he never takes me up on them.'

'Then why not ask him outright?'

I shrugged. 'I get the feeling that he's already written our marriage off.'

'Has he said so?'

'He did say he wasn't sure we could live together again. He says he feels he doesn't really know who I am any more.'

'*And do you?*'

I stared at her. 'What do you mean?'

'It takes a crisis like the one you've both just lived through to make you start taking stock of yourself,' she said. 'The girl Rex fell in love with is still there, Sophie. I'm quite sure that he saw more in you than the way you dressed and all those left wing student views you used to have. He must have seen past those things a long time ago if he's truthful. It's not the superficial things that make a person. It's what's inside that counts.'

'So why was he so upset when I changed my dress and hairstyle?'

'Because it was all so sudden. You were already letting that house occupy your life, putting all your energy and passion into it at the expense of your marriage. When you decided to change your appearance he panicked, began to wonder if you'd outgrown him. That was why he came to us and asked us for a loan. It was to stop you worrying about money so that you could get back to normal. Unfortunately it had the reverse effect. Can't you see, Sophie, he was desperate to get you back then and I'm sure he still is.'

'He's got a funny way of showing it.'

'He's got his pride, love. It's already taken a battering. I think the ball is in your court now.' When I was silent she changed the subject. 'So, what about Christmas? Are you going to spend it with us?'

'I'll come for Christmas Day,' I told her. 'I won't be able to stay because of Albert.'

She frowned 'Who?'

'Albert, my new charge — Mrs Lowe's cat.'

She smiled and handed me the tray. 'Of course. Fine then. Christmas Day it is. Better than nothing, I suppose.'

★ ★ ★

I moved into Mrs Lowe's flat the following Saturday. All my furniture was safely in storage and all I needed for the weeks to come was packed into two suitcases. When I arrived, Mrs Lowe was waiting in the hall for her taxi. She wore a smart red coat and a jaunty little hat and she looked quite excited at the prospect of her winter holiday.

'I always stay at the same hotel,' she told me as

she handed me the keys. 'And on Christmas Day there's always a red rose on my breakfast tray. They look after me so well.' She looked at me, her face serious. 'Now, you know where everything is, don't you, dear? And if anything should go wrong I've left the number of the handyman on the telephone pad. His name is Fred Gray and he can turn his hand to anything.'

'I'll remember,' I promised. 'Just you go and have a fabulous time. Albert and I will be fine.'

Outside the taxi hooted and I saw her into it and waved her off then went inside to unpack. The last of my things put away, I felt at a loss. I'd have to go out and do some shopping, stock up with food for the coming week. There'd be no time during the last week of term, what with the concert and everything. My eyes suddenly alighted on the telephone and I thought of Rex and what Mum had said. Maybe I should take the bull by the horns and invite him round. Without giving myself any more time to think about it I lifted the receiver and dialled his number.

'Hello, Rex Turner.'

'Rex, it's me, Sophie. I've just moved into this temporary flat and I was thinking — wondering — if you'd like to come round and have a meal with me this evening. A sort of house warming.' I held my breath.

'Oh, Sophie, that would have been nice.' My heart sank. He was going to knock me back yet again. 'It's just that I was just about to leave,' he went on. 'I'm going up to see my folks for Christmas and as there's nothing to keep me here I thought I'd make an early start, spend a couple of weeks with them as I haven't seen them in ages.'

'I see,' I said trying hard to keep the disappointment out of my voice. 'Well, give them my best won't you?'

'Of course.' He paused. 'If I known sooner I could have gone tomorrow,' he went on. 'But they'll be expecting me.'

'Yes of course. It was just a sudden impulse,' I said quickly. 'It doesn't matter. Have a lovely time.'

'Maybe we can meet when I'm back,' he said.

'Yes, maybe.'

As I replaced the receiver I felt something soft bump against my leg and I looked down to see Albert rubbing his head against me, purring like an engine. I bent down and picked him up, burying my face in his soft fur. 'Well, looks like it's just you and me, Albert,' I told him.

★ ★ ★

The carol concert and the nativity play went off without too many hitches and on the last day of term the staff gave a small informal leaving party for John. The new head and his wife came too so we were all introduced. We said our final good-byes but in the car park, John caught up with me.

'Sophie, can I have a word?'

'Of course, is there something I can do for you, John?'

'It's just that I went to put the house on the market yesterday but on the way home I suddenly thought of you,' he said. 'I know you're looking for somewhere permanent to live. Any chance that you might be interested?'

'I don't know, John,' I said hesitantly. 'There's not a lot I can do about it until after Christmas.'

'No, of course not. I'll tell you what though, I'm leaving the keys with the agent. It's Bruce and Freeman in North Street.' He took out his wallet and handed me one of their cards. 'I'll tell them that you might be interested and if you felt like it after Christmas you could go and have a look round.'

My heart gave a lurch. I'd always liked John's house, a three bedroom, detached villa in a quiet, leafy road quite close to school. It was just the kind of place that Rex had always fancied. But it would be too big for me to live in alone. If only . . .

'Thanks for thinking of me, John,' I said. 'It's certainly something to think about.'

* * *

Christmas Day with Mum and Dad was quiet but enjoyable. I told them about John leaving and how he'd suggested that I have a look at his house. Mum was enthusiastic.

'That's a good idea. Why don't you go and look at it over the holiday?'

I shrugged. 'A small flat would do for me,' I said. 'What would I do with a whole three bedroom house on my own?'

'Well, you never know . . . '

I silenced her with a look. 'I've got to be

realistic, Mum,' I said. 'I have to face the fact that from now on I'm on my own.'

When I got back to the flat Albert was waiting for me, or rather for his supper, which he attacked with gusto the minute his dish touched the floor. As I switched on the TV and prepared to watch the evening film I wondered what Rex was doing. I imagined his family with the whole tribe of aunts, uncles and cousins crammed into his parents' lounge playing silly games and exchanging news and I felt nostalgic and quite envious. I wondered what excuse he had made for going home on his own, or if he had told them that our marriage was over.

On Boxing Day I stayed in bed late, getting up to make myself some breakfast and taking it back to bed. The sooner the prolonged holiday period was over, the better. I felt in a kind of limbo.

The following day I remembered what John had said about looking round his house and wondered if the estate agents would be open. At least it would be something to do. I fished the card John had given me out of my handbag and dialled the number. To my surprise a girl's voice answered almost at once.

'Bruce and Freeman's, estate agents. Can I help you?'

'Hello. You have a house on your books — twenty-three Lime Avenue. Would it be convenient for me to take a look round today sometime?'

'The vendor has already moved out,' she said.

'I know, actually Mr Harrison was a colleague of mine. He suggested I might be interested.'

'I see. Well, you can pick up the keys at any time. At the moment we're running on a skeleton staff so would you mind going on your own?'

'Not at all. I'll pick up the keys after lunch.'

John's house looked abandoned and rather forlorn without him. He had removed all his furniture into storage and as I opened the door and stepped inside there was an empty, impersonal feel about the place. Before the hall had been carpeted and for the first time I realized that the floor was made of stripped oak. I pictured what it would look like polished and scattered with bright rugs. Upstairs I peered into the three bedrooms, all nicely decorated and well proportioned. The bathroom had been updated recently and so had the kitchen. Both were sleek and modern with no garish colours or gimmicky trimmings.

As I went from room to room on the ground floor I was surprised at how different the house looked devoid of furniture or fittings. It was as though it had been reduced to a blank canvas, ready for a new owner to put their personal stamp on it. I pictured our own furniture, imagining how I'd arrange each item; inventing colour schemes and lighting for each room. Looking out through the French windows into the garden I saw myself sitting on the decked patio on a summer evening with a glass of wine. Then with a sigh I reminded myself that if I bought this house I'd be doing everything alone. I turned away. Anyway it was too large and too expensive for one.

As I turned back into the room I heard the scrape of a key in the front door and stopped dead. The girl at the agents hadn't mentioned that someone else would be viewing today. How embarrassing. Surely she should have waited till I'd returned the keys before handing out the spare set. I hastily gathered up my coat and bag, planning to explain that I was just about to leave anyway. In the doorway I stopped in my tracks, the blood rushing to my cheeks as I stood face to face with the new viewer. He was as surprised as I was.

'*Sophie!*'

I shook my head. 'Rex! What — what are *you* doing here?'

'The same as you, I imagine.'

'This is John Harrison's old house, my headmaster. He's left and . . . '

'I know.'

I shook my head. 'You know, but how? It's only just been put on the market.'

'It doesn't matter how. So, you've looked round?'

'I've finished now. I was just going.'

'What's your verdict?'

'It's nice,' I said. 'Very nice. Not for one though. It's a family house.' I made a move towards the door. 'I'll go and let you look round in peace. I think you'll like it. It's just your sort of house.'

'Don't go,' he said. 'You don't have to. In fact I'd be glad of your opinion. You always pick up more details than me.'

As we toured the bedrooms again I thought

how bizarre this whole situation was. We descended the stairs and Rex inspected the kitchen.

'I like this,' he said. 'Nice clean lines and no unnecessary trimmings.'

'I thought a striped blind would look nice,' I said. 'Orange and white. The house faces south-west so there must be sun for most of the day.'

He nodded in agreement. 'I like the ceramic tiled floor too.'

'There are French windows in the living room,' I told him, 'leading on to a deck. It'd be perfect for eating out on summer evenings.'

He looked at me. 'You really do like it, don't you? Even though it's less than a hundred years old.'

I shrugged. 'For a suitable family it would be ideal,' I said guardedly. I frowned. 'I thought you were spending Christmas with your family.'

'I was. I came back to look at the house.'

'You still haven't said how you knew about it?' But even before he replied I knew the answer. 'It was Mum, wasn't it? She rang and told you I was going to view it.'

He smiled. 'Something like that, though I had no way of knowing you'd be here today.'

I shook my head exasperatedly. 'Why can't she leave things alone? I'd never have told her if I'd thought . . . '

'I was coming back anyway,' he interrupted. 'I say *back* because where I'm living now could never be called *home* in a million years.' He took a step towards me. 'I'd go as far as to say that nowhere is home to me without you.'

I held out my hand to stop him coming any

further. 'And yet you said we couldn't live together any more.'

'I said I wasn't sure because I felt you didn't really know what you wanted.' He took my hand. 'Do you know now, Sophie?'

I swallowed hard. 'I think so.'

'No more ancient monuments to restore.'

'I think I have to admit that wasn't one of my brightest ideas.'

'And no more makeovers?'

'We all have to grow up sometime, Rex.' I thought of Mum's remarks on the subject. 'Anyway, surely you saw more in me than mere clothes. It's what's on the inside that matters.'

He took a step closer, still holding my hand. 'And what is on the inside, Sophie? Now, I mean.'

His eyes held mine and I couldn't hold back any longer. 'I haven't changed,' I said, a huge lump in my throat. 'All I really know is that I miss you. It's supposed to get better but it doesn't. It just gets worse.'

'You don't have to tell me. We could always give it another try,' he said. 'Somewhere new.' He pulled me close. 'Somewhere like this, if you really want to, if you're prepared to give us another chance.'

Before I could reply his lips were on mine, his arms holding me breathlessly close in the embrace that I'd longed for till my heart ached. I had no words to describe what I felt at that moment but I think my response told him all he wanted to know.

Outside it was already growing dark when we

locked the front door securely behind us. In the dusky half light we stood and looked at each other.

'Shall we take the keys back to the office and make an offer?' Rex asked me.

Reaching up I touched his cheek. 'Maybe tomorrow,' I said. 'Let's go back to the flat for now. We could . . . '

He looked at me enquiringly. 'We could what?'

I stood on tiptoe to kiss him and felt him smiling under my lips. 'Catch up,' I said, returning his smile. 'There's an awful lot of it to do. It could take all night.'

25

FRANCES

Harry was discharged from hospital later that morning and I drove him home. He still seemed very tired and a little disorientated so I tucked him up in bed and left him to sleep, promising his favourite meal when he wakened.

When we arrived home the house was still empty but Charles arrived soon after four o'clock.

'Where's Harry?' he asked without preamble.

'Up in his room. He's asleep so I'd rather you didn't disturb him at . . . ' But he'd already turned on his heel and by the time I'd followed him into the hall he was already halfway up the stairs. When I arrived in Harry's room Charles was sitting on the side of his bed.

Harry still looked sleepy and slightly disorientated. 'Dad — hello,' he said.

'Hello there,' Charles said briskly. 'What's all this I hear about you, eh? Sliding down the banisters!'

Harry glanced apprehensively across to me. 'I — I fell,' he muttered.

'So I hear. That was a pretty silly thing to do wasn't it?'

'He was being bullied,' I put in.

Charles shot me a look of pure venom. 'Of course he wasn't,' he snapped. He looked at

285

Harry. 'What was it, a dare?'

'I didn't want to do it,' Harry protested. 'We're not supposed to but they're older and bigger than me. They laughed and said if I didn't do it I was a wimp and I'd get a thrashing.'

Charles laughed. 'Well, that's what boys do, isn't it? When you're a bit older you'll be doing it to the new boys too.'

'I sincerely hope not!' I crossed to the bed and laid a hand on Harry's forehead. He felt hot. I glanced at Charles. 'I think Harry has had enough. I suggest we go downstairs and let him rest.'

Charles followed me out of the room and I closed the door. On the landing he turned on me, 'You're molly-coddling the boy again. It's no wonder he gets called a wimp.'

'He's nine years old, Charles,' I said. 'He could easily have been killed. We should sue the school.'

He laughed. 'I've never heard such a ludicrous over-reaction. St Eldred's is one of the best schools in the country and . . . '

'He's not going back,' I interrupted.

He stared at me. 'Of course he is, as soon as he's fit and well again. I won't have my son missing out on his education. I telephoned the head by the way, and apologized for the scene you made.'

'Any protest I made was justified,' I told him. 'The doctor at the hospital was appalled at the bruises on his body. I'm sure he would back me up if necessary.'

'He won't get the chance. We're not dragging

some wet behind the ears young doctor into this. It's hysterical nonsense!'

'It's almost the end of term. During the break we can find another school — preferably one nearer home where he can go as a day boy.' He opened his mouth to argue but I said firmly, 'I'm not letting this go, Charles. I should never have allowed him to go back after the summer holidays. This time I'm adamant.'

'Huh! We'll see about that!'

He set off down the stairs and suddenly I made up my mind. It was now or never. Following him downstairs and into his study I closed the door and stood with my back to it. 'I'm leaving you, Charles,' I said quietly. 'I've had enough. Our marriage is clearly over. I'll be taking Harry with me too. You've been seeing Celia behind my back and now I'm giving you the chance to go back to her if that's what you want. Harry and I will be better on our own.'

He swung round. 'I don't need your permission to see Celia if I want to. Go if that's what you want,' he said coldly. 'But don't think you're taking my son.'

'Harry is my son too,' I pointed out. 'And I won't have him abused any longer.'

'Abused!' he snorted. 'What rubbish! You'd rather bring him up as a snivelling little mummy's boy, wouldn't you? Well, I don't think so! My son is going to grow up a man — learn to face the world and deal with its trials and tribulations.'

'You mean you want him to grow up a cold, insensitive boor with no thought for anyone but

287

himself,' I said. 'That's what St Eldred's teaches, isn't it? And they certainly made a good job of you!'

For a moment I thought he was going to hit me. I saw his fists clench and unclench at his sides then he said, 'All right then, if that's what you want, go, and take him with you — for now. You've turned him into a blubbing little brat so you may as well reap the benefits. But don't think you've heard the last of it, Frances. I'll fight you through the courts for custody.'

'I wouldn't waste your money. You won't get it!' I heard myself standing up to him as never before but I had no idea where all this was coming from. Even though I was shaking like a leaf inside I'd somehow found the courage to stand my ground at long last and there was no way I was going to cave in now.

'I'll go and pack,' I said. 'I don't like taking Harry out again tonight but we can't stay here another night with you.'

'Don't worry you won't have to, I'm going,' he said. 'I'm leaving now and the next time you hear from me will be through my solicitor.'

He stormed back upstairs and for a moment I was afraid he might try to take Harry but he didn't. I heard him opening and shutting drawers and cupboards. Clearly he was packing — presumably he would go back to Celia's. A wave of relief flooded through me. I went back into the kitchen and after an interval I heard the front door slam and, a few minutes later, the sound of his car roaring down the drive.

I finished making Harry's meal and went

upstairs to see if he was fit to come down. I found him sitting up in bed looking anxious.

'Mum, I won't really have to go back to St Eldred's, do I?'

'No, I promise.'

'I heard Dad say I had to. He sounded so cross.'

I sat down on the side of his bed. 'Do you feel like coming downstairs for supper?' I asked.

'Is Dad there?'

'No. Dad had to go out again. He won't be back tonight.'

His face cleared and he pushed back the duvet. 'All right then.' He reached for his dressing gown.

'It's fish fingers,' I told him.

He grinned. 'With chips and beans?'

'If you want.' I smiled. It was so great to see him back to his normal self again.

* * *

When Harry was safely tucked up in bed again later I decided to ring Adam. I explained the situation as briefly as I could.

'Perhaps you'd better take this as my notice,' I said. 'I've no idea when I'll be able to work again.'

'Where are you going, Frances?' he asked. 'To relatives — a friend?'

'To be honest, Adam, I haven't a clue at the moment,' I confessed. 'I have no relatives I'd ask for help and my two closest friends are in the middle of changes of their own at the moment so

I suppose it will have to be a bed and breakfast somewhere.'

'Listen. I've got a holiday cottage in Norfolk. You could go there if you like, at least until after Christmas. As for work, don't worry about it. This is our slack period anyway and after the holiday, when you've got Harry sorted out, we can talk further about it.'

'Oh, Adam, that's so kind of you,' I said. 'I'd like to get away from here as soon as possible.'

'Of course. If you've got a pen and paper I'll give you the address.' I wrote it down as he dictated it to me. 'A lady from the village keeps an eye on it for me,' he went on. 'I'll ring her and let her know that you're coming so that she can turn on the heating and get some shopping in for you.'

'Thank you so much.'

'And give me a ring when you've arrived. I'll try and drive down and see you at the weekend. Oh, and Frances,'

'Yes?'

'How did you get on down in Dorset?'

Although it was only a couple of days earlier recent events had almost managed to wipe it from my mind. 'Oh, it worked out very well,' I told him. 'I don't think I'll be hearing from the woman who claimed to be my mother again.'

'Claimed to be?'

'Yes. It turned out to be a lie, but I'll tell you more about it when I see you.'

'Poor Frances. Life hasn't been easy for you lately has it?'

'You could say that.'

Harry and I drove to Norfolk the following day. I packed all our things, including Harry's Christmas presents, so that we wouldn't have to return to Melford. For my part, I never wanted to see the place again.

Brinkley was a tiny fishing village and I found Puffin Cottage without too much trouble. It had once been a fisherman's cottage which had been tastefully updated with all the modern comforts. Just as Adam had said, Mrs Jones, his caretaker had turned on the heating and also lit a cheery fire in the living room so that the place was warm and welcoming. Harry was enchanted and ran upstairs to claim his bedroom.

'Mum, I can see the sea from my window,' he called excitedly, as he ran down the stairs. 'There are boats down there and everything. Can we go and see?'

I laughed. 'I think we should unpack first and have something to eat. Then we'll go exploring.'

Away from Melford, Harry was a different child. I too felt as though a weight had been lifted from my shoulders and I knew that I had made the right decision. Getting right away was what we both needed. The thought of what Charles might do to get the better of me was a worry, but I decided that all I could do for the moment was wait and hope for the best.

Adam joined us that weekend, arriving on Saturday morning. He and Harry quickly made friends and got along famously. The weather was fine and mild and he took us on a tour of the village that afternoon, introducing us to all the places and local people he knew so well.

'I used to come here on holiday with my parents when I was a kid,' he told me as we walked along the quay. 'I've always loved the wild, unspoiled Norfolk coast. It has a wonderful atmosphere of freedom and it's a great place to unwind.'

Later, when Harry was in bed, he asked me what I planned to do.

'I haven't really had time to make plans yet,' I confessed. 'The priority is to find somewhere permanent to live and get Harry settled in a new school.'

'Any idea where?'

I shrugged. 'I haven't a clue. It doesn't much matter where we go as long as there's a good school nearby for Harry.' I looked at him. 'And as long as I can still work for you.'

'That's a foregone conclusion.' He paused for a second. 'What about your marriage; is it really over, Frances? Are you sure this is really what you want?'

'More than sure. Charles certainly is. He said that the next time I hear from him it will be through his solicitor.'

His eyebrows rose. 'Surely it should be down to you to divorce *him*. After all he's the adulterer. You've done nothing wrong.'

It was something that hadn't occurred to me. 'I suppose you're right,' I said. 'He's talking of applying to the courts for custody of Harry.'

He looked sceptical. 'I doubt very much if he'd get it. If I were you I'd get yourself some legal advice as soon as possible.' He looked at me. 'Have you had any thoughts at all about where you'd like to set up home? Obviously somewhere central, where there's a good school?'

'That would be ideal.'

'If you like this area there's King's Lynn, or, a little further away there's Stamford. Both have good schools for Harry and both are within easy reach of London.'

I shook my head. 'I don't know either of those places. Frankly, Adam, I don't know where to begin. It's all a bit overwhelming.'

'Well, no need to choose right away. I could drive you over to see both places tomorrow if you like. There's nothing much you can do till after the Christmas break anyway.'

'Why don't you join us here for Christmas?' I suggested, then, sensing his hesitation I added, 'Unless you have something else planned of course.'

'No, I haven't and it's sweet of you to invite me. It's just that . . . ' He looked at me.' 'With Charles planning to find grounds for divorce . . . '

I blushed, realizing what he was getting at. 'Oh! Of course. I didn't think of that.'

He smiled. 'No, you wouldn't, Frances. You haven't got that kind of mind. And that's probably just what Charles is banking on. But from now on you're going to have to be very careful.'

I forced a laugh. 'I've got enough to think about, finding a place to live and the right school for Harry.' I looked at him. 'I have to be honest, Adam. I've no idea when I'll be able to work for you again.'

'That's not a problem,' he assured me. 'Once

Harry is settled in school you could work around whatever area you're living in. Meantime, don't worry about your salary.'

'Oh! I couldn't take money if I'm not working,' I said quickly.

He laughed. 'Oh, don't worry about that! I'll send you some paperwork to be getting on with at home.' He grinned at me. 'Can't have you sitting idle, can we?'

The following day Adam drove Harry and me to see both of the towns he'd recommended. I fell in love with Stamford at first sight, loving the elegant Georgian houses, built of local dove-grey stone, and the beautiful surrounding country-side. Looking in one of the estate agent's windows we saw some small two bedroom apartments advertised to rent on the outskirts of the town.

'One of those would suit Harry and me down to the ground,' I said. 'But they'd want rent in advance and it's out of the question at the moment.'

'I could always make you a small loan,' Adam said. 'Just until your divorce settlement comes through.' I opened my mouth to protest but he continued, 'Don't argue, Frances. You have to be practical. The sooner you can settle in, the sooner you can find a solicitor and start planning a future for the two of you.' He took my hand. 'Come on, the agent's office is open. No time like the present. Let's go and view those apartments straight away.'

By the time we arrived back in Brinkley I was the tenant of one of the new apartments. I could hardly believe it. The flat I chose had been recently completed and had the most wonderful view of the river and surrounding meadows. Harry had been so excited, looking round and choosing his own bedroom.

'Are we really coming to live here, Mum?' he asked. 'And can I really go to a school where I can come home every day?'

'I hope so, yes,' I said, laughing.

He squeezed my arm. 'So when can we move in?'

'On New Year's Day,' I told him.

He grinned from ear to ear. 'Oh, Mum. I can't *wait!*'

I persuaded Adam to stay until first thing on Monday morning so that he could have a relaxing evening. Back at the cottage I made a meal for the three of us and then Harry went off to bed, tired but excited by the prospect of his new future.

Once he was settled I joined Adam beside the blazing log fire he had lit in the living room.

'I really wish I could spend Christmas here with you both,' he said wistfully.

I looked at him and for the first time since we'd met I realized how lonely he must have been since the tragic loss of his family.

'We'd have loved to share Christmas with you too, Adam,' I said.

He nodded. 'But best to be careful under the circumstances. I daresay Charles will be looking out for any little hint of misconduct he can find to use against you. Best not to give him any ammunition.'

It was something I hadn't thought of but I immediately saw the sense in what he was saying.

I looked at him for a long moment. In the firelight he looked pensive and sad. 'Thank you so much for all you've done to help me, Adam,' I said quietly.

He looked up. 'Not at all. Glad to have been of help.'

'Why are you so good to me?' I asked him softly.

He smiled ruefully. 'Are you really telling me you haven't guessed?'

'I know you're the best friend I've ever had.'

'But you must have sensed that I'd like to be more than that?' When I didn't answer he leaned forward to take my hand and said quickly, 'I'm sorry. I don't want to spoil things between us, Frances.'

'You're not — you won't.'

'You're just coming out of a damaging marriage. Your emotions must be shot to pieces. It's going to take time for you to start examining your feelings. I know that.'

'You're right. But having your support means a lot.'

'Thank you. So, for the time being I promise not to mention my own feelings again.'

Part of me was disappointed. At that moment, his hand still holding mine, I wanted nothing more than for him to take me in his arms and kiss me, but was he right, was what I felt just a rebound thing? Was I merely grateful for someone strong to lean on? Somehow I didn't think so, but time would tell. For now he was right. There was a big bridge to cross. The months to come would be difficult and trying. We should wait for life to settle down again.

26

As always at the beginning of a new year, business at Fantaisie was slow. The previous week Imogene had gone on a buying trip, leaving Katie in charge. She'd had plenty of time to jot down some of the many ideas she'd had about the exciting new future she and Imogene were planning for the business but now it was her turn to spend some time away from the shop so she was working at home, creating two new wedding dresses for Fantaisie's hire service.

So much had happened since Christmas. The new lease for the shop had been signed and to their surprise they had been offered the first refusal of the premises next door. She and Imogene had spent a long time talking about it and at last had decided to take the risk, using the second shop for their hire business.

As she sat stitching, Katie's thoughts went to Frances and Sophie. It seemed an age since the three of them had made their trip to Dorset. To her surprise and disappointment Fran hadn't even sent her a Christmas card. She couldn't help wondering if something had happened. She'd had a card from Sophie who had scribbled a note inside, saying that she'd had to move out of Greenings at short notice but had found temporary accommodation.

Sitting by the window to catch as much natural daylight as she could, Katie noticed that there were a lot of children about. It must be half-term, she mused, picking up another sequin with her needle. That meant that Sophie would be free and as she was working at home there couldn't be a better time to arrange a meeting. Maybe the three of them could get together this week and catch up with all the news.

Setting her sewing aside she went into the kitchen and put the kettle on for coffee, while she waited for it to boil she took out her phone and selected Sophie's number. She picked up at once.

'Hi, Katie. Long time no speak.'

Well at least Sophie sounded cheerful. 'Hi. How are you?'

'Great thanks. Enjoying a few days off.'

'I thought it must be half-term, that's why I'm ringing. Did you have a good Christmas?'

'Not too bad. You?'

'Super. Look, it's ages since we got together. I'm working from home at the moment so I'm more or less free. How about meeting for lunch?'

'Sounds lovely. Have you heard from Fran?'

'No. Have you?'

'Not for some time. I feel guilty, I keep meaning to ring her but such a lot has happened and somehow I haven't got round to it.'

'Shall I ring her now — or will you?'

'I will,' Sophie said. 'But shall we say it's a date anyway. Tomorrow — same time, same place? I'll book our usual table.'

'Lovely. See you there then.'

★ ★ ★

Napolitano was quiet when Katie arrived. She was a little early so she wasn't surprised to find that she was first. She ordered herself a glass of white wine and settled down to wait, sitting where she could keep an eye on the door.

She spotted Sophie the moment she arrived. She was laden with bags and had obviously been shopping. Spotting Katie she waved cheerily as she made her way across the restaurant.

'Phew!' Dumping her bags on to a spare chair she sank into the seat next to Katie. 'I don't come into Town very often so I thought I'd kill two birds with one stone.'

Katie laughed. 'Looks as though you've bumped off a whole flock if that lot's anything to go by.'

Sophie grinned. 'I'm going on a Mediterranean cruise at Easter,' she said. 'So I needed a few things.'

'Wow, a cruise! Lucky you. By the way, did you manage to contact Fran? Is she coming?'

'Yes. She's moved — living in Lincolnshire now. I don't know any details but she says she'll explain everything when we're all together.' She beckoned a waiter and ordered a glass of wine for herself and one for Frances.

'She'll be here in a minute,' she explained. 'I think she's been through quite a tough time. She didn't say a lot but she's obviously not living at Crayshore Manor any more.'

When Frances arrived a few minutes later it was clear to both of them that she had lost weight. Katie greeted her warmly.

'Fran! Lovely to see you. Hey, you've been on

a diet. Are you going to tell us the secret of your success?'

Frances sat down wearily. 'No secret,' she said with a wry smile. 'Divorce is the answer. That'll do it every time.'

Katie winced, 'Fran love, I'm sorry. Me and my big mouth. I'd no idea.'

'Of course you hadn't. Don't be sorry. It's all for the best anyway.' Frances pulled off her gloves. 'I'm sorry not to have been in touch with either of you. It was deliberate, I'm afraid. I didn't want to burden either of you with all my troubles, not at Christmas.'

'That awful woman hasn't been giving you more problems, has she?' Katie asked.

Frances took a sip of her wine and shook her head. 'No, thank goodness. I haven't heard another word from her, and anyway she'll have no idea where I am now that I've moved.'

'So you and Charles have split up?' Sophie ventured.

'Yes and not before time. I'd already found out that he was seeing his ex-wife again. He didn't try very hard to hide the fact. But what finally tipped me over the edge was that Harry had an accident at school and fractured his skull.'

The other two gasped. 'Oh God, Fran, how awful!'

'It was the same day that we went to Dorset. When I got home several messages had been left for me on the phone telling me that he was in hospital.' She looked at the other two. 'It turned out to be no accident but the result of more bullying but the school did their best to cover it up. I tried to reach Charles and my suspicions were confirmed when I found out that he was with her, Celia. When he eventually came home he refused again to accept that Harry was being bullied and insisted that he would be going back to school as soon as he was fit enough. That was when I made up my mind. Harry and I left the following day.'

'Poor Fran.' Katie touched her arm. 'You must have felt so alone. Where did you go?'

'We were lucky; Adam — my boss — has a cottage in Norfolk. He let us stay there until after Christmas. Then I found a flat in Stamford — again with Adam's help. As soon as we moved I got Harry into a good school, found a solicitor and filed for divorce.'

Sophie and Katie exchanged looks. 'It all sounds very organized,' Sophie said. 'But I'm sure you're playing it down. It must have been such a traumatic time for you.'

'Naturally, but not as bad as I thought,' Frances said. 'Charles had hinted that he would apply for custody of Harry and for a while I was terrified that he might get it. He has a lot of influence. But thank God it didn't happen.' She paused to finish her wine. 'I must admit that I wouldn't have known where to start if it hadn't been for Adam. It was his suggestion that I applied for a divorce first. I was expecting fireworks but to my surprise Charles neither contested it nor mentioned applying for custody of Harry. I rather suspect that Celia had a hand in that. She's hardly the motherly type. Charles does have access though. The arrangement is that he'll see Harry every other weekend.'

'So in the end it all worked out better than you expected?' Sophie said.

Frances smiled. 'Yes, thank goodness. Harry loves his new school and we both love the flat and living in Stamford.' She paused. 'None of it would have been possible without Adam. I don't know what I would have done without him.'

'So, are you still working for him?' Katie asked.

'Yes. I hardly dare believe it but everything seems to be on course for us at last.' She looked up. 'But enough about me.' She looked at Sophie. 'You're looking fantastic. To what do we attribute that glow?'

Sophie smiled. 'I told you that Greenings was finally sold,' she said. 'I had to move out in a hurry in the end but I found a temporary flat so I wasn't exactly out on the street.' She regaled them with the story of Mrs Lowe's flat and her custody of Albert, which meant she was stuck at the flat over the Christmas break.

'But I didn't mind,' she said. 'Albert is a poppet and I really missed him when his owner came home.'

'Don't tell me it's a cat that's given your eyes that sparkle?' Katie enquired mischievously.

'Not exactly, no.' Sophie avoided their eyes, playing with the stem of her glass. 'Actually Rex and I have decided to give our marriage another go.' Both girls gave a whoop of delight that had other customers turning to look. 'And we've found the perfect house,' she went on. 'As it happens we both turned up to view it at the same time, which isn't quite the coincidence you might think. I suspect my mother of having a hand in that. To cut a long story short we both liked the house and we put in an offer which was accepted. We'll be moving in a few weeks' time but before that happens we're going on a second honeymoon during the Easter break.'

'That's fantastic!' Katie said, but it was Frances she was watching. Finally, unable to contain her curiosity any longer, she said, 'Fran, Adam — your boss — seems to have gone to an awful lot of trouble for you. Do we take it that you and he are . . . ?'

'*Katie!*' Sophie looked shocked but Frances shook her head.

'It's OK. I'm not free anyway until my decree comes through, remember.'

'He does sound lovely though.' Katie observed.

Frances smiled. 'He is.'

'Oh, come off it. He's obviously head over heels in love with you,' Katie said. 'So how do *you* feel about him, Fran? Come on — give!'

Sophie quickly put in, 'As Fran says, it's early days and she still isn't free. We shouldn't press her. I don't suppose she knows what she feels at the moment.'

'I do actually,' Fran said suddenly. 'Since Christmas Adam has been a tower of strength, helping us and keeping my job open for me. At first I thought I felt the way I did about him because of his kindness and understanding, but for a few weeks after Christmas he kept his distance because of the divorce and it was then that I realized how much I missed him. I did some work for him at home during that time and we spoke on the phone regularly but as the days and weeks went by I found myself longing to see him. That was when I knew.'

'That you shared his feelings?' Katie asked.

Frances nodded. Looking up, she grinned ruefully at Katie. 'Satisfied? Any more you'd like to know?'

Seeing that Katie was about to ask the inevitable question and unwilling to see her friend pressed further Sophie put in quickly, 'So, what about you, Katie? We haven't heard a word about you so far and last time we were all together things looked pretty bleak for you. I take it you eventually confessed to Imogene about the devious Drew.'

'Funny you should mention him.' Successfully diverted, Katie couldn't keep the grin off her face. She leaned forward, eager to impart her recent piece of good luck. 'I told you how he was trying to con me into leaving Imogene and Fantaisie. That was bad enough and the thought of confessing to Imogene was even worse. It took me ages to screw up enough bottle. My knees were knocking that morning, I can tell you. I was quite prepared for her to sack me on the spot but to my surprise she was amazing about it. She knows her ex pretty well and she knows what he's capable of. She finished up asking me to become a full partner.'

'Really?' The other two looked at her in amazement. 'After what had happened — how come?'

'Well, you see, the lease on the shop was in both their names and it was up for renewal, which was why Drew was hoping to see her go bust. He planned to take over the business and run it himself. Imogene suggested that we let him think she was bankrupt. She pulled out of the lease and I took it on in her place.'

'Sounds great, but is it all above board?' Sophie asked cautiously.

'Oh yes. The lease is in my name now, but it's only a formality. Everything was legally arranged before Christmas, and guess what — I — well we have been offered the shop next door so we're actually expanding; using the new shop for the hire service. We're going to call it Something Borrowed. When we open in a few weeks' time we're going to have a grand opening day with champagne and everything. I'll make sure you both get invitations.'

'So what about Drew,' Sophie asked. 'Did you ever hear any more from him?'

Katie laughed. 'Oh yes! Obviously he was hopping mad when he realized Imogene had turned the tables on him, but his curiosity got the better of him and he couldn't resist coming round to see for himself. Imogene let him think she was working for me. I don't think he was fooled for a minute but there was nothing he could do about it. He actually congratulated us but you could see how much it pained him.' She chuckled. 'The words came out sort of *shredded*, as though he was straining them through his teeth.'

Sophie laughed. 'So all's well that ends well then. I think all this calls for a celebration.' She caught a waiter's eye. 'We'll have a bottle of bubbly and toast the success of Something Borrowed.' She looked at the other two. 'Just think, this time last year we'd almost forgotten one another existed. It's thanks to the school reunion that we met up again and it seems to have been lucky for all of us.'

'Not without all of us going through the mill first though,' Frances reminded them. 'Let's hope that we've all managed to learn something from it.'

Sophie nodded. 'And let's hope that next Christmas will be better for all three of us than the last one.'

'Actually *I* had a fantastic Christmas,' Katie said with a grin. 'Imogene took me to this fantastic health spa and we spent four days being seriously pampered. The best Christmas I ever had!'

The waiter brought their champagne and drew the cork with a loud pop. The girls laughed as they watched the champagne fizz into their glasses. Sophie raised hers.

'To us,' she said. 'Here's to marriage, divorce and Something Borrowed.'

'To us,' the other two responded. 'The best of good luck to all of us!'